BONES UNDER THE
BEACH HUT

SIMON BRETT

BONES UNDER THE BEACH HUT

A FETHERING MYSTERY

MACMILLAN

First published 2011 by Macmillan
an imprint of Pan Macmillan, a division of Macmillan Publishers Limited
Pan Macmillan, 20 New Wharf Road, London N1 9RR
Basingstoke and Oxford
Associated companies throughout the world
www.panmacmillan.com

ISBN 978-0-230-73638-2

Visit www.panmacmillan.com to read more about all our books
and to buy them. You will also find features, author interviews and
news of any author events, and you can sign up for e-newsletters
so that you're always first to hear about our new releases.

To Bruce and Ros

And also to Sonja Zentner
who, at the 2010 Chichester Cathedral
fundraising Festival of Flowers, won the right
to have her name included in this book.

Chapter One

There weren't many proper beach huts on Fethering Beach. Just a few ramshackle sheds once owned by fishermen, which had been converted for use by holidaying families. For proper regimented beach huts, with pitched roofs and the proportions of large Wendy houses, you had to go west along the coast to the neighbouring village of Smalting. And it was there that Carole Seddon had the use of a beach hut for the summer.

Smalting was a picturesque – very nearly bijou – West Sussex village, whose inhabitants thought themselves superior to the residents of Fethering. In fact, they thought themselves superior to the residents of anywhere. Like many of the villages along that stretch of coast, the earliest extant buildings were fishermen's cottages, which had been refurbished many times, ending up as elegant well-appointed dwellings, mostly bought by comfortably pensioned people downsizing in retirement. A couple of large houses had been added to the village in the eighteenth century, and a few more spacious holiday homes had been built by the late Victorians. In the first decade of the twentieth century, Smalting had become a fashionable seaside resort and rows of neat Edwardian terraces had sprung up. In the nineteen thirties two private estates had been developed either side of the village, and with that further building stopped. Unlike Fethering, Smalting did not spread northwards and so did not have room for any of what was still disparagingly referred to as 'council housing'. The army of cleaners and home helps who serviced the needs of its residents all came from outside the village.

Nobody did any basic shopping in Smalting. There was nothing so common as a supermarket. The newsagent was the nearest to a practical shop in the village, selling milk and bread as well as more traditional stock and beach items for holidaymakers. The other retailers were highly expensive ladies fashion boutiques, tiny craft galleries and antique dealers. Facing the promenade stood a row of dainty tea shops. Smalting's one pub, The Crab Inn, had such a daunting air of gentility about it and such high prices for food that it was rarely entered by anyone under thirty. But it did very well from the over-sixties.

The beach huts conformed to the high standards that were de rigueur for everything else in Smalting. There were thirty-six of them at the back of the beach, just in front of the promenade, and they were divided into three slightly concave rows of twelve. Eight foot in height and width, each one was ten foot deep and set on four low concrete blocks. They were painted identically – the bitumenized corrugated roofs green, the wooden walls and doors yellow and blue respectively. Touches of individualism were clearly discouraged, though a considerable variety of padlocks was on show, and some of the owners had indulged in rather elaborate name signs. These tended to feature anchors, coils of rope, shells and painted seagulls. The names chosen – *Seaview, Salt Spray, Sandy Cove, Clovelly, Distant Shores* and so on – didn't demonstrate a great deal of originality.

The beach hut of which Carole Seddon had use was called *Quiet Harbour*, and she felt rather guilty about her new possession. This was not unusual for Carole. Despite her forbidding exterior and controlled manner, inside she was a mass of neuroses, though this was something that she would not acknowledge to anyone, least of all herself. She had been brought up to believe that everyone should be self-sufficient, that turning to others for help was a sign of weakness. Afraid of revealing her true personality, Carole had always tried to keep people at arm's length, not allowing anyone to get close to her. This had certainly been her practice during her career at the Home Office. She had also tried to keep her distance within marriage, which was perhaps the reason why she and David had divorced.

And when she had moved permanently to Fethering in retirement (early retirement) Carole Seddon still kept herself to herself. She had acquired a Labrador called Gulliver for the sole purpose of looking purposeful, so that her walks across Fethering Beach did not appear to be the wanderings of someone lonely, but the essential behaviour of someone who had a dog to walk.

So intimacy was not a natural state for Carole Seddon. Even Jude, her neighbour and closest friend, sometimes found herself shut out. Carole was hypersensitive to slights, quick to take offence. And she worried away about things.

Just as she was now worrying away about her use of *Quiet Harbour*. Like many people who lack confidence, Carole was wary of breaking even the most minor of regulations. There were many things in her life that she couldn't control, but one thing she could was keeping the right side of the law. Her work at the Home Office had encouraged her natural law-abiding tendencies, and she would try to avoid even tiny infringements, like keeping out a library book beyond its due date or being twenty-four hours late in applying for the road tax on her Renault. And Carole wasn't convinced that her using the beach hut was entirely, 100 per cent legal.

The contact had come through Jude, inevitably from one of her clients. In Woodside Cottage, the house next to Carole's High Tor, Jude worked as a healer and alternative therapist. Neither of these job descriptions cut much ice with her neighbour, who regarded as suspect any medical intervention that wasn't carried out by a traditionally qualified doctor. Whenever the subject of Jude's work came up in their conversations, Carole had to keep biting her lips to prevent the words 'New Age mumbo-jumbo' from coming out of them. But she had to admit the benefits of her neighbour's work when it came to broadening their social circle. And on more than one occasion, it had been through a client who had come to Woodside Cottage for healing that Carole and Jude had become involved in criminal investigations.

It was in the role of client that Philly Rose had come to Jude. She was crippled by back pain and, as was so often the case, the cause of the agony lay in her mind rather than her body.

Philly, in her early thirties, and her older boy-friend Mark Dennis had moved down from London to Smalting some six months before, just at the beginning of January. For both of them it had been a new start, Philly giving up employment as a graphic designer to go freelance and Mark chucking his highly paid City job to do what he'd always wanted and be a painter. Cushioned by his savings and recent huge bonus, the two of them had embraced country living, involving themselves in everything that the South Coast had to offer. Their two sports cars were traded in for a Range Rover. They acquired two cocker spaniels, bought a sailing dinghy, planted their own vegetables. Both took a lot of exercise. Mark lost the extra weight put on by his City lifestyle. Their make-over seemed complete.

Renting one of Smalting's beach huts was just another symbol of how deeply they were digging their roots into the new environment.

And then one day at the beginning of May, Mark had walked out. That was all the information Carole had. Maybe Jude knew more, but client confidentiality or perhaps a wish to protect the woman's privacy had stopped her from revealing anything else. What

Carole did gather, though, was that her boyfriend's departure had not only shattered Philly emotionally, but also left her in dire financial straits. There hadn't turned out to be much freelance work for a graphic designer in West Sussex and, having lost Mark's substantial contribution to their mortgage payments, Philly felt the threat of repossession looming.

As a result, she was trying to realize the value of any assets she could. The Range Rover was sold and replaced with an eight-year-old Nissan. The sailing dinghy was advertised for sale, but had yet to find a buyer. And Philly had confided to Jude that if she could recoup any of the annual rental they'd paid for the beach hut – some six hundred and fifty pounds – that too would be welcome.

Needless to say, it was Jude who'd suggested the idea to her neighbour. Up until that point Carole would have reckoned she had no need for a beach hut. She could never see herself as a 'hutter' (as the users were inevitably called). Beach huts were for visitors, families from London perhaps, who needed somewhere to store all their impedimenta for days at the seaside. For someone like her, living only a few hundred yards from the sea at High Tor in Fethering High Street, renting a beach hut would be a pointless indulgence.

But that was before Carole knew that her granddaughter Lily was coming to stay in Fethering for a week that summer. Lily was the new element in Carole's life, whose existence had gone some way to thawing the permafrost of her grandmother's emotions. Not blessed with natural maternal instincts, Carole reckoned she had failed in the upbringing of her only child Stephen. He had reacted to her emotional distance – and perhaps to his parents' divorce – by building up a carapace of his own. Burying himself in his work (which involved money and computers in a relationship his mother could never quite understand), he too had minimized engagement with his fellow human beings. But marriage to the vivacious Gaby had changed all that, and the arrival of Lily had also contributed to the humanization of Stephen Seddon. He was never going to be the relaxed life and soul of any party, but family life had saved him from the route of total desiccation on which he seemed to have been set.

And though Carole was very cautious in assessing her emotional reactions to everything, what she felt for Lily did seem wonderfully spontaneous. Somehow, without the worries about her competence as a parent, which had dogged her during Stephen's childhood, Carole did have the feeling of starting something new, the possibility that her instinctive attraction to her granddaughter represented something that she had never experienced before – uncomplicated love.

A visit from Stephen and family to High Tor on Christmas Day had been successfully achieved, and now a pattern had emerged of their meeting up every six weeks or so, either in Fethering or at Stephen and Gaby's house in Fulham. At times Carole still couldn't believe how well she got on with her daughter-in-law, but Gaby had a generous and inclusive personality.

While recognizing that Carole was not necessarily easy, she managed to achieve a relaxed relationship with her mother-in-law, whose basis was their mutual adoration of Lily.

Happy with the way things were going, Carole was still amazed when Gaby proposed that she and Lily should come and stay in Fethering for a whole week. At the end of June Stephen had a work commitment that was going to take him to New York, and his wife reckoned Lily was just at the age to appreciate a seaside holiday. The little girl was starting to toddle and although the flat, slow gradient of Fethering Beach didn't offer any rock pools, it still offered sufficient riches of wavelets and worm casts and seaweed to fascinate a two year old.

Carole made no prevarication when the suggestion was made. She told Gaby it was a great idea, but once everything had been agreed she went through much anxiety about the forthcoming visit. Carole Seddon was one of those people whose forays into society had to be shored up with periods sequestered in High Tor with only Gulliver for company. The thought of someone – even someone as easy as Gaby – sharing her home for a week was a troubling one. Would the two of them still get on after such sustained exposure to each other? And would there be enough going on in Fethering to satisfy the demands of a toddling two year old?

It was just after she had begun to ask herself these questions that Jude suggested her taking over Philly Rose's beach hut. The timing was perfect. Philly had proposed her paying for just a month to see how the arrangement worked out, but Carole, in an atypical moment of extravagance, had said no, she'd pay for the whole year. Given her financial situation, it was no surprise that Philly didn't argue.

These negotiations had been conducted through Jude. Carole had yet to meet Philly Rose, and she was happy about that. She suffered from that very English unwillingness to conduct financial dealings face to face, which is of course why estate agents in England do so well.

But, with the agreement made and her cheque safely in Philly Rose's bank account, Carole felt she could treat *Quiet Harbour* as her own. Though she still had some anxiety about the legality of the subletting arrangement, she did not ultimately regret her decision. According to local Fethering gossip, beach huts along that part of the South Coast were highly sought after, and there was a long waiting list of aspiring purchasers and renters.

And now, rather to her amazement, Carole Seddon was about to become a hutter.

Chapter Two

The deal with Philly Rose was concluded at the beginning of June, but it took a couple of weeks before
Carole plucked up the courage to visit her acquisi-
tion. A new owner of a beach hut in Smalting must of
necessity be an object of curiosity for the more estab-
lished users. Everyone would be bound to look at her.

But eventually Carole had to overcome her misgiv-
ings and bite the bullet. It was a Tuesday in mid-June.
Gaby and Lily would be arriving for the start of their
seaside holiday on the following Sunday week. If
Carole was going to look vaguely competent as the
denizen of a beach hut (would she ever get to the
point of thinking of herself as a hutter?), she needed
to have a few dry runs. And she had nearly a fortnight
to make it look as though beach-hut life was second
nature to her.

Because of her disquiet about potential illegality,
Carole had spent much time consulting the website of
Fether District Council to check local by-laws. (Having
for a long time resisted the lure of computers, she had
finally succumbed, and with the zeal of a convert was
now in a relationship with her laptop which made

many happy marriages look inadequate.) She was relieved not to find on the website any ruling that specifically prohibited subletting of beach huts, and her researches also brought her another bonus piece of information. Dogs were allowed on Smalting Beach.

She was quite surprised by this. Carole knew there were beaches in Bognor, Felpham and Littlehampton where no dogs were allowed during the summer. And she would have expected a place as refined as Smalting to be very strict in such matters. The idea of dogs fouling their precious sand must have been anathema to the gentry of the village. But according to the website there were no restrictions, even in the summer months when the beach would be crowded with visiting families. Carole eventually decided the reason for this anomaly. Most of the inhabitants of Smalting probably were dog owners themselves and so would lobby against anything that might curb their own pets' movements.

Anyway, she was cheered by the thought that she could have the support of Gulliver during her first experimental day at the beach hut.

Carole had once again fallen into the error so common among shy people – the idea that everyone is watching their every movement. But when she pitched up at Smalting Beach with her tote bag and Labrador, nobody took a blind bit of notice. Though the beach was quite full, mostly families with very small children taking advantage of the relative calm before the schools broke up, they were all too preoccupied with their splashings and sandcastles to register the new-comer undoing the padlocks of *Quiet Harbour*.

The blue double doors at the front went virtually the entire width of the hut. Across them a stainless-steel bar was fitted into slots and padlocked at either end. There was also a padlock on the staple and hasp where the two doors met, so there were three keys on the yellow plastic-tagged ring that Jude had got from Philly Rose. In spite of the protective rubber covers that fitted over the slots, the salt air had got in and the keys were hard to turn. When she had finally – and with difficulty – opened the doors, she fixed the hooks that hung from them into the rings at the sides of the hut.

Carole dared to let Gulliver off the lead while she examined her property. Though he was unfamiliar with Smalting Beach, she knew he wouldn't stray too far away from her.

The interior of *Quiet Harbour* was very neat and not a little poignant. Everything in it seemed to be designed for two: a pair of folded director's chairs, a small camping table. From pegs on the wall hung two snorkels, flippers, large for him, small for her, and a set of two plastic rackets with a foam ball. On a shelf at the back stood a Camping Gaz double burner and a row of sealed plastic containers, which turned out to contain cutlery and basics such as tea bags and sachets of instant coffee. There were two large and two small bright red plastic plates and a pair of mugs with humorous inscriptions: 'MR STUD' and 'SEXY LADY'. Everything in the hut was a celebration of the relationship between Philly Rose and Mark Dennis; the relationship he had walked out of.

The floor was covered by an offcut of newish-looking, clean green carpet, on which Carole's flip-flops left sandy marks when she entered the hut. She opened up one of the chairs and set it just inside the doorway. In time she would venture out on to the beach, but she wanted to make an unobtrusive start. And the position where she'd put her chair would get plenty of sun. It was a beautiful June day, one of those which should have presaged a perfect summer. But Carole Seddon had lived in England too long to be over-optimistic about that hope being realized.

Not knowing that the burner would be there, she had brought a thermos of hot black coffee with her and she poured herself a cup. Out of her tote bag she drew her copy of *The Times* and turned to the back of the main section for the crossword. She felt the familiar tug of annoyance at the positioning of the puzzle. In the old days, before *The Times* went tabloid, the crossword was always on the back page with the clues beside it, so that the paper could be folded to reveal both elements at the same time. Whereas now, it was on the penultimate page with the grid and the clues on separate halves so that, unless you had the paper flat on a table you had to keep turning the folded sheets. Why was it, wondered Carole in exasperation, that people keep wanting to change things that were already working perfectly well?

Even as she had the thought, she realized how crusty she would have sounded if she'd said the words out loud. But it didn't worry her too much. Carole Seddon was getting to the stage in life when she reckoned a little crustiness was entirely justified. And of all the things in the world to which a crusty response was justified, meddling with *The Times* crossword stood head and shoulders above the rest.

'Tristram, do stand up straight. Just because you're in your bathers, there's no need to be slovenly.'

From her perch inside *Quiet Harbour*, Carole could not see the owner of the over-elocuted female voice that issued this command from the adjacent beach hut – called *Seagull's Nest* – but its addressee was in clear vision. A boy of about five, wearing bright red shorts and a martyred expression, straightened his shoulders. 'Yes, Granny,' he said balefully.

'And Hermione's right down by the sea! You really should keep an eye on her, Nell.'

'Yes, Deborah, all right.' A harassed-looking, chubby young woman in a one-piece swimsuit appeared in Carole's eyeline, hurrying down to the edge of the wavelets where a blonde-haired toddler in a swimming nappy sat doing no harm to herself or anyone else. The child was absorbed in patting at the sand with a plastic spade and seemed uninterested in her mother's appearance by her side. Soon her brother, the one saddled for life with the name of Tristram, joined them and the three got into a routine of splashing games. Carole began to feel almost excited at the prospect of Lily doing the same, in less than a fortnight's time.

The voice of the unseen female from the next

beach hut started up again. 'You know, Gavin, Nell really has let herself go since she had Hermione. She hasn't made any attempt to get her figure back, has she?'

'Well, she's kept pretty busy,' an upper-class male voice protested, 'what with the two little ones and—'

'Mothers have always been busy,' the woman steamrollered on, 'but that doesn't mean that they should lower their standards. I was busy when I had you and Owen to look after, but I still made sure that when your father got home from work, you were both in bed and I was made up and looking my best for him.'

'Yes, but the fact is, Mummy, you didn't have a job. Nell works full time and still—'

'Your father would have been appalled by the idea of any wife of his having a job. He would have regarded it as a criticism of his abilities to look after his own family.'

'Maybe, but times have changed, Mummy, and—'

'At least your father didn't live to see you married to Nell. He always had very high hopes for you, Gavin. I wouldn't have liked to see him disappointed.'

'But, Mummy—'

'Oh, look, Tristram and Hermione are throwing sand at each other now. And Nell's doing nothing to stop them. In fact, she's positively encouraging them.'

'They're just kids and—'

'I'd better go and sort this out,' the voice said ponderously, and Carole watched as its owner came into view and processed down the beach. The woman called Deborah was probably seventy, but she'd kept her figure well. She wore a predominantly white bathing costume with a design of red flowers on it, and her tanned skin had the texture of shrivelled leather. Over well-cut white hair she wore a broad-brimmed straw hat with a thin red and white scarf tied around it. Carole recognized the type. There were plenty of them on the South Coast. Well-heeled widows, pampered, soigné and utterly poisonous.

Unwilling to witness Deborah's latest attack on her daughter-in-law, Carole returned her attention to her crossword. And as she did so, she had the thought: that is an object lesson in how not to be a grandmother. Please, please, God, may I never behave even vaguely like that towards Lily.

Chapter Three

Carole was filling in the crossword clues almost as fast as she could write them down, when suddenly her rollerball ran out of ink. She tried pressing harder but the point only gouged holes into the flimsy paper. Oh no. She knew from experience that, however well the solving was going, she couldn't do it without seeing the letters.

She riffled hopefully through the contents of her tote bag for something to write with, but without success. She sat in frustration, drumming her fingers on the arm of her director's chair. Putting the crossword to one side and completing it when she got back to High Tor was not an option. When she was on a roll like this, she just had to finish the thing as soon as possible. She had to find a pen from somewhere.

A lot of people might have asked to borrow one from someone in a nearby beach hut. But not Carole Seddon. She always tried to avoid asking questions that offered the possibility of refusal. No, her first thought was to walk up the beach to find Smalting's newsagent and buy a ballpoint.

But before she put that plan into action, it occurred

to her that Philly Rose and Mark Dennis might well have used a pen for something while they were in *Quiet Harbour*. It would be worth checking out the beach hut before taking the long traipse up the beach to the village. Perhaps on the cutlery shelf, in or near one of those neat plastic containers.

When she reached the back of the hut, she felt the solid surface give under her. She stepped back quickly and then gingerly probed at the carpet with her toe. Yes, there was definitely something that felt like a hole in the wooden floor.

She peeled back the corner of the carpet and soon enough saw what had nearly made her trip. There was a hole in the corner, spreading across two of the planks that made up the hut's floor. Its edges were black and charred.

Someone appeared to have lit a fire under *Quiet Harbour*.

Chapter Four

Carole inspected the outside of the hut to see if there were any clues as to what had happened. The structure, presumably prefabricated elsewhere and assembled on Smalting Beach, was set on four concrete slabs to prevent damp from the ground seeping up into its woodwork. And yes, under the back corner of the hut, there was evidence of a small fire having been lit.

Using a children's spade, which she had found inside, Carole poked at the charred debris, releasing a smell of petrol that had been trapped in the folds of what appeared to be cloth. Inspecting it more closely, she saw that strips of old rag had been bundled together. Outermost were the remains of a tea towel, with a design of ponies on it, maybe a souvenir from the New Forest. The minimal evidence of flame damage on the rags suggested to her that the fire hadn't been lit too long ago, and also that it had been extinguished before the flames could spread and burn down the whole beach hut.

Going back inside, she also deduced that the green carpet in *Quiet Harbour* must have been put down after the fire had been discovered. There was no sign even of scorching on the underside, which might – though not necessarily – suggest that the same person who had put out the fire had also covered up the evidence of it.

Another deduction: the lack of sand on its surface suggested that the carpet hadn't been in position for that long.

Before she flipped it back into place, she noticed that, though most of the nails fixing the floorboards to the struts beneath were old and deeply hammered in, the silver round heads of a few stood almost proud of the wood. It looked as if some running repairs had been done, but clearly before the fire had happened. Otherwise surely the burnt planks would have been replaced . . . ? Odd, she thought, as she flattened the carpet back down.

Carole had decided that she needed to talk to Jude about her discovery, so she packed up her thermos and tote bag. In spite of her promising start she hadn't got far on *The Times* crossword. Have to finish it back at High Tor.

As she clicked the padlocks shut on *Quiet Harbour*, she heard the voice of the matriarch in *Seagull's Nest* pontificating. 'You really shouldn't give in to the child so much, Nell. If you spoil Tristram now, he'll grow up without any backbone or moral values.'

Jude had all the windows open, which meant there was enough breeze to set her bamboo wind chimes going. When she had first heard them, Carole had dismissed the chimes as just more evidence of her neighbour's New Age idiocy, but now she had come to find the sound rather comforting. Not, of course, that she would ever have told Jude that.

The sitting room of Woodside Cottage looked as it always did: throws and drapes and cushions disguising the precise outlines of its sofas and armchairs. Scarves and floaty tops, as ever, did the same service for the house's owner. Even in the summer, Jude was bedecked in extras that blurred the contours of her substantial, comfortable body. Her blond hair was piled up on top of her head, tentatively secured by an array of pins and clips.

Carole had always envied the ease with which Jude carried herself. Spontaneity seemed to come spontaneously to her, in her choice of clothes and in every other area of her life. Whereas Carole, whose sartorial ambition was not to draw attention to herself, still agonized over the extent to which she was achieving that desired effect. She avoided bright colours, wearing unpatterned shirts, jackets and skirts. Though she frequently wore trousers, she never wore jeans. Her shoes were sensible enough to chair an official inquiry.

Every six weeks Carole had her grey hair cut into exactly the same helmet-like shape, and her pale blue eyes always took in the world suspiciously through rimless glasses. She was thin – to her mind, angular – and it never would have occurred to her that she actually had rather a good figure.

To Jude life always seemed a natural state of affairs, to Carole something of an imposition.

But over coffee that Tuesday morning in Woodside Cottage she was too excited by her news to indulge her usual anxieties. 'And there was quite a lot of petrol-soaked rag under the corner of the beach hut, so I think there must have been a serious attempt to burn the whole thing down.'

'Yes, but it could just have been vandals,' said Jude. 'I mean, even in a place as up itself as Smalting I'm sure there's a rough element.'

This idea didn't accord with Carole's image of the neighbouring village. 'Or they could have come in from somewhere else,' she said darkly.

'Perhaps. Anyway, I'm sure there's a lot of vandalism to everything on the beaches. Young people have a few too many drinks, feel like a bit of wanton destruction, there's no one there protecting the beach huts . . . I don't quite see what you find sinister about it, Carole.'

'Not sinister so much as intriguing. Not the attempted burning of the hut – that, as you say, could be just mindless vandalism – but the fact that a new bit of carpet had been put inside to cover the evidence.'

'There could be a perfectly innocent explanation for that too. Philly Rose wanting the hut to be usable until it got repaired?'

'Who would she get to repair it?'

'I would imagine there'd be someone from the Fether District Council who'd deal with that sort of thing.'

To Carole's mind, Jude wasn't getting nearly as excited as she should be about the charred hole in the floor of *Quiet Harbour*. 'But maybe Philly Rose didn't want to tell anyone from Fether District Council about the fire? Maybe she has a secret to hide?'

'Maybe she has, but if that secret is to do with the fire, you wouldn't have expected her to agree to let out the beach hut if the new occupant was going to discover it as quickly as you did.'

Carole felt disgruntled. Her neighbour was being uncharacteristically negative. 'Listen, Jude,' she continued, 'I was wondering whether the fire had anything to do with the disappearance of Philly Rose's boyfriend?'

'Mark? What, are you suggesting she burnt him to death in the beach hut?'

'No, of course I'm not. I just do think that there's something odd about the fact that there had been a fire under the hut, someone had put it out and someone – possibly the same person or maybe another – had covered the hole up with a bit of carpet. And I would like to ask Philly Rose if she has any explanation for what happened.'

'All right,' said Jude casually. 'Then let's ask her.'

'What?' Carole was taken aback by such a direct suggestion. 'Can we do that?'

'Yes, of course we can.' Jude looked at the large-faced watch secured to her wrist by a broad red ribbon. 'I'll call Philly and ask her if she'd like to join us for lunch at the Crown and Anchor.'

'Today?' Carole had an instinct that any kind of social meeting should always be arranged a few days in advance. 'Will she be free?'

23

'I don't know. If she isn't she won't come. And if she is she will.'

'How can you be so sure?'

'Three reasons. A) She's become a good friend of mine. B) She's very hard up and would love to have lunch bought for her. And C) She's very lonely since Mark left and needs people to talk to.'

'Oh,' said Carole, 'fine then.'

Chapter Five

They arrived at Fethering's only pub, the Crown and Anchor, before Philly, and were greeted in his usual lugubrious manner by the shaggily bearded landlord Ted Crisp, dressed in his summer uniform of faded T-shirt and jeans. He was actually now having difficulty in justifying his customary air of gloom. In the past he could always put it down to bad business. At times the Crown and Anchor's finances had been quite rocky and once the pub had nearly had to close, but those days were gone. The fine June weather was bringing the holidaymakers in in droves and Ted now had a very efficient staff to back him up. His Polish bar manager Zosia had taken away all his anxieties about staffing, and his chef Ed Pollack was going from strength to strength. The landlord responded very sniffily to the word 'gastropub', but in the view of many restaurant guides and well-heeled clients, that was what the Crown and Anchor was becoming known as throughout West Sussex. Anyone who wanted evidence of that should have tried booking a table for a Saturday evening or Sunday lunchtime. Often there would be nothing available for a month ahead.

Ted Crisp had even extended the premises. At one side of the sea-facing frontage there now stood what looked like a Victorian conservatory. Though used by the pub's ordinary customers – particularly on a fine June day when all the doors and windows were open – it could be shut off from the main bar area. This was now the 'Function Room', available for wedding receptions and other private parties. There was no way round the fact: the Crown and Anchor was doing really good business.

Though deprived of his traditional excuse for grumpiness, Ted Crisp was not about to change his habitual mien. From behind the bar he looked up gloomily at Carole and Jude's entrance. 'Two large Chilean Chardonnays, I assume,' he pronounced, in the manner of a newsreader reporting a tsunami.

'Cheer up, Ted, it might never happen,' said Jude.

'How d'you know it hasn't already?' he demanded, as he handed the glasses across.

'Getting a lot of bookings for the Function Room?'

'Mustn't grumble.'

'But you still will, won't you, Ted?' That was rewarded by a grunt.

'What's good for lunch?' asked Carole.

'Ed says the Dover sole's to die for.'

'Ooh, that sounds nice.'

'Shall I take your order?' Ted reached for a pad of paper.

'Not quite yet. We've got a friend joining us,' Jude explained.

'Please yourself,' said Ted, in a manner that people

who didn't know him so well would have regarded as rude, and he turned to serve another customer.

In spite of the sunny weather Carole and Jude decided they'd sit inside. The alcove tables in the bar were less full than those in the sun and, although their conversation with Philly Rose was not exactly confidential, a degree of privacy would be welcome.

They had hardly sat down before she arrived, looking around the bar and waving when she saw Jude. Philly Rose was small, thin as a whippet, with almost ash-blond hair and surprisingly dark brown eyes. She wore a sleeveless *eau de Nil* top over white jeans and red Converse trainers.

Once they'd been introduced, Carole went to get the woman a drink, just a mineral water with ice and lemon. And they thought they might as well order food at the same time so all three opted for the recommended Dover sole.

As she returned from the bar, Carole saw that Philly and Jude were deep in conversation. She felt a familiar pang that was almost too resigned to be jealousy, just a wish that she had her neighbour's ability to put people at their ease. For Carole dialogue rarely flowed, it was something that had to be carefully constructed and worked at.

But whatever intimacies the two women may have been sharing up until that point, Jude immediately moved on to the subject of *Quiet Harbour*. Carole began by saying how grateful she was for the opportunity to use the beach hut.

'No problem,' said Philly wryly. 'I'm afraid I'm not

going to need it now. And I need the money.' So she wasn't attempting to hide her financial problems.

'But Carole did find something odd in the beach hut when she got there,' prompted Jude, and Carole repeated exactly what she had seen in the place.

'A fire?' asked Philly in puzzlement.

'Yes. A fire which had been lit underneath the floor. And which could have caused a lot of damage if someone hadn't put it out. You didn't notice that when you were last there, did you, Philly?'

'No, certainly not. Mind you, it is a month or so since I was at *Quiet Harbour*. We only went a few times after our rental had been confirmed. We went to kit it out with everything, but then . . . I mean, I've walked past it often enough since then with the dogs, but I haven't gone inside. Not since . . .' Her silence was eloquent of the pain she still felt about her boy-friend's departure.

Jude broke in gently, asking, 'Have you heard much talk in Smalting about vandalism to the beach huts?'

Philly shook her head. 'Nothing specific I can think of. I mean, there are always plenty of old farts sound-ing off in The Crab Inn about the disgraceful, loutish behaviour of the young, but it all seems to be pretty generalized, you know, how the country's gone to pot since the war and how they should bring back national service. Anyway, that lot of old fogies would regard dropping a lolly stick on the prom as vandalism.'

'How many keys are there to *Quiet Harbour?*' asked Carole suddenly.

'We were given two when we signed for it. I presume the Council keep duplicates in case they need access.'

'Jude only passed one on to me.'

'Yes, well . . .' The blush on the girl's cheeks stood out against the whiteness of her hair. 'I had one and, er, Mark had the other.'

'So you reckon he went off with his when he left?'

'I don't know. I expect he did.'

'Haven't you looked through his things?'

'He didn't leave that much and . . .' Emotion threatened. 'No, I haven't looked through his things.'

'So he probably still has got his key?'

Jude, whose brown eyes had been flashing messages to Carole to soften up her interrogation, interceded. 'I don't see that who had keys matters much, because the fire was clearly started from outside the hut.'

'Yes, I'm sorry. I was just asking for information.' Carole had got the bit between her teeth and was not about to back off from what she was beginning to think of as her investigation. 'So, if you haven't been in *Quiet Harbour* recently, Philly, presumably it wasn't you who put down the carpet?'

'Carpet?' the young woman repeated wretchedly.

'Yes, the green carpet that was laid over the floorboards.'

'Oh, *that* carpet,' said Philly, although Carole felt sure she was hearing of it for the first time. 'Yes, we had it ready to put down there.'

'But you didn't put it down?'

'What do you mean?'

'It had been put down after the fire, because the carpet was unmarked. So, if you haven't been to the beach hut since the fire, it means you can't have put it down.'

'Oh, I'm sorry, you had me confused,' said Philly, apparently relieved that she now understood the line of questioning. 'Yes, I did put the carpet down. I'd forgotten. I just dropped in one morning last week when I was walking the dogs, and the carpet was rolled up in there, so I unrolled it and laid it down.'

'And you didn't notice that the floorboards had been burnt through?'

'No, I didn't,' replied Philly, having regained her self-possession.

Carole opened her mouth for another question, but caught the deterrent look in Jude's eye and restrained herself. At that moment the direction of the conversation was diverted by the arrival of their Dover soles, served by a grinning and pigtailed Zosia who greeted Carole and Jude warmly.

When talk resumed, it was about the differences between Smalting and Fethering, a subject on which Philly Rose had some amusing insights. Though even humour could not disguise her underlying melancholy. She was in a state of shock, nearly two months on and still unable to come to terms with no longer having Mark in her life.

'Sometimes,' she admitted, 'I do find the gentility of Smalting almost suffocating. It's like being permanently at a posh dinner party. I'm constantly afraid of saying the wrong thing. And as a result there's a strong temptation to say or do something totally outrageous.'

'Fethering can be a bit like that too,' said Jude.

'Can it?' asked Carole, genuinely surprised.

'Oh, come on, some of the types round the Yacht Club are pretty stuffy, not to mention all the old biddies who play bridge every afternoon.'

'Yes, I suppose so.'

'Anyway, Carole and I aren't like that,' said Jude with a grin. 'We are representatives of the Bohemian sector of Fethering.'

Her neighbour didn't think that was probably true, not of herself anyway. It was certainly the first time in her life that anyone had ever described Carole Seddon as 'Bohemian' and though she suspected that Jude was teasing, she found she was rather attracted to the idea.

'Do you find that the locals in Smalting have accepted you, Philly?' asked Jude.

'Oh, I don't think "accepted" quite. That takes a good few years.'

'And they'd feel happier if your family had been there for three generations,' suggested Carole.

'Well, no, not really, because none of the people in Smalting have actually been there that long. House prices are far too high for the locals. The place has been bought up mostly by retired couples with whacking great pensions. Mind you, even if they've only been there a couple of years, they still make you feel your lowly status as an "incomer".'

'Does it get you down?' asked Jude gently.

That prompted a rueful grin from Philly. 'It used not

too. We used to find it quite funny, giggle about it. But that was . . . well . . . It does get me down a bit. Doesn't take much, I'm afraid, to get me down these days.' Again Carole and Jude could sense the depth of her pain.

Conversation flowed easily enough for the rest of the meal, but they kept to uncontroversial subjects of local interest. When Jude raised the question of dessert or coffee, Philly Rose looked at her watch and said, 'Sorry, I must dash. I have actually – thank God – had a commission designing a brochure and I'm up against a deadline.'

'Good you've got some work,' said Jude.

'Yes. Anyway, must be off.' She reached for a wallet in the back pocket of her white jeans. 'Now how much will my share be?'

'No, my idea, my treat,' said Jude.

'Well, if you're sure . . .' But Philly didn't take much convincing. 'I'm very grateful, because things—'

'It's fine,' Jude interrupted sensitively. 'By the way, when we last spoke you said you were thinking of selling the house. Is that still your plan?'

'I think it must be. I can't really see much alter-native.' And a new level of bleakness came into her brown eyes.

'Things'll sort themselves out,' said Jude.

'Yeah.' Philly's response was almost brusque, as if she was embarrassed by having shown how much she was hurting. 'Well, I can't thank you enough, Jude. And lovely to meet you, Carole. I must be off.'

'Oh, one thing,' Carole interposed. 'About the fire at *Quiet Harbour* – will you report that?'

'Report it?'

'To whoever it should be reported to. Someone at the Fether District Council, presumably.'

'Oh.' Philly seemed nonplussed. Clearly the idea didn't appeal to her. 'Would you mind doing that, Carole? I mean, you're the one who's renting the beach hut now.'

'Yes, but am I renting it officially? I mean, as far as the Fether District Council is concerned?'

'They are aware that I've made an agreement with you.'

Are they? thought Carole. I wish I'd known that earlier. It would have saved me a good deal of anxiety. 'So it's all official, is it?'

'Well . . . sort of.'

'What does that mean?'

'The guy who looks after the beach huts for the Council – his name's Kelvin Southwest – said he shouldn't really allow it, but he'd stretch a point.'

'Why?'

Philly Rose blushed. 'Well, I'm almost embarrassed to say this, but I think it was because he took a shine to me.'

'Oh?'

'Yes, I'm rather afraid our Kelvin sees himself as something of a "ladies' man".'

'Oh?'

'Anyway, Carole, would you mind contacting him about the fire? His number's on the Fether District Council website. Go into "Leisure" and he's under "Outdoor Recreation Office".'

After Philly had left the Crown and Anchor, Carole looked beadily at Jude. 'She's hiding something.'

'What do you mean?'

'That business about the carpet in *Quiet Harbour* . . . She had no idea that it was there.'

'So?'

'Well, that means, as I say, that she's hiding something.'

'Look, Carole, the poor thing's in a bad state. She's been recently dumped by the man she thought she was going to spend the rest of her life with. The last thing she needs at the moment is you badgering her.'

'I didn't badger her.'

'I don't know what else you'd call it – asking her how many keys there were to the beach hut. It was like an interrogation.'

'Hm,' said Carole rather grumpily. 'Usually you're supportive when we're involved in one of our investigations.'

'Yes, I usually am. And I would be in this case too but for the fact that at the moment we don't have an investigation.'

'I wouldn't be so sure about that,' said Carole darkly.

Chapter Six

Carole could see what Philly Rose had meant when she described Kelvin Southwest as 'something of a ladies' man'. It was definitely how he appeared to view himself, though the jury was out on how most other people might see him.

He was tubby, probably early fifties, and had taken the ill-advised course adopted by so many men going thin on top. He had grown a goatee. His remaining hair was fair and fluffy and so was the beard. It weakened rather than strengthened the line of his jaw.

He wore a light blue polo shirt with the Fether District Council logo embroidered on to it, and tightly cut navy shorts, which somehow seemed wrong to Carole. All right, he was part of the Council's Leisure Department, but she still had difficulty in taking seriously an official in shorts. Kelvin Southwest's chubby legs were hairless and pale and ended in leather sandals worn over short white socks. The combination made it even more difficult to take him seriously.

On the phone they'd arranged to meet at *Quiet Harbour* at eleven o'clock on the following day, the Wednesday. The idea of Jude joining Carole had not even been mooted. For one thing, she had a client booked in that morning for treatment to painful knee joints. And for another, Jude didn't share her neighbour's conviction that they were at the commencement of another investigation.

Pathologically punctual as ever, Carole had the Renault parked by the promenade and was standing outside the beach hut at ten to eleven. Gulliver wandered down by the shoreline, intrigued by a whole new palette of smells.

Of course Carole could have unlocked the hut, but something told her she should wait until Kelvin Southwest's arrival. She felt rather foolish, just standing there, particularly as she knew that anyone less uptight than Carole Seddon would have kicked their shoes off and sat down on the sand to wait. She wished she'd brought *The Times* crossword with her.

Kelvin Southwest arrived about ten minutes past eleven, carrying a plastic-covered clipboard. He made no apologies for his lateness, but stretched out a hand, saying, 'Carole, how nice to see you. Now I didn't get it on the phone. Am I talking to Mrs or Miss Seddon?'

'Mrs,' replied Carole, a trifle frostily.

'Lucky Mr Seddon,' said Kelvin Southwest with what he must for some reason have thought was a seductive smile.

'I'm divorced.' That was even frostier.

'Ah-hah, on the market again. That's going to be good news for someone.' If there was one masculine quality Carole Seddon disliked it was roguishness. And she would have thought her expression made that clear. But evidently it didn't, as Kelvin Southwest continued, 'So you're the lovely lady who is now the tenant of *Quiet Harbour*.'

'Yes. Miss Rose assured me that you knew all about the handover and were quite happy about it.' He looked at her with an enigmatic grin. 'I mean that you said it was quite legal.'

'Ooh, I wouldn't go so far as to say "legal", Mrs Seddon.' He then compounded his roguishness by winking. 'Let's say I was happy to sanction the arrangement. I won't tell on you.' He punctuated this piece of schoolboy slang with a chuckle. 'I can never say no to a pretty woman, you know.'

'Ah.'

'Still, unfortunately I can't spend my morning gazing into your blue eyes – much as I would like to.'

Carole very nearly made a sharp rejoinder to that and might well have done so, had not Gulliver, curious about who his mistress was talking to, at that moment bounded up to her.

'Is this your dog?'

'Yes.'

'Ah.' He raised a plump finger and shook it in mock reproof. 'Naughty, naughty.'

'What?'

'During the summer months dogs should be kept on a lead on Smalting Beach. Fether District Council regulations.'

'There's no sign up to say that.'

'No, I agree there isn't. It's just one of those things that everyone who uses the beach knows.'

'Well, I don't.'

'Clearly, Mrs Seddon. And I'd love to make an exception to the rule – especially when it concerns such a lovely lady as yourself – but I'm afraid in this instance my hands are tied. It's not like you taking over the rental. With dogs it'd be the other beach users who'd object, you see. They'd accuse me of favouritism, and I can't have that, can I?'

'I'll put his lead on,' said Carole shortly. 'Come on, Gulliver, come here, boy.' Once a rather miffed dog was secured, she turned back to the Fether District Council official. 'I believe we were discussing the legality of my having taken over the rental of this beach hut from Philly Rose, Mr Southwest.'

'Yes, of course we were. And I have already told you I have no problems with that. Waiting lists can always be circumvented, you know, for the right person.' He leered at her. 'But I am here this morning as a result of your phone call yesterday. I am employed by the Fether District Council to do a job, and that is what I must do.' He somehow managed to make it sound as though Carole was preventing him from discharging his duty. 'Now, Mrs Seddon, you spoke of a fire having been lit under this beach hut . . .'

'Yes. Do you want to see inside?' She reached into her trouser pocket for the key.

'Don't worry, I have a set of my own. If you don't mind, I'd rather examine the damage from the outside first.'

'Fine.' Carole led the way to the back of the hut. 'As you see, it's here, under this corner.'

Kelvin Southwest sank into a crouch, a movement which threatened to split his tight blue shorts. He inspected the burn marks and poked a stick at the scorched rags beneath.

'Vandals, do you reckon?' asked Carole.

He stood up self-importantly to his full height, about level with her shoulder. 'Possibly,' he replied. 'I will complete my examination of the damage before committing myself to a theory as to what actually happened.'

He moved back to the front of *Quiet Harbour*, took a bunch of keys out of his pocket and selected one. 'This was meant to be the master key for all of the Smalting beach huts. Originally all of the padlocks were from the same manufacturer, so although they all had individually different locks, this little baby opened all of them. Still, after a time the salt gets into some of the mechanisms and they sieze up. People who replace the padlocks on their huts – and I can understand why they sometimes have to do that – are meant to lodge a spare key with me at the Council offices. But do they? Do they hell!'

'Fortunately, *Quiet Harbour* still has its original padlocks.' Sure enough, they gave easily to his master key. 'Now I will examine the interior.'

In his official, professional mode Kelvin Southwest clearly imagined himself to be the archetype of reliability and efficiency. That wasn't how he came across to Carole, though. To her he was just a pompous little jobsworth.

She stayed outside watching as he entered the hut

and, following her movements of the previous day, moved across to the corner and flipped back a triangle of carpet. He again crouched, giving her a further unwanted view of straining shorts and builder's crack. On rising, he was smugly silent as he made notes on his clipboard.

'Someone put the fire out,' reiterated Carole. 'Someone must've—'

Kelvin Southwest raised a hand to silence her and she was duly – though somewhat irritatedly – silent while he completed his notes. Then he looked down at the floorboards and squatted, offering yet more builder's crack.

He rose to his feet and looked at Carole sternly. 'You haven't been fooling with these floorboards, have you?'

'No, of course I haven't.'

'Because someone has hammered some new nails into them.'

'Yes, I noticed that. I was going to—'

He raised his hand again and, to Carole's annoyance, she was again silent.

'I think I know what we should do next,' he announced.

'What?'

His chubby face crinkled again into the expression that he believed to be charming as he said, 'I think we should go and have a cup of tea and talk about things, Mrs Seddon. Or may I call you Carole?'

She wanted to say, 'Mrs Seddon to you,' but hadn't quite got the nerve. Instead, she heard herself saying, 'Yes, of course, Mr Southwest.'

'My friends call me Kel.'

Well, if you think I'm going to call you Kel you've got another think coming, was the thought in Carole's mind as, to her fury, she said, 'Oh, right you are, Kel.'

Kelvin Southwest clearly prided himself on his local knowledge. Assuring Carole that he knew the best tea shop in Smalting, he led her straight to The Copper Kettle on the promenade. She did not think that the guiding hand he occasionally put on her hips was strictly necessary, but he did it in such a way that it could have been accidental. In each instance the contact was so brief that it would have looked excessive for her to have made a fuss.

The flirtatious way with which he greeted the owner and staff of The Copper Kettle showed him to be a regular, and he made such a big deal of the treat he was offering Carole that he could have been taking her to the Savoy Grill.

'Best cup of tea in Smalting,' he assured her. 'And the prettiest waitresses,' he added with a wink to one particularly drab specimen. 'So, a pot of tea for two then.'

'I'd rather have coffee,' said Carole.

'Oh, very well. How would you like it?' he asked. 'A tall skinny latte?'

'Just ordinary coffee, thank you. Black.'

'Right you are.' He favoured the waitress with one of his roguish smiles. 'So, beautiful, that's a pot of tea for one and a black coffee. And would you like something to eat, Carole? Best cakes and pastries in Smalting here, you know.'

'Just the coffee, thank you.'

'Oh. Well, I'll have one of your Swiss buns, angel cake. Because I'm not sweet enough already,' he simpered to the waitress.

This tiresome little ritual concluded and when the girl went off to get their order, Carole became brisk and businesslike. 'Was there some reason why you wanted to talk to me further?'

Kelvin's face took on an expression of mock hurt. 'Does there have to be a reason? Isn't it enough that I should want to spend time with a beautiful woman?'

Her first instinct was to say that she wasn't a beautiful woman, but Carole curbed it. She couldn't face the inevitable blandishments and reassurances that such an assertion would provoke. 'So what is it you want to talk to me about?'

He again looked offended by her directness. 'Well, of course, about the beach hut. About *Quiet Harbour.*'

'Yes?'

The order arrived, so Kelvin Southwest broke off for a smirk at the waitress and a 'Thank you, my lovely'. He then took a large bite from his Swiss bun, whose icing was soft and left a pink frosting on the moustache of his goatee.

'So what about the beach hut?' Carole went on gracelessly.

'Well, the fire damage will have to be repaired.'

'Obviously. And I assume the repairs will be organized by someone from Fether District Council?'

'Not just someone, Carole.' He beamed as he pointed a chubby finger at his chest. 'By me. By yours truly, Kelvin Southwest.'

'Oh, well, good. How long do you think it'll take?'

'I'll have to get on to the contractors. Depends how busy they are. But with a bit of luck they'll get it done within the month.'

'Within the month? That's no good to me. My daughter-in-law and granddaughter are coming to stay with me on Sunday week.'

'Oh dear, oh dear. I suppose I could tell the contractors it was top priority.'

'If you would, I'd be most grateful.'

He shook his head sceptically. 'I still doubt if they could do it before Sunday week, though.'

'But that's the main reason I took over the beach hut from Philly Rose. So that I'd have it for my granddaughter.'

'Well . . .' Kelvin Southwest stroked his wispy goatee with deliberation. 'We are presented with rather a dilemma, aren't we? And that dilemma is not made easier by the fact that your taking over the rental of *Quiet Harbour* from Philly Rose was not entirely within the strict rules of Fether District Council for the letting of beach huts.'

'But you told me that—'

He raised a placatory hand. 'Don't worry. It's down to me to make that kind of decision. The beach huts are really my empire, you know.'

This was said without irony. He really did believe what he was saying. Carole got the feeling that, to his own mind, the most suitable adjectives to describe Kelvin Southwest might include 'Napoleonic' and 'Churchillian'.

'So,' he went on, 'if I've given my approval of Philly Rose's transfer of the rental to you, that is a decision by which I will stand.'

'Oh, thank you so much, Mr Southwest.'

'Kel, please, Kel.'

'Very well,' said Carole, hiding her distaste, 'Kel.'

He looked at her with an expression of winsome complicity. 'As I may have mentioned, I'm a bit of a sucker when there's a pretty woman involved.'

Carole didn't know whether he was referring to Philly or to her – or to both of them – so her only reaction was a little nervous giggle.

Enjoying the teasing out of his narrative, Kelvin Southwest put the last piece of his Swiss bun into his mouth and masticated it thoroughly before he went on, 'Now I'm a reasonable man, Carole, and when I can I like to help people out – particularly of course when they're pretty women – and I think I can see a way round your little problem . . .'

'Oh?'

'Yes, indeed. You scratch my back and I'll scratch yours.' Carole could only think at that moment of one prospect that appealed to her less than scratching the plump back of Kelvin Southwest. And that was having hers scratched by him.

'You see, Carole, as I said, the beach huts are my empire, and in that empire what I say goes. If I get an applicant for a beach hut who I don't think to be a suitable tenant – and it does happen more often than you might imagine – then I tell them to get lost. Well, no, I don't, not in so many words. I tell them that

44

there are sadly no beach huts available, even if there are. So you see, though I'm employed under the broad umbrella of Fether District Council, within my empire I make my own rules.'

He paused, as if expecting some commendation for this statement, and Carole found herself asking rather fatuously, 'And why not?'

'So, in the same way, Carole, if I were to decide to offer you the use of another vacant hut here on Smalting Beach while *Quiet Harbour* is being repaired, well, that could be done . . . just on my say-so. It would be up to me to make that decision.'

'Good. Well, I mean, if you could see your way to—'

Again he raised a podgy hand and she was deferentially silent. 'As I said, I'm always happy to oblige when there's a pretty woman involved.' Yes, as you said rather a lot of times, thought Carole. 'So I think that could be the solution, don't you?'

'That you give me the use of an empty beach hut?'

'Yes.'

'Well, that would be very generous of you.'

'I would regard it as the least I could do, Carole. You took over *Quiet Harbour* from Philly Rose in the belief that you were taking over a perfect working beach hut. You then discovered that it had a hole burned in its floor. Repairing that is within the remit of Fether District Council – or, to be more specific, of me, Kelvin Southwest. It is not your fault that your beach hut has been damaged and you have paid the rental money to Philly Rose in good faith. I would be in dereliction of my duty were I not to attempt to make amends to you.'

We know all that, thought Carole impatiently. Will you please get on with it, you boring little man? 'I would, as I say, be very grateful—'

'Leave it with me,' he said magisterially. 'I will find you another beach hut here on Smalting Beach. It may not be precisely what I should do, according to the terms of my employment by Fether District Council, but it's what I'm going to do. Rules are there for the unimaginative foot soldiers of life. For a maverick free spirit like myself, they are there to be broken. And I'm always prepared to break the rules . . .' He brought out his roguish smile again '. . . particularly when there's a pretty woman involved.'

'Well, thank you,' said Carole, thinking that now he had announced what he was going to do, there was nothing to stop him doing it as soon as possible and ending what she was finding a rather awkward tête-à-tête.

But Kelvin Southwest was not yet ready to relinquish his hold on her. He wanted to luxuriate for a while in his magnanimity and her gratitude. So he favoured Carole with tales of other occasions when he'd seen his way to bending Fether District Council's rules in the matter of beach huts.

Eventually, when her eyes were in serious danger of glazing over, he paused long enough for Carole to ask, 'Will you be investigating?'

'Investigating what?' he asked, the wind temporarily taken out of his sails.

'The fire at *Quiet Harbour*. Will you be trying to find out who was responsible for it?'

'I will try. I will ask around. But without much confidence that I'll find the answer. I'm sure it was done by some kids after dark. I doubt if there were any witnesses.'

'But it looks as though someone put the fire out before it could do any more damage.'

'Maybe, but I shouldn't think anyone witnessed that action either.'

'Perhaps not.'

'And while we're talking of investigation, Carole . . .' A new beadiness came into his eyes '. . . you can assure me, can you, that you had nothing to do with the hammering in of the new nails in the floor of *Quiet Harbour*?'

'Of course I can. Yesterday morning was the first time I'd been in the place.'

'Yes, yes, right you are.' Finally he rose to his feet, saying, 'Well, Carole, would you like me to show you your new beach hut?'

'Yes, please . . . Kel.'

As she rose, he guided her out of The Copper Kettle, again with a proprietary hand on her lower back. He grinned saucily at the waitresses as they left.

'Oh, what about the bill?' asked Carole when they reached the door. 'For the tea and coffee.'

Winking at her and then at the waitress who'd served them, Kelvin Southwest said, 'Oh, I have an arrangement here. I have an arrangement in a number of places in the area, actually. I do favours for a lot

of people and they're happy to do favours for me . . .
if you know what I mean. As I said, you scratch my
back . . .' Rather than finishing the phrase, he let out a
fruity chuckle.

Carole recoiled inwardly. She hated to think what
kind of favour Kelvin Southwest might think was his
due in exchange for the favour he was doing her.

Chapter Seven

It was the kind of blazing June that got the residents of Fethering talking darkly of global warming. Mind you, every kind of climatic change got the residents of Fethering talking darkly about global warming. A thunderstorm, a heavy fall of snow, a sudden frost, even an unusually high wind, could start a lot of heads shaking in the Crown and Anchor or the local supermarket Allinstore. Like most of the English, the residents of Fethering had always used the weather as a conversational staple. But whereas the fisherman who once peopled the village would look gloomily up at the sky when they discussed it, the current inhabitants, who had just parked their 4x4s, would take on the same gloomy expressions and mention global warming. Not all of them actually believed in it, but they knew that in Fethering mentioning global warming was de rigueur.

The Thursday dawned even brighter than the previous days and Carole decided that she ought to go and investigate her new beach hut. The one to which Kelvin Southwest had given her the key had the name *Fowey* spelled out in whorls of rope on a board above its doorway. It was in every structural particular identical to *Quiet Harbour*, but Carole still felt she should check the place out. Her main aim was that, when she introduced Gaby and Lily to the delights of Smalting Beach, she should appear completely relaxed, *au fait* with the beach hut and its location. Almost an authentic hutter. She had already marked down The Copper Kettle as a good place to fill Lily up with ice creams and fizzy drinks. (She'd never allowed Stephen to have fizzy drinks when he was growing up, but her attitude to her granddaughter was more relaxed. After all, one of the essential clauses in the grandparents' charter was the right to spoil.)

There was also something new she wanted to introduce to *Fowey*. In common with *Quiet Harbour*, the hut only contained two chairs, also director's chairs, suggesting that perhaps they were equipment supplied by Fether District Council for the original renters. And it had so happened that, driving her Renault past a garden centre the previous day, Carole had seen on display a tiny child-size director's chair. Its wooden structure was painted pink and the seat and back were made of pink canvas.

The normal reaction of Carole Seddon to such an object would have been to snort while the phrase 'overpriced rubbish' formed in her mind, but the existence of Lily was having strange effects on her normal reactions. In the control of an irresistible power, she found herself parking her Renault outside the garden centre, going straight in and buying one of the small pink director's chairs. It was indeed overpriced, but Carole didn't let that worry her. She just knew that her granddaughter would love her own personal seat.

On a heady roll, she also found herself going to the Fethering Allinstore and buying a Big Beach Bucket Bag. Inside the red net sack was a big red bucket, which contained a smaller red bucket with crenellated indentations, a blue plastic spade and a selection of brightly coloured sand moulds in the shapes of a fish, a crab, a boat and a star.

Carole didn't want to risk the danger of Lily seeing these new purchases before they got to Smalting Beach, deciding that their maximum effect would be produced if her granddaughter found them when she entered the beach hut. So they needed to be planted there. Which was another reason for her to pay a visit to *Fowey* that Thursday morning. Also Gulliver could do with a change from Fethering Beach for his walk.

Just as Carole was about to leave, Jude appeared at the front door of High Tor. In deference to the weather, she only wore one chiffon scarf over her yellow T-shirt and denim skirt. Perched on her blond topknot was a battered straw hat.

'Hi, Carole,' she said. 'It's so hot I'm about to go down to the beach. I've knocked together a bit of a picnic. Do you and Gulliver fancy coming?'

'We were just about to go to the beach ourselves. But not Fethering Beach.'

'Oh?'

'Smalting. To check out my substitute beach hut.'

'And follow up on your investigation?' asked Jude teasingly.

'Who knows? Anyway, why don't you come with us?'

Fowey was not in the same row of beach huts as *Quiet Harbour*. It was in fact as far away as it could be. The three slightly curved rows of twelve units each were set in a bigger curve, forming a crescent shape, so that from their director's chairs outside *Fowey* Carole and Jude had a perfect view of the damaged hut.

It was, of course, locked shut, as were about half of the others. In front of the remainder, families spread themselves while small children made endless journeys up and down to the water. Like the nearby Fethering Beach, the one at Smalting sloped very gradually, so that at low tide a couple of hundred yards of sand were exposed. When the tide was high, it came up to the bank of shingle that protected the beach huts and the promenade.

Carole and Jude found themselves looking at a perfect English seaside scene, as featured on vintage railway posters; one that hadn't changed much for the previous fifty or sixty years, except for the ubiquitous mobiles and the white earphone leads of iPods. Another difference from the normal reality of English seaside scenes was that it wasn't raining.

Thinking back to her own childhood, Carole was also struck by the brightness of the swimwear on display. Her recollection was of a navy woollen bathing costume that clung embarrassingly to her developing figure, that tickled and felt clammy when it got wet. Watching the pubescent girls in tape-thin bikinis cavorting on Smalting Beach made her feel very old.

She wasn't made to feel younger by the behaviour of her neighbour. As soon as they'd got the director's chairs out and Carole had settled down to her crossword, Jude proceeded to remove her T-shirt and skirt. What was revealed was a turquoise two-piece costume, which did little to disguise its owner's generous proportions. Carole, who didn't carry a spare ounce of weight, still worried about her wobbly bits, but clearly Jude had no such inhibitions. And as ever, in spite of the volumes of flesh exposed, she managed to look good. A couple of passing boys in microscopic Speedos viewed her with considerable interest.

Jude caught Carole's eye and, as she so often could, seemed to intuit her friend's thoughts. 'If you've got it, flaunt it,' she shrugged. 'Haven't you brought a bathing costume with you?'

'No,' replied Carole in a manner that suggested she had been asked something much more offensive. That teenage awkwardness about her body had never quite left her, and now as a post-menopausal woman she felt far too old to start showing it off. She didn't even really like showing her legs without tights and her chosen beachwear for the day was a pair of grey slacks, a sleeveless white shirt, white socks and blue canvas shoes.

'You'll have to get hold of one before next week,' said Jude.

'What do you mean?'

'Lily's going to want her Granny to go into the sea with her, isn't she?'

'Oh. I hadn't thought of that.'

'I'm going down for a paddle,' Jude announced impetuously. And she ran over the flat sand towards the sea, setting everything jiggling, but again attracting some admiring male glances.

Carole tried to focus her mind on *The Times* crossword, but without success. She was continually distracted by the sounds and sights of the beach. And her eyes kept wandering across to the locked frontage of *Quiet Harbour*, prompting further speculations about what she had seen inside the hut.

To distract herself, she went into *Fowey* and took the small pink director's chair out of its plastic wrapping. She set it on the sand between its two grown-up counterparts and indulged in a moment of soppiness. She couldn't wait to see Lily sitting in it. She somehow just knew her granddaughter would love the thing. Then, not wishing Jude to witness her sentimentality, she folded the little chair and put it back inside.

Still restless, she gave in to the reproachful look from Gulliver, who took a pretty dim view of being tied up by his lead to a hook on the outside of the beach hut. So Carole took him for a little stroll along the curved rows of beach huts, observing as much as she could without being seen to be snooping. The one right next door to *Fowey* was called *Shrimphaven*. The doors were open, but the hut looked to be empty. As a result Carole peered in more obviously than she might have done, and was embarrassed to meet the bespectacled gaze of a young woman sitting in the shadows over an open laptop. Making an awkward cough of apology, Carole scuttled off along the line of huts.

Some of the owners she recognized from her previous visit. Outside a hut called *Mistral* an elderly couple sat on candy-striped loungers. The woman, plump, white-haired, with powdered skin like pink meringue, was contentedly working her way through a book of word searches. She looked up as Carole passed.

'Morning,' the old woman said in a comfortable, homely voice. 'I gather you've got problems with *Quiet Harbour*.'

'A bit of fire damage. Not too serious. Vandals, I suppose.'

The woman shook her head gloomily. 'Too much of that going on these days. By the way, my name's Joyce Oliver.'

'Carole Seddon.'

'And that's Lionel.' The husband she gestured to looked unsuitably dressed for the beach. Though he was in shirt sleeves, the shirt was a formal white one, and his charcoal trousers with neat creases looked as though they were the bottom half of a suit. Over the back of his lounger hung a matching jacket. His shoes, black lace-ups with toecaps, were highly polished. Beside him on the sand was a copy of the *Daily Mail*, but he wasn't reading it. He was just looking out to sea with an expression of infinite bleakness.

'In a world of his own, as ever,' said Joyce Oliver with a little chuckle, as Gulliver tugged on his lead to get moving. 'Well, I'm sure we'll see you again, Carole.

We're here most days in the summer, and particularly at the moment because we're in the process of moving house. Place where we brought up the kids is far too big for us now. It's a wrench leaving the house, but has to be done. Lionel can't manage the garden any more. It's his pride and joy – the work he's put into the landscaping and the water features you wouldn't believe. But it's too much for him now and he hates the idea of having someone else doing it for him, so the move does make good sense.

'Anyway, we're not quite out of the old house, and there's lots of work needs doing on the new one – well, you can't really call it a house, it's only a flat – so coming down here to the hut is quite a relief, let me tell you.'

'Yes, it's a lovely spot,' said Carole, providing a predictable comment on Smalting Beach. Then with a nod to Joyce Oliver, she continued along the line of beach huts.

Chapter Eight

Carole was surprised that the man in the next hut appeared to recognize her. She had no recollection of ever having seen him before. Rising from a wooden folding chair, he said, 'Good morning. You must be Mrs Seddon.'

His beach hut had not been open on her previous visit, because Carole would certainly have remembered it if it had been. The opened doors revealed, fixed on to their interiors and continuing on all three walls of the hut, a huge array of naval memorabilia. Highly polished brass port and starboard lights were attached to the inside of their appropriate doors. There were also anchors, ancient quadrants and sextants, watercolours of ships, model ships, ships in bottles, framed hat ribbons, wooden dead eyes, cleats, badges, flags, boards with demonstration knots pinned on them, and green glass floats for fishing nets. In pride of place at the back of the hut stood a brass-studded wooden ship's wheel. Over the doors was fixed a worn brass plaque bearing the name: *The Bridge*.

Slightly fazed by the display, Carole acknowledged that she was indeed Mrs Seddon. The gentleman who'd asked the question was of a piece with the contents of his hut. Probably in his early seventies, he had a full grey beard in the style of George V. He wore a blazer with embossed brass buttons and on its breast pocket a badge featuring a lot of woven gold wire. His dark blue tie also bore some naval insignia.

Offering a hairy hand to Carole, the man identified himself. 'Good morning, my name is Reginald Flowers and I am President of the Smalting Beach Hut Association.'

It was then that Carole noticed he was not alone. Sitting on another folding chair beside him was a chubby little woman with faded red hair and thick-lensed glasses. Open on her lap was a folded-back spiral reporter's notebook in which she'd apparently been writing shorthand.

'And this is Dora,' said Reginald Flowers with the utmost condescension, 'who is my secretary.'

'Well, Reginald, that's not strictly accurate,' the woman objected rather feebly.

'What do you mean?'

'Well, I'm not *your* secretary. I'm secretary of the Smalting Beach Hut Association.'

'It comes to the same thing, Dora.'

'No, it doesn't really.'

'Yes, it does. Anyway, I need to speak to Mrs Seddon. So could you please go off and type up those letters as soon as possible?'

'I'll do them this evening. I only came down this morning to have a nice day in my beach hut.' She smiled myopically at Carole and pointed along the row. 'Mine's the third one along. It's called *Cape of Good Hope.*'

'Oh. How nice,' said Carole.

'And obviously my full name isn't just Dora. It's Dora Pinchbeck.'

'Ah. Well—'

'Dora,' said Reginald Flowers firmly, 'I would be very grateful if you could do those letters straight away, and *then* you can enjoy your day in the beach hut.'

'Well, I'd really rather—'

'*If* you would be so kind,' came the implacable order.

'Oh, very well.' And Dora shuffled her notebook and pen into her bag. 'I'll have to lock up *Cape of Good Hope* before I go.'

'That will be quite permissible,' her magnanimous boss assured her.

With a long-suffering sigh, Dora Pinchbeck scuttled off to her beach hut.

'And bring the letters here for me to sign as soon as you've finished them!' Reginald Flowers called after her. Then he turned back to bestow a gracious smile on Carole. 'As I say, I am the President of the Smalting Beach Hut Association. As such, I do of course know everything that goes on in these beach huts.'

'I'm sure you do. Anyway, nice to meet you.' Nodding towards the collection in the hut, Carole said, 'An ex-naval man, I assume?'

His face darkened. 'No, I did not myself in fact serve before the mast, though many of my ancestors did. Let's just say that the history of the British Navy has been a lifelong interest of mine and one that in retirement I have been able to pursue more thoroughly.'

Carole was about to respond: 'I'd never have guessed,' but decided it might sound flippant to someone who was as clearly obsessed as Reginald Flowers. So instead she commented on the splendour of his hoard. 'Do you really leave it here all the time? Isn't there a terrible risk of it all being stolen?'

'No, Mrs Seddon. Although I do take the collection home during the winter months, there is in fact no danger of any of it being stolen. That is what the Smalting Beach Hut Association is there for.'

'Oh?'

'During the summer months the SBHA – as we call it – appoints a security officer, whose job it is to patrol the beach huts and ensure that their security is maintained.'

'What a good idea. Isn't that rather expensive, though?'

'The SBHA has funds to cover the costs.'

'And where do those funds come from?'

'Some from Fether District Council.' A shadow crossed his face, as though he regretted having to take help from that source. 'One of the first actions of the SBHA when I formed it was to lobby the Council for a security officer. And I won that little battle, as I have won many other set-tos with Fether District Council.' His face darkened again. 'Though sadly they would not let me sit on the selection board when the security officer was appointed.'

'So are you saying that the Council supports the SBHA financially?'

'Only a very little. They do no more than they absolutely have to, and even that is after a lot of lobbying from us . . . well, from me usually. No, the costs of running the SBHA are raised largely from subscriptions.'

'Oh.' Suddenly Carole realized how she should respond to this prompt. 'Well, I should pay a subscription, shouldn't I?'

'Yes, that would be a good thing. The SBHA exists to look after the concerns of all beach hut users. And your subscription also entitles you to receive our regular newsletter, *The Hut Parade*.'

'What an amusing title,' Carole lied.

'Well, we like it.' The smile that accompanied these words left no doubt that it was Reginald Flowers who had thought up the name for the newsletter. Carole reckoned he was probably its editor too. 'Your subscription also secures for you a complimentary annual tide table. All new members get that.' There was disapproval in Reginald Flowers's voice as he continued, 'I gather you have taken over the rental of *Quiet Harbour* from Miss Rose.'

'Yes, but it's all been cleared with Kelvin Southwest from the Fether District Council.'

A cynical light came into Reginald Flowers's watery blue eyes. 'Oh yes, well, it's very easy to get things cleared with Mr Southwest, isn't it? Particularly if you're a woman.'

Now she had formed an estimation of Reginald

Flowers's character, Carole was unsurprised to find there was friction between him and Kelvin Southwest. Two control freaks for a single beach is probably one too many.

'He was very reasonable about it,' she said.

That prompted a sardonic chuckle. 'Oh yes, I'm sure he was. Always ready to do little favours for people, our Kelvin, isn't he? Provided of course that the people are prepared to do little favours for him.' Carole didn't think any comment was appropriate; she mustn't be seen to be taking sides in what was clearly an ongoing conflict. 'One day,' Reginald Flowers continued ominously, 'one day our Kelvin is going to take one favour too many . . .'

'Oh?'

'There's a very fine line, Mrs Seddon, between co-operation and corruption, you know. Still, it wouldn't be the first time a local government officer has taken a backhander, would it?'

Once again Carole decided not to comment. She moved the subject on. 'If you let me know how much I owe you for the subscription, I'll write you a cheque straight away.'

'The subscription is twenty pounds per annum.'

'Oh well, I think I've probably got that in cash. I'm just going for a little walk, but when I get back to my hut I'll find my handbag and bring the money over to you.' Carole suddenly realized that, in spite of Reginald Flowers's reassurances about the security of the Smalting Beach, she had been very foolish to leave her bag in the hut. She looked over to *Fowey*, but was relieved to see that Jude, still dressed only in her bikini, was sprawled in one of the director's chairs.

'There is a form for you to fill in,' announced Reginald Flowers. Oh yes, of course there would be. Carole somehow got the feeling that becoming a member of any organization run by him would involve a lot of form-filling. He bustled about inside his naval museum and emerged holding a badly printed form covered with lots of boxes that Carole could see would be too small for the information they were meant to contain. And the form was three pages long.

But she took it with appropriate gratitude and said she'd bring it back with the money when she'd filled it in. 'I'll do it the moment I get back to the hut,' she said, gesturing in the direction of *Fowey*.

Reginald Flowers looked puzzled. 'I understood that you were taking over Miss Rose's hut. That's over there.'

So he doesn't know everything that goes on in the beach huts, does he? Carole guessed he didn't know about the fire under *Quiet Harbour*, and for some reason she didn't feel inclined to tell him about it. All she said was, 'There was a bit of a problem with that one, so while it's being sorted out, Kelvin Southwest's let me use *Fowey*.'

'Has he?' said Reginald Flowers, as if hearing of another example in the long list of the Council official's transgressions.

Carole continued her walk. The hut adjacent to *Quiet Harbour* was still being ruled by the poisonous matriarch whom Carole had seen on her previous visit. The downtrodden glumness on the faces of her son Gavin, his wife Nell, and their children Tristram and Hermione, showed that their stay with Granny was proving to be a very long week indeed. Carole once again made all kinds of vows to herself about the way she was going to behave to Lily.

And then she was once again outside *Quiet Harbour*. She didn't want to make a show of inspecting it, so she walked on past. But there was still something intriguing about the place, oddities that needed explanation, a sense of unfinished business.

Chapter Nine

The picnic lunch that Jude had prepared was very
good. A chicken salad with some nice crusty bread,
suitably light for the hot weather. And, needless to say,
being Jude, she'd brought a bottle of Chilean Chardonnay in a cool bag. Carole said she'd just have one glass,
but somehow they managed to finish the bottle. And
sitting outside *Fowey* in their director's chairs in the
sunlight, both women found themselves dozing off.
To Carole it all felt titillatingly decadent.

She hadn't slept for long when she woke with
a start. There had been no sound, nothing to wake
her but her Calvinist conscience. In the other chair
Jude still slept, her large, sagging body as relaxed as
a child's. Carole looked across Smalting Beach with
half-closed eyes, the sunlight glowing red through her
lids. And noticed to her surprise that the doors to *Quiet
Harbour* were open.

Wide awake now, she saw Kelvin Southwest
emerge from the hut with another man dressed in
jeans and a worn T-shirt, who was carrying a clipboard
and a tape measure. They had a little discussion on
the sand, then the other man moved purposefully up

the beach to the promenade. Kelvin Southwest didn't follow him. With trepidation Carole realized that he was coming straight towards *Fowey*. She straightened in her chair and picked up *The Times* crossword, unwilling to look as if she'd just woken up.

Reginald Flowers was still sitting on his wooden chair outside *The Bridge* and Kelvin Southwest had to walk directly in front of him, but neither man made any gesture of recognition or greeting.

The beach hut emperor of Fether District Council was dressed in the same uniform of polo shirt and shorts as he had been on Tuesday, but this afternoon he looked hot and bothered. He still greeted Carole with another of his roguish smiles, however, together with a hearty, 'Good afternoon, good afternoon.'

'Good afternoon, Mr Southwest.'

'Kel. Remember, you're Carole and I'm Kel.'

'Yes . . .' she forced herself to say it '. . . Kel.'

Their voices had woken Jude from her doze and she looked around blearily. Carole hoped her friend hadn't heard her using the word 'Kel'.

'And I am the bearer of glad tidings,' he went on. 'Because it's for *you*, Carole, that I have moved heaven and earth to get the repairs to *Quiet Harbour* done as soon as possible. In fact, I've just been talking to the contractor who's doing the job – someone local I've known for a long time. I put a lot of work his way and he . . . well, let's say we scratch each other's backs, just as I said it would give me great pleasure to scratch yours.'

Behind him Jude had clearly managed to identify

Kelvin Southwest from Carole's description, and she was grinning like a Cheshire cat. Carole tried to avoid catching her friend's eye, fearful of starting to laugh.

'Well, anyway, my friend the contractor has had a look at the damage to *Quiet Harbour*. He reckons it's only three boards that'll need replacing and not much more than touching up the paint on the outside. So he's just going to get his tools and he'll be starting the job straight away.' He gave her a wink, which fortunately Jude couldn't see, or that would have really set them off. 'So who says Kel doesn't sort things out quickly for his favourites, eh?'

'I'm sure nobody's ever said that, er . . . Kel.'

'Well, let me tell you, Carole, having moved heaven and earth for you, I could do with a little break. How would you like to join me again at The Copper Kettle?'

'Well, that's very kind, but I have just had lunch. And then again I am here with my friend.'

He turned around to where Carole indicated, apparently noticing Jude for the first time. She rose from her director's chair, grinned at him and said, 'I'm Jude.'

'Kelvin Southwest,' he responded, almost brusquely, then turned straight back to Carole. 'So . . . do you fancy something in The Copper Kettle?'

'As I say, I've just had lunch. I really don't want anything at the moment, thank you.'

'Oh. All right. Very well. I'll see you soon no doubt, Carole.' And, clearly put out, the little man stumped on his little legs up towards the promenade.

Carole now dared to catch Jude's eye and both of them burst out laughing. And Carole was faced with the amazing fact that she had finally met a man who fancied her more than he fancied Jude.

But the thought didn't comfort her as much as it might have done. After all, the man in question was Kelvin Southwest.

The Times crossword was a particularly tough one that day. Or maybe the wine and the distractions of the beach prevented Carole from giving it her full concentration. She kept looking over to see what was happening at *Quiet Harbour*.

The contractor's van must have been parked nearby, because he was back with his toolbox and some planks very soon after Kelvin Southwest's departure. He went inside the hut, occasionally reappearing to prop up against its frontage the roll of carpet and the floorboards he'd removed.

Then he came out empty-handed and talked on his mobile phone. Shortly after this Kelvin Southwest returned to *Quiet Harbour* – maybe the contractor's call had been to him. The two men went inside. It was some minutes before they re-emerged. By now the little man from Fether District Council seemed very agitated. He paced up and down as he too made a call on his mobile.

It was less than a quarter of an hour before the police arrived. Two uniforms in a patrol car. They joined up with Kelvin and the contractor, and all four went into the hut.

It was half an hour before the other police vehicles, which must have been summoned, started to appear. Some of their occupants began erecting white screens around *Quiet Harbour*, while four polite but firm WPCs walked along the shoreline asking all the holidaymakers to leave Smalting Beach.

Chapter Ten

Human remains. That was all that was announced on the local television news the following morning, the Friday. Police had been summoned to Smalting Beach in West Sussex following the discovery of what turned out to be human remains under a beach hut there.

The minute the bulletin had finished Carole went straight round to Woodside Cottage. Jude looked bleary and voluptuous in a floaty, yellow silk dressing gown, having just stumbled out of bed. Still, catching her at that time meant she'd got the coffee on.

'Did you see the news?' asked Carole.

'No. I'm still hardly awake.'

Carole relayed the minimum of information the television had provided. 'But it must have something to do with the fire,' she went on. 'If there were human remains in *Quiet Harbour*, then someone must've tried to set fire to the place to remove evidence of their crime.'

'What crime?'

'Well, murder obviously.'

Jude smiled indulgently at her friend. 'You don't think you're getting a bit ahead of yourself here, do you? Human remains don't have to be the result of a murder.'

'Oh, but in this case they must be.'

'Why?'

'Well, because . . .' Carole was nonplussed, but only for a moment. 'Because that's why there were new nails in the floorboards. The murderer had taken the floorboards up so that he could reach down to bury his victim in the sand and shingle underneath the beach hut, then he'd replaced them and lit the fire to destroy the evidence of what he'd done.'

Jude grinned in a rather infuriating way. 'Just a minute, Carole. I thought you were supposed to be the logical one in our relationship, and the logic in what you've just said contains serious faults.'

'No, it doesn't,' protested Carole, frustrated by Jude's atypical unwillingness to catch her enthusiasm.

'Listen. Let's just for a moment accept your unlikely assertion that there is a murder – and therefore a murderer – involved. Now he could have done one of two things. He could, yes, have taken up the floorboards to bury his victim in the sand and shingle under the beach hut. But if he'd done that, the last thing he would have wanted to do would be to set fire to the place. By doing that he would immediately be drawing attention to where he'd hidden his victim.'

'Well, I—'

'Oh, come on, Carole. If the fire had taken hold and *Quiet Harbour* had gone up in flames, whoever cleared up the debris would almost definitely have discovered evidence of recent digging and investigated that – and found the body.'

'So what are you saying?' asked a rather disgruntled Carole. She knew Jude was right and felt sheepish about having let her excitement outrun her logic. It was a very un-Carole Seddon thing to do.

'I would say that there are definitely two perpetrators involved. That the person who lit the fire was not the same as the one who buried the human remains.'

'I suppose you're right,' said Carole grudgingly. 'Oh, it's very frustrating not to have more information.'

'It's early days. At this stage I doubt whether the police have any more information than what's been on the news bulletin.'

'And even if they have, I don't think they're about to share it with us.'

'No. As we've found out before, they're funny that way, the police, aren't they?'

'So all we can do,' said Carole grumpily, 'is to sit and wait for the next news bulletin.'

'Oh, I wouldn't say that's *all* we can do.'

'What do you mean?'

'I'm going to ring Philly.'

'What a great idea. See if she's got any more information.'

'I had actually thought,' said Jude with a hint of reprimand in her tone, 'of checking whether she's all right. The news about the human remains being found in the beach hut that she's only recently vacated must have been a terrible shock to her.'

'Oh yes, fine. Check that she's all right, of course,' said Carole solicitously. But her tone changed as she went on, 'Then see if she's got any more information.'

'I assume you've heard the news about *Quiet Harbour*,' said Jude on the phone to Philly.

'Yes. It's horrible. It makes me feel . . . I don't know . . . spooked out.' The girl did sound very emotional, almost as though she were in shock.

'What, the thought that the human remains may have been under the floorboards while you were actually in the hut?'

'Not that, really, no. As I say, I haven't been inside *Quiet Harbour* for about a month.'

'You did say you'd been in to put down the carpet,' Jude reminded her gently. 'You said you went in there last week when you were walking the dogs.'

'Yes.' There was a silence from the other end of the line, as though Philly Rose was trying to decide what to say. 'The fact is, Jude, that wasn't true.'

'Oh?'

'I only said it because your friend Carole was kind of badgering me about it.' Jude would make a point of telling her neighbour that. Philly had accused Carole of the same thing as she had – 'badgering'.

Jude said nothing, waiting for the explanation. Which duly came. 'I haven't actually been in *Quiet Harbour* since Mark left. I just . . . somehow, I don't know . . . We'd been so happy there. It all seemed too . . . I couldn't.'

'So you hadn't seen the piece of carpet Carole mentioned?'

'No. The fact is, I wanted Carole to take over the rental, not just because I needed the money, but also because I never wanted to see the place again. I don't take the dogs for their walk on Smalting Beach now. I try to avoid it.'

'And that was because it contained *happy* memories?'

'As opposed to what?'

'*Quiet Harbour* didn't prompt unhappy memories? You and Mark didn't have rows in there?'

'No.'

'It wasn't in there that he told you he was leaving?'

'No. Anyway, he didn't tell me he was leaving. He just left. That's what made it doubly hurtful.'

'Well, are you sure he has left you?'

'What do you mean?'

'Are you sure Mark hasn't had an accident? If he didn't discuss leaving you, perhaps you should report him as a missing person?'

'I know he walked out on me.'

The words were said with such pained certainty that Jude didn't attempt to seek further explanation. Philly Rose must have had reasons to know that she had been dumped by Mark Dennis.

'I suppose you should prepare yourself, Philly,' Jude suggested tentatively, 'for the possibility that the police will want to talk to you.'

'They have already.'

'Oh?'

'Last night. Obviously they came to me as the person who was renting *Quiet Harbour*.'

'So they didn't know you'd handed it over to Carole?'

'No. And I didn't tell them.'

'Why not?'

'Look, I don't particularly like Kelvin Southwest – or indeed the little games he plays – but I'm not about to get him into trouble with his employers.'

'You mean Fether District Council didn't know about the change of rental?'

'I'm sure they didn't. It's just a little deal he set up privately.'

'Right. But the police are sure to speak to Kelvin Southwest, aren't they? Since he's in charge of all the beach huts. He's bound to tell them about the handover to Carole, isn't he?'

'Not if he can help it. He called me yesterday evening before the police arrived and swore me to secrecy about the arrangement.' Jude looked across her cluttered sitting room to her neighbour, grateful that Carole couldn't hear Philly's end of the conversation. It would have started up again all her anxieties about the legality of her using the beach hut.

'And did you get much information out of the police, Philly?'

'They were doing the questioning, not me.'

'I know that. I just wondered if they let slip anything of interest.'

'What kind of thing?'

'Well, whether they had any suspicion as to the identity of the human remains that were found, whether the remains were of a male or female, how long they'd been there, that kind of thing.'

'If they did have that sort of information, they certainly didn't share it with me.'

Jude thought it had been too much to hope for. 'By the way,' she said, 'do you know if Smalting Beach is open to the public again? They can't keep the whole area as a crime scene for long, can they?'

'No, it is open. When I was walking the dogs this morning I met someone who'd been down there. She said the row of twelve beach huts including *Quiet Harbour* is cordoned off, but the rest of the beach is open.'

'And will no doubt, as the day goes on, gather its share of snooping locals, indulging their curiosity.'

'Yes.' Apparently that idea was repellent to the young woman. She seemed to shudder as she spoke.

'Are you all right, Philly?'

'Well, as you know, I wasn't feeling great even before all this. And Smalting is such a gossipy area. With what's happened now . . .' She sounded perilously close to tears.

'Would you like me to come round? I could do you a massage or—'

'No. Thanks. It's sweet of you, Jude, but I'll be fine.'

Philly Rose sounded far from fine, however. And after their conversation finished, Jude had the feeling that the discovery beneath *Quiet Harbour* had stirred some very deep dread in the girl.

Kelvin Southwest's attempts to cover up the arrangement he had made about passing on the rental of the beach hut had clearly been unsuccessful, because within the hour Carole had had a call from the police. They understood she had been the first person to find the charred floorboards in *Quiet Harbour* and they would be at High Tor shortly to talk to her about exactly what she'd seen.

There were two of them, a Detective Sergeant in very dressed-down plain clothes and a uniformed WPC. The woman didn't say much, and Carole wondered whether she was just there as some kind of regulation chaperone to her senior colleague. Or maybe to provide a compassionate touch should their interviewee become hysterical.

Though Carole was far from hysterical. She felt very controlled as she recounted what she had found on the Tuesday when she opened up *Quiet Harbour*. She told the Detective Sergeant about her conversation with Philly Rose in the Crown and Anchor, and about her dealings with Kelvin Southwest. As she completed each section of her narrative, she waited for the Detective Sergeant to volunteer some comment or let slip some vital piece of information. But he was a pro. Each time he just finished making a note of her last answer and moved on to his next enquiry.

Eventually, as he seemed to be winding up the interview, Carole had to resort to direct questioning.

'So do you know yet how long the human remains had been under the beach hut? And indeed whether they are the remains of a man or a woman?'

'I can assure you, Mrs Seddon, that when it is appropriate for such information to be released to the general public, you will hear about it in the news media.'

'But I just wondered whether—'

'I am sure a lot of people – particularly in the Smalting area – are wondering a great deal about what's just happened. I am sure the coffee mornings of Fethering are busy with gossip and speculation. But I would remind you, Mrs Seddon, that when an official police investigation is under way, we are not in the habit of reporting on its progress to anyone who happens to be interested.'

Well, that was a fairly unequivocal put-down. And Carole hadn't liked the reference to 'coffee mornings', which seemed to consign her to the category of 'gossipy old woman who has nothing better to do with her time'. What spoilsports the police could be.

Chapter Eleven

'Look, this is very hush-hush,' said the voice at the other end of the phone. It took Carole a moment to recognize that the speaker was Kelvin Southwest.

'Oh, really?' she responded without much intonation.

'Yes. The fact is, Carole, that . . . well, I'm sure you will be aware from the news bulletins about the unfortunate discovery under *Quiet Harbour*.'

'I think I'd have had to be bricked into a cell like some unlucky medieval saint not to have heard about it.'

'True.' His tone suggested he wasn't used to people using that kind of analogy. 'Well, look, Carole, the fact is . . . the police are investigating the circumstances which may have led to . . . the discovery.'

'I would be very surprised if they weren't. When human remains are found it is quite common for the police to take an interest. They would be failing to do their duties if they didn't.'

'Yes. Yes.' The little man at the other end of the phone sounded awkward and rather wretched. 'Now, Carole, it's entirely possible that the police will want to talk to you about the discovery, since you were the one who . . .'

'I would expect that, yes.' Some instinct stopped her from revealing to Kelvin Southwest that she had already been questioned by the police. Wait and see what he had to say first.

'Well, look, Carole, there are certain things that in certain circumstances appear in one way, but in other circumstances appear in another light altogether, if you know what I mean.'

'What on earth are you talking about?' Carole didn't feel inclined to make the conversation any easier for him. She didn't mind hearing the little worm squirming for a minute or two.

'Well, erm, the fact is that while doing people favours is an admirable expression of all that's best in human nature, one doesn't necessarily want everyone to know when such favours are done.'

'Are you saying that you don't want the police to know about you arranging for me to take over Philly Rose's rental of *Quiet Harbour*?'

'Well, I, er . . . Yes, that's exactly what I'm saying.'

'I don't see why the police should be interested. What you have done isn't criminal.'

'No, I agree. It's not criminal per se, but if the information of what had happened were to get back, via the police, to my paymasters at Fether District Council . . .'

'I think I get your drift, Mr Southwest.' It was a measure of his agitation that he made no attempt to get her to call him Kel. 'Hm, well, I suppose I could keep it quiet . . .'

'I'd be very grateful if you could, Carole.'

'. . . but then again I'm not sure why I should.'

'Do you want to get me into trouble?'

The answer to that was probably yes. The more she had to do with Kelvin Southwest, the less Carole liked him. But rather than replying to his question, she saw a way of using the situation to get more information. 'I would be prepared to keep quiet about what happened . . .'

'Oh, thank you so much.'

'. . . but I would want something in return.'

'I beg your pardon?'

'Oh, come on, Mr Southwest. I'm sure you of all people know what I mean. A favour in return for a favour? You scratch my back and . . . ?'

'What do you want me to do?' he asked ungraciously.

'I just want you to tell me how to contact the Smalting Beach Hut Association security officer.'

'And if I do that you won't mention to the police about the arrangement I made over transferring Philly Rose's rental to you?'

'You have my word on it. You tell me and I will not in the future mention anything about that arrangement to the police,' said Carole, choosing her words with scrupulous care.

The security officer's name was Curt Holderness. Kelvin Southwest gave her a mobile number for him.

He also gave her his own mobile number, 'Just so's you can warn me if the police start getting nosey about the change of rental agreement . . .'

Arriving as a stranger to Smalting Beach on the Sunday morning you would not have known about the grisly discovery made there only a few days before. True, *Quiet Harbour* was shrouded in a sort of white tent and the rest of the row of beach huts was still cordoned off by police tape, but that didn't stop holidaymakers from continuing to enjoy themselves. A lot of the other huts were in use, extended families had set up little colonies surrounded by stripy windbreaks, and the air was full of the delighted screams of small children.

Shrimphaven, the hut immediately adjacent to *Fowey*, was closed and locked up. Maybe the mysterious girl with the laptop took Sundays off.

Carole had feared that appearing back on Smalting Beach with Jude so soon would make them look like crime-scene ghouls, but that worry was soon dissipated. Though a few people walking along the beach might linger in front of the site of the macabre discovery, there was no crowd or unseemly rush. Smalting was far too genteel for that kind of thing.

The previous evening, when they had decided to return to *Fowey*, Carole had suggested that it was her turn to provide them with a picnic, but Jude had demurred, suggesting that they should try the Sunday roast in The Crab Inn the following day.

'It's supposed to be very expensive,' Carole had said.

'Well, I'm sure we can afford it.'

'But it's supposed to be very popular too. I'm not sure we'd get in on a Sunday.'

'We'll find out when we get there, won't we? And if they don't have a table for lunch, well, we can just have a drink.'

'You seem very keen to get into The Crab Inn, Jude.'

'It's the only pub in Smalting. Could be a useful source of information. We might get into conversation with some locals. See what the gossips of Smalting are making of the crime.'

'Ah, so you admit there is a crime now, do you?'

'With human remains having been found it'd be hard for me not to, wouldn't it?'

Carole had grinned with quiet satisfaction. 'So, Jude, if you admit there's a crime, you must also admit that we're engaged in another investigation.'

The Sunday dawned another glowing June morning, prompting more mutterings about global warming from the doom-mongers of Fethering. When they arrived at *Fowey* Carole was surprised to find a brown A4 envelope tucked into the stainless-steel bar across the front of the hut's doors.

'Getting love letters already?' suggested Jude.

'Don't be ridiculous.' Carole slid her finger along inside the top of the envelope and produced a membership card and a newsletter. 'Ah, now I am a fully fledged member of the Smalting Beach Hut Association.

And aren't I lucky? I've got my very own copy of *The Hut Parade*.'

She held up for Jude's inspection the two rather smudgily printed sheets stapled together. It came as no surprise that the newsletter demonstrated the fatal giveaway of the amateur in artwork: a tendency to use too many fonts and colours in any document. She now felt pretty certain that Reginald Flowers did his own editing – and probably wrote the bulk of the news-letter's content too.

Carole looked across to *The Bridge* to see if he was there to be thanked, but of course that block of huts was still shut off by police scene-of-crime tape.

There was something else in the brown envelope. She shook it out. Of course – her promised compli-mentary tide table for new members.

Once they'd opened up *Fowey*, Jude took the bright sunlight as an invitation to strip off again. The bikini was vibrant yellow this time, and once again she had run off across the sand to the sea. Carole took Gulliver – on his lead of course – for a walk along the shoreline.

When she drew level with the tented *Quiet Harbour* she looked surreptitiously towards it, checking for police activity. There didn't seem to be anyone on the site, though a couple of patrol cars were still parked up on the promenade, their occupants presum-ably keeping the crime scene under surveillance.

It was just after twelve when Carole and Gulliver got back to *Fowey*. They found Jude dried off and once again dressed in what looked like a white Victorian nightdress, set off by a pink chiffon scarf. 'I was thinking we might as well go to The Crab Inn straight away.'

'Isn't it a bit early?'

'You were worried about it being too full. Sooner we're in there, the better the chance we have of getting a table for lunch.'

'But what about Gulliver?'

'I'm sure The Crab Inn will have somewhere you can tie him up in front of a nice big water bowl.'

And so it proved. Gulliver was so busy lapping up water, he was hardly aware of his mistress going into the pub.

Chapter Twelve

The Crab Inn was so up itself it almost came out through the top. It was a pub only in name; the interior seemed to breathe the words 'expensive restaurant'. Though there was a bar, it was not large, and the idea of someone coming in just to down a few pints seemed incongruous. The walls were painted in subtle shades of cream. The pictures hung on them mostly looked like – though probably weren't – original nineteenth-century maritime scenes. There were also some very chocolate-boxy watercolours of local views – the gentle undulations of the South Downs, Cissbury Ring, a distant prospect of Chichester Cathedral, Smalting Beach at low tide. In the bottom corners of the frames of these were cards with prices and a contact number. Clearly the work of a local artist.

The Crab Inn staff, male and female, were dressed in black trousers and black shirts with nothing so vulgar as a logo on them. A man in black behind the bar looked up at Carole and Jude's entrance. 'Good afternoon. May I help you?' His accent was French and he spoke with that kind of obsequiousness that borders on disapproval.

'Good afternoon. Do you have a table for two for lunch?' asked Jude. It wasn't how Carole would have phrased the question. She tried to avoid saying things that could be slapped down with a firm 'No'. She would have favoured some circumlocution beginning, 'I wondered if by any chance it was possible that you might . . . ?'

'I'll check the book,' replied the young man, with a scepticism that suggested they'd be lucky to find a vacant lunch table for two in this millennium. He looked almost disappointed as he was forced to admit that there was a table free. Nor was the table he pointed out to them tucked away in some unfavoured corner next to the door to the kitchen. It was actually set in one of the bay windows at the front, commanding a splendid sea view.

'If you'd like to order drinks, I will have them taken over to your table.'

'No, thank you,' said Jude to Carole's considerable surprise. 'We'll have our drinks at the bar and then go over to the table.'

'Very good, Madame.' The young man looked slightly put out as he asked what they would like to drink. Checking The Crab Inn's extensive wine menu, Carole and Jude were pleased to see that they had the same Chilean Chardonnay that Ted Crisp served in the Crown and Anchor, though The Crab charged nearly 50 per cent more for it.

While their drinks were being poured, Carole raised an interrogative eyebrow. Jude understood that an explanation was required for her insisting they should have their drinks at the bar, and nodded her head towards one of the other tables. There, sitting with a (no doubt overpriced) pint of bitter in front of him, sat Reginald Flowers.

He had yet to see them and both women were struck by the expression of desolation on his face. He looked terribly lonely. Maybe everything he cared about was in *The Bridge* and the police cordon that prevented him from getting there was the cause of his misery.

When they'd got their drinks and agreed with the young man in black to put them on a tab, Carole moved purposefully towards Reginald Flowers. After all, they'd come to The Crab Inn in the hope of gaining local information, and there in front of them sat the person who probably knew more about the hutters on Smalting Beach than anyone else. What's more, his having left the envelope for her at *Fowey* provided the perfect conversational opening.

She thanked him profusely. 'So splendid to have my first copy of *The Hut Parade* – not to mention my complimentary tide table.'

'Glad to welcome you to membership of the SBHA.'

'Honoured to be a member.'

'Did Dora hand over the envelope to you personally?'

'Well, no. I found it tucked into the bar of my beach hut.'

'Oh dear. Black mark, Dora.' Reginald Flowers took a small police notebook out of his blazer pocket and wrote something in it with a fountain pen. 'I've told her before she should always hand such documents over personally. If she leaves them on the beach huts, they could be taken by anyone – stolen by people who aren't even members of the Smalting Beach Hut Association.'

Carole's instinct was to ask what ordinary member of the public might possibly be interested in the newsletter of the SBHA, but she restrained herself. There was something vulnerable about Reginald Flowers at that moment, and she didn't want to dent his fragile self-importance. Instead she said, 'Now I don't think you've met my friend Jude . . .'

'I've seen you on the beach.'

'Probably with rather fewer clothes on.' Jude grinned at him and he grinned back. Carole was once again struck by the instinct her neighbour had for putting people at their ease.

He rose and stretched out a hand. 'My name's Reginald Flowers. I'm President of the Smalting Beach Hut Association.'

'Oh yes, Carole's mentioned you. Are you a regular here at The Crab Inn?'

'Not really. Normally I take a packed lunch down to *The Br*— my beach hut – but, er, given the current circumstances . . .'

'Yes, it must be wretched for you not being able to get into your place,' said Carole. 'Have the police given any indication of how long it'll be before they grant you access again?'

'No, they haven't.' And from Reginald Flowers's tone of voice this was clearly a bone of some contention.

'Mind you, I've left them in no doubt that I should be the first to be informed when they do vouchsafe us any news. I am, after all, President of the Smalting Beach Hut Association.'

'Yes.'

'And, all right, I understand that when there's been a crime committed, the police have a job to do.'

'Are we sure there has been a crime committed?' asked Jude.

'I think it's a reasonable assumption. Dead bodies are not, in my experience, in the habit of burying themselves.'

Continuing to play slightly dumb, Jude asked, 'So the bones were actually buried under the beach hut? Not just stuffed in the space between the floor and the shingle? Because on the news they just said that the remains had been found *under* the beach hut.'

'Oh no, they were buried.' Reginald Flowers was clearly enjoying his role as the one with privileged information.

'Did the police tell you that?' asked Carole.

'I intuited it from them,' he replied rather grandly.

'And did you intuit anything else?'

'Like what?'

'Well, how long the remains had been there? Whether they were the remains of a male or a female body? What age of person they belonged to?'

Reginald Flowers wilted a little under Carole's wave of interrogation. 'They did give me some other information,' he said, saving face a little, 'but they requested that I should keep it to myself. There's quite enough gossip going round Smalting at the moment without my adding to it.'

'Of course,' said Jude gently. 'By the way, you said you normally have a packed lunch. Is that what you're doing today?'

'That's what I would be doing if I could get into my bally beach hut – pardon my French. So I've ordered the Sunday roast here.' Clearly the idea of eating a packed lunch anywhere other than inside *The Bridge* was not one that he could countenance. 'Regardless of their ridiculous prices,' he went on.

'We're eating too,' said Jude. 'I say, you wouldn't like to join us, would you? I mean, unless you're expecting someone . . . ?'

He wasn't expecting anyone, and he would like to join them. The alacrity with which he accepted the invitation told Carole, who knew a bit about being on her own, just how lonely he was. In subsequent conversation he revealed that he had never married and, before taking early retirement, had been a schoolteacher.

The young man in black behind the bar conceded somewhat grudgingly that he could add another chair to their table, and soon the three of them were ensconced in the bay window of The Crab Inn, consulting its lavishly produced menus. Their contents were predictable. Television chefs, thought Carole, have a lot to answer for. The Sunday roast appeared to be about the only thing on the menu that wasn't accompanied by something drizzled, wilted or glazed, and wasn't served with a *jus*, a *confit* or a *coulis*.

The prices were, as anticipated, extortionate, but what the hell? Now they had ensnared Reginald Flowers, Carole and Jude reckoned they could consider their lunches as legitimate investigative expenses. They didn't dwell on the fact that they didn't have an expenses budget and had never made any money out of any of their detective activities.

The young man in black was, it seemed, just the pub's greeter. Jobs as menial as taking people's orders were delegated to girls in black, who were clearly his underlings. One approached the table in the bay window. She reeled off a list of daily specials, most of which included something seared, steamed or pan-fried, but her customers weren't tempted and all opted for the Sunday roast. Carole and Reginald Flowers ordered the beef, while Jude chose pork.

Picking up the conversation, Carole reminded Reginald that he'd been talking about the gossip recent events had prompted in Smalting.

'Always the same in small villages,' he said. 'Everyone's got their own theory – and they're all rubbish.'

'And do you have a theory of your own?' asked Jude.

'Well, I wouldn't be surprised if drugs were at the bottom of it. Or immigrants. Or both,' he concluded ominously.

'In what way?'

'Look, if there's one thing everyone can agree on these days, it's that since the Second World War, this country has gone to the dogs.' Jude was not as convinced as Reginald about the universality of this view, but she didn't interrupt. 'And the reason this country has gone to the dogs is down to two things: drugs and immigrants. Young men in my day didn't have time or money to buy drugs. They were all trying to rebuild our country after the disasters of the war, they were doing national service, they were—'

'Did you do national service?' asked Carole.

'Well, no, I didn't actually, as it happens, but that doesn't change my point. We still had some concept of service in the those days, the idea that we owed something to the generations before us, to the generations that followed us, that we owed something to our country, for God's sake. Patriotism wasn't a dirty word when I was growing up, you know. We were proud of being British and yes, we were jolly grateful to the chaps from other countries who helped us in the war, but that didn't mean we wanted to have our country overrun by them. Now I'm the last person in the world who could be accused of having any racial prejudice . . .'

And, in the manner of everyone who begins a sentence, 'Now I'm the last person in the world to . . .' Reginald Flowers went on to demonstrate just how much racial prejudice he did have. Living on the South Coast for as long as they had, Carole and Jude had heard it all before.

Reginald Flowers was still in full ranting mode when their food arrived and he continued while they were eating. The food was actually pretty good though loyally neither Carole nor Jude reckoned it matched the quality available at the Crown and Anchor. Only when they came to order their afters did the President of the Smalting Beach Hut Association mercifully run out of political steam. The dessert menu was an intriguing mix of the exotic: clafoutis, panna cottas and syllabubs, and English nursery puddings – bread and butter, Eton mess, spotted dick and custard. Once they had given their orders – plain fruit salad for Carole, spotted dick and custard for Jude and Reginald – they did finally manage to get him back on to the subject of the police investigation on Smalting Beach.

But when they did, all he could offer was rather meagre pickings. Apart from the one unknown that he'd already revealed to them – the fact that the remains had been buried under *Quiet Harbour* rather than just lying there – he had no other new information. The police were evidently as unwilling to share their findings with the President of the Smalting Beach Hut Association as they were with other mere mortals. So Carole decided to change tack and to pick his brains about the regular users of the Smalting beach huts.

It wasn't difficult to get him on to the subject. Since his retirement from teaching it was clear that his whole life now revolved around *The Bridge* and the Smalting Beach Hut Association. And perhaps being temporarily barred from the centre of his world, he was prepared to be less discreet than he might have been on his home turf.

Carole asked him first about the elderly couple she'd twice seen in front of the hut called *Mistral*. 'Ah yes, Lionel and Joyce Oliver,' said Reginald Flowers.

'They're there practically every day. He must be in his eighties now, long retired.'

Carole remembered the expression of bleak misery she had seen on the man's face, as she asked, 'What did he do?'

'He was an undertaker. Family firm in Fedborough. Took the business over from his father, and I think his grandfather had been in the trade as well. Lionel got bought out, though, when he retired. The firm's now owned by one of the big chains, I think.'

'And his wife?'

Reginald Flowers shrugged. 'Wife and mother. Never done much else of anything I don't think. Always there on the beach, though, with her magazines. No, the Olivers are friendly enough, but they don't really mix.'

'What do you mean?'

'They don't support the SBHA social activities as much as one might wish.'

'I didn't know the SBHA had social activities,' said Carole with some trepidation.

'Oh yes, always trying to get people involved, you know. We've got a quiz night coming up next week.'

'Have you?' Carole was already marshalling her excuses to get out of that.

'On the Thursday. We used to do them here in The Crab Inn, but what they charge for their function rooms is now totally exorbitant. So it'll be in the St Mary's Church Hall. Dora's booked that for us. Do you know where it is? Just off the High Street.'

'Oh.'

'Still, I don't know why I'm telling you all this. You will've seen the details in your copy of *The Hut Parade*.'

'Of course.' Carole wasn't about to admit that she hadn't yet had a chance to open the pages of that esteemed periodical. It was entirely characteristic of Reginald Flowers, though, that he would assume everyone's first action on receiving a copy of his news-letter would be to read it from cover to cover.

Carole got the conversation back on track. 'But you were saying the Olivers tend to keep themselves to themselves?'

'Yes, I think they were probably more outgoing before . . . but things change. People get older.'

'Why, what happened?' asked Jude, alert to the slight hesitation in his voice.

'What do you mean – what happened?'

'You said the Olivers were more outgoing *before*, which suggests to me that something happened to make them less outgoing.'

'No, I didn't mean that. I didn't mean anything. Just that they've got older.'

'Right.' Carole and Jude exchanged looks. They both knew that Reginald Flowers was holding some-thing back. Equally they both knew that they wouldn't get it out of him at that moment. But in time they would try to find out more about the Olivers.

Carole moved the conversation on. 'Then there's that grandmother, the one in the beach hut called *Seagull's Nest*.'

'Ah yes.' Reginald Flowers spoke without enthusiasm. 'Her name's Deborah Wrigley. Lives in one of those big houses on the Shorelands Estate, you know, over in Fethering.' The two women nodded. They knew all about the exclusively gated Shorelands Estate. People there were even more up themselves than the inhabitants of Smalting.

'Anyway, Deborah Wrigley's husband was something big in the City. Banker I think. Died maybe six years ago, very soon after retirement, probably the poor bastard succumbed to the effects of twenty-four hour nagging when he was at home all the time. Left his wife as rich as Croesus, and she now devotes her life to bitchy bridge parties, that is when she's not playing her children off against each other about their potential inheritances . . . oh, and bullying her grandchildren.'

Carole awarded herself an inward nod of satisfaction. Her initial assessment of Deborah Wrigley's character seemed to have been 100 per cent accurate.

'She's extremely put out at the moment,' Reginald Flowers continued with relish. '*Seagull's Nest* is in the row that's still cordoned off by the police. Like *The Bridge* . . .' But he only allowed himself a brief moment of wistfulness. 'Deborah Wrigley's been bending the ear of that jumped-up little jack-in-office Kelvin Southwest about the situation. But of course he can't do anything. He just has to wait till the police decide the huts can be opened again. Like the rest of us. So the lovely Deborah must be continuing to antagonize her family somewhere else at the moment.'

Carole and Jude didn't reckon they were going to

get much more out of him on Deborah Wrigley, but Jude made a mental note to check whether Philly Rose had had anything to do with the grandmother from hell. After all, *Seagull's Nest* was directly next door to *Quiet Harbour*.

Carole had meanwhile moved on to the subject of the SBHA's security officer. 'You haven't had any insights from him, have you, Reginald, you know, about what happened at *Quiet Harbour*?'

'No. And I don't expect any.' Curt Holderness was clearly another on the list of people disapproved of by Reginald Flowers. 'I regret that his powers of vigilance leave a lot to be desired. Not very punctilious in the discharge of his duties, I'm afraid. But then Kelvin Southwest had a considerable influence on the appointment.'

Carole immediately picked up the subtext of this. 'A bit of mutual backscratching involved – is that what you're saying?'

'It's exactly what I'm saying, yes.'

Interesting how whenever Kelvin Southwest's name came up, it brought with it the slight whiff of minor corruption.

There was a hiatus while their sweets were delivered, but after a brief discussion about the enduring appeal of nursery foods like spotted dick, Carole resumed her fact-finding mission. 'Actually, Reginald, there's another hut user I—'

'Not "hut user", Carole, "hutter".'

'Hutter,' she repeated, unconvinced that the word would ever trip naturally off her tongue. 'Anyway, there was another one I wanted to ask you about. I don't know if you'll know who I mean . . .'

'I think, Carole,' he said with quiet complacency, 'you will find that, as President of the Smalting Beach Hut Association, I know about the people in *all* of the huts.'

'Yes, well, the hut I'm interested in is called *Shrimphaven*.' Slight annoyance crossed his face at the name. 'It's right next door to *Fowey*, the one I'm currently using. There's a young woman in it.'

'Yes, I know the one you mean. Sits there all day and half the night with one of those laptops.'

'Do you know what she's doing there?'

'No. I've asked her on more than one occasion and she won't tell me.' It clearly irked him that he couldn't provide a more complete answer. 'I think I may have to take my enquiries further. You know, as President of the Smalting Beach Hut Association. I may even have to involve Kelvin Southwest.' He spoke the name with distaste. 'I mean, there are regulations about the proper uses of these beach huts. If we were to discover that someone was running a business from one of them . . . well, action would have to be taken.'

'What kind of action would there—?' But Carole's question was interrupted by the sound from the bar of a glass smashing.

Reginald Flowers looked across to the source of the noise, shook his head knowingly and said, 'Oh dear, here comes trouble.'

Chapter Thirteen

The cause of the commotion at the bar of The Crab Inn was a tall man with long, greying hair. Dressed in paint-spattered denim shirt and jeans, he was swaying slightly as he took issue with the black-clad French greeter.

'Look, all I want to do is buy a drink,' he was remonstrating in an aggrieved, languid upper-class accent.

'And I've told you, Mr Czesky, that I can't allow you to do that. The manager has banned you from this pub.'

'Yes, but you're not the manager. I bet the manager isn't even in today.'

'No, he isn't as it happens.'

'See, taking Sunday off. Your manager doesn't want to let work spoil his weekend, does he? So, since he's not here, he need never know that you've let me buy a drink.' The man pulled a crumpled pile of banknotes out of his pocket and scattered them on the counter. 'Look, my money's as good as anyone else's. Legal tender, got Her Majesty's face plastered all over it.'

'Mr Czesky, you've already broken a wine glass. There are a lot of other people waiting to be served.' It was true. While Carole and Jude had been talking to Reginald Flowers the pub had filled up considerably. 'I must ask you to leave.'

'Well, where else am I supposed to go? This is the only pub in Smalting, and pubs, you know, by tradition used to be places that would welcome anyone, particularly locals. Everyone in the village would come in and have a pint, the toffs mixing with the fisherman. Now suddenly The Crab Inn has become the exclusive preserve of the tight-arsed upper middle class – is that what you think is happening? Well, it isn't. This lot . . .' he gestured wildly round the bar ' . . . this lot haven't got any real class. Add all the real class in the bar together and the lump you'd come up with would be smaller than my little finger.'

The greeter in black kept trying to interrupt, but the tall man seemed only just to be getting into his flow. 'This whole area is so bloody up itself. Oh, it's all right if you've spent your life in some bloody office, working in insurance or banking or some other way of screwing money out of people. But no one has interest in the individuals who really add something to the value of this world. Look at all these people . . .' Another uncoordinated gesture round the bar. 'Forget their class – if you added together all the artistic talent they've got, it wouldn't be enough to cover my bloody fingernail. But you're happy to sell drinks to these talent-free clones, aren't you? Whereas someone like me, someone who's slightly different, someone with a bit of artistic talent, who doesn't fit into one of the moulds that you've—'

How long he might have gone on who could say – he certainly seemed to have got into his groove – but he was at this point interrupted by a woman who had just entered the bar. She was a short plump blond in her forties of rather faded beauty and with permanent worry lines between her eyebrows. Her dress was blue cotton with white broderie anglaise trimmings.

'Gray,' she said, with a hint of a foreign accent. 'Come on, you must come home.'

'Why should I?' he asked truculently. But it was the truculence of a little boy who had already conceded victory. He could have protested to the pub's greeter all day, but this woman – presumably wife or girlfriend – had instant control over him. With a gesture of contempt to everyone in the room, the man turned and meekly followed the woman out of The Crab Inn.

Carole and Jude, who had been too absorbed by the scene at the bar to speak up until this point, both turned to Reginald Flowers for some explanation.

'Gray Czesky,' he announced. 'Calls himself an artist.'

'And has he got one of the beach huts?' asked Carole.

'Good heavens, no. We don't want people like that in the Smalting Beach Hut Association. He's got a house on the front.'

'What, here in Smalting?' asked Carole, surprised.

'But those houses on the front are all rather splendid. He doesn't look the sort to own one of them. Unless he's a very successful artist.'

'So far as I know,' said Reginald Flowers, 'he's completely unsuccessful. I've no idea whether he has any talent or not.'

'Those are his watercolours on the wall over there. I noticed the name while we were getting the drinks.'

'Are they? Well, maybe he makes a few bob selling those.'

'Perhaps he's got a private income?'

'Of a kind. You see, the one thing Gray Czesky does have is a rich wife. That's why he can afford to live on the seafront at Smalting.'

'Presumably it was his wife who took him out just now?'

'Yes. Helga. Constantly having to bail him out of somewhere. God, what some women are prepared to put up with.'

'It must be *lurve*,' Jude suggested.

That got a very dismissive snort from the President of the Smalting Beach Hut Association. The two women got the impression that love in any of its forms did not register highly on his list of priorities.

For the rest of their meal Reginald Flowers moved back into ranting anti-immigrant mode, so that Carole and Jude were quite relieved when it was time to settle up and return to the beach. Their lunch companion didn't leave at the same time. He had been nursing the contents of his second pint and clearly planned to eke it out a little longer. Saying their goodbyes, both women were again aware of the deep loneliness in his eyes. He couldn't really function properly without his haven of *The Bridge* to go to.

As they walked back towards *Fowey* with Gulliver, Carole looked up at the three or four splendid houses on the Smalting promenade. Someone who lived in one of them – like Gray Czesky – had a perfect observation point to see everything that happened on the beach. It was worth bearing in mind.

The other thought that struck her was that in just a week's time she'd have Gaby and Lily with her.

They didn't stay long in front of *Fowey* after lunch. With sad British predictability, the weather had turned. While they had been inside The Crab Inn the cloudless sky of the morning had become overcast with dull clouds and the rain was starting to spit down.

In the Renault on the way back to Fethering, Carole and Jude assessed the new information they had got from Reginald Flowers and were forced to admit it wasn't very much. They were faced by an impasse, which would probably remain until the police revealed more about the human remains that had been discovered. Carole felt a bit headachey after the lunchtime wine and the two women parted at the gate of High Tor. By then it was raining heavily.

Once she'd brushed the sand off Gulliver, Carole sat down in her front room with the *Sunday Times*, and was annoyed to find half an hour later that she had dozed off. She disapproved strongly of going to sleep during the day, regarding it as one of the many slippery slopes towards old age that must be avoided at all costs.

She tried to concentrate on the paper, but couldn't. Her headache was worse and she went upstairs to take a couple of paracetamol. While up there she switched on her laptop and checked the BBC website in the forlorn hope that there might be some more news about the discovery on Smalting Beach. Needless to say, there wasn't.

She felt restless, slightly anxious about the following Sunday. The frustration she and Jude had come up against in the car was still with her. Despite the poverty of their information on the subject, her mind kept circling round what had been found under *Quiet Harbour*. She felt she needed to do something to move their investigation forward, but she couldn't think what.

Then she remembered the mobile phone number that she had squeezed out of Kelvin Southwest. A contact for Curt Holderness. She didn't know what hours security officers worked, but she could at least leave a message asking him to call her. She rang the number.

To her surprise, it was answered instantly. 'Curt Holderness,' he said in a voice of lazy confidence.

'Good afternoon. You don't know me. My name's Carole Seddon.'

'Oh, I think I've heard the name. Wasn't it you who discovered the charring at the bottom of the beach hut at Smalting, you know, the one where a rather nasty discovery was made?'

'Yes, that was me.'

'Well, what can I do for you?'

'It was actually in connection with the beach huts that I was calling you.'

'Did Kelvin Southwest put you on to me?' The way he said it, the question was clearly an important one.

'Yes.'

Curt Holderness's voice seemed to relax. 'Good old Kel. We work very well together, you know, Kel and me.'

'Oh?'

'Anyone's got a problem with the beach huts, we can usually sort it out between us.'

'Good.'

'Rules are there to be bent, after all, aren't they?' Carole wasn't quite sure what he was talking about, so she waited while he elucidated. 'Someone needs something done – or something not done. A blind eye turned perhaps . . . ? Kel and I can usually sort something out. Someone wants to stay overnight in one of the huts, maybe use it as an office . . . well, it's not doing anyone any harm, is it? Kel and I can usually see our way to being accommodating about things.'

'So you bend the rules in exchange for favours from people?' asked Carole, remembering Kelvin Southwest's favoured method of doing business.

'Yes, favours.' He relished the word, then chuckled. 'Sometimes favours of the folding variety. So, what is it you would like me to fix for you, Carole? Want to install a little generator, do you, so's you can run a little fridge off it? That's what a lot of people ask for this time of year. Strictly against the Fether

District Council rules, but when you come down to it, what harm's it going to do anyone? Why shouldn't people be comfortable in their beach huts?'

Illuminating though this diversion had been, Carole thought she should perhaps get back to the real purpose of her phone call. 'I don't actually want you to bend any rules for me, Mr Holderness.'

He looked puzzled. 'Oh? But I thought you said Kel put you on to me.'

'I did.'

'But usually when Kel puts people on to me . . .' Embarrassed about how much of himself he had given away, the security officer changed tack. 'What is it you want from me then, Carole?'

Carole thought of various subterfuges, but rejected them. Try the direct approach first. 'I just wondered if you had any more information about what happened?

'How do you mean?'

'Well, whether you had been told anything by the police, you know, anything that isn't public knowledge.'

The man at the other end of the phone laughed. 'You don't ask a lot, do you? You are aware that I have a part-time job as security officer for the Smalting Beach Hut Association?'

'Yes, of course.'

'Well, some people might reckon the word "Security" covers keeping schtum about anything the police might have told me that isn't public knowledge.'

'So are you one of those people, Mr Holderness?'

'Sometimes I am, yes. Depends on the circumstances.' There was a teasing quality in his voice.
'What are you really asking me to do, Mrs Seddon?'

She took her courage in both hands. 'I'm asking
whether you'd agree to meet up for a drink and talk to
me about what happened.'

He laughed again. 'I see. It's the Miss Marple Mafia
of Fethering, is it?'

'Well, it's—'

'All right, I'll meet up with you.'

Chapter Fourteen

It turned out that Curt Holderness also lived in Fethering and was happy to meet in the Crown and Anchor. He said he quite often dropped in there on a Sunday evening for a pint, so if Carole cared to join him . . .

Rather ashamed of the muzziness she had felt after lunch, she was determined not to have any more alcohol, but somehow that resolve vanished when she was faced by the lugubrious face of Ted Crisp behind the bar. She succumbed to a Chilean Chardonnay, though she did ask him to make it a small one.

'I'm meeting someone called Curt Holderness. Do you know him?'

'Goodness, yes. He's been a regular for quite a while. Sometimes used to drink in here back when he was a copper.'

'Oh well, if you can point him out to me when he comes in—'

'He's come in.' Ted nodded his shaggy head towards one of the alcoves. 'Over there. And he's drinking a pint of Stella.'

Carole looked across. There was no drink on the

table in front of the man Ted had pointed out. 'No, he isn't.'

'What I meant was that you are buying him a pint of Stella.'

'Oh, right, I see. A pint of Stella too then, Ted.'

As he pulled the pint, the landlord observed, 'I don't think I've ever seen Curt buy a drink. There's always someone there to buy it for him.'

'Like who?'

'Someone who perhaps wants a favour from him.' Yes, and I know how he likes to be repaid – with a favour of the folding variety, thought Carole as Ted went on, 'Can't imagine what favour you might be wanting from Curt – and I'm not going to ask.' Then, to Carole's annoyance, he winked at her.

The afternoon's rain had cleansed the air and Fethering was enjoying a beautiful summer evening. As a result, most of the pub's customers were once again at the tables outside, which pleased Carole. She didn't want people eavesdropping on her conversation with Curt Holderness.

He was a thickset man with thinning hair cut very short, and he still looked like the policeman he had once been. In spite of the warmth he wore black leather trousers and there was a matching blouson lying on the seat beside him. Presumably outside in the Crown and Anchor car park was a motorbike.

He half-rose in his seat when Carole introduced herself. His handshake was almost aggressively strong. But despite his macho manner, there was a wariness about him, almost an anxiety.

'Ted said a pint of Stella would be appropriate, Mr Holderness?'

'How right Ted was. Thanks.' He took a long draught of the lager. 'And please call me Curt.'

'Thank you. Please call me Carole.' She sat down and took a sip of wine. Now she was actually at a table opposite him, the burst of self-assertiveness with which she had set up the meeting had dissipated. She couldn't think where to start.

He seemed to sense her discomfiture and smiled a teasing smile. 'I know Miss Marple was famous for just sitting on the sidelines and observing everything, but I think you're going to have to be a little more proactive than that, Carole.'

'Yes. I'm sorry, Curt. Well, first, thank you very much for agreeing to meet me.' He inclined his head graciously. 'And yes, as you implied, I'm probably just another nosey middle-aged woman, but because it was my discovering evidence of the fire in *Quiet Harbour* that led to . . . well, you know . . .' His steady gaze unsettled her, and he seemed to know it. Carole got the feeling that he was playing with her, but also assessing the situation, trying to work out what she really wanted from him. 'I mentioned on the phone,' she floundered on, 'that you might have some new information from the police that—'

'And what made you think that might be the case?'

'Well, I gather you used to be in the force yourself.'

'Yes, and so you think I might ring one of my old muckers who would give me the up-to-date SP on the exact stage their investigations have reached?'

His response was deliberately couched in a kind of all-purpose police argot, still sending her up.

He shook his head. 'Sorry, Carole, that kind of thing doesn't happen outside of telly cop shows. Once you're out of the force, you're out of the force. They don't want ex-coppers hanging around – particularly ex-coppers who've gone into the private security business.'

'So you retired early, did you?'

She seemed to have touched a nerve there. 'What do you mean?' he almost snapped.

'Well, I mean you don't look of an age to have gone the full distance.'

That mollified him. 'Yes, I did retire early.'

'Me too.' Carole didn't often volunteer details of her departure from the Home Office. Its earliness still rankled. But she thought identifying her experience with his might relax him.

'A lot of cops get out early,' he said. 'It's stressful work and when I was coming up for fifty I asked myself: do I want to go on doing this or do I want to develop some other career while there's still time?'

'So did you get the SBHA job immediately?'

'No. I lounged around for a few years, enjoyed the freedom. My pension wasn't that bad, I wasn't responsible for anyone else, so I didn't really need to work. Then I was offered the SBHA job—'

'By Kelvin Southwest?'

He gave her a curious look. 'Yes, as it happens, it was. Of course, you know the fragrant Kelvin.'

'When I discovered the evidence of the fire, it was him I got in touch with.'

Curt Holderness nodded his head, as if to acknowledge that her answer made sense. Carole thought it slightly odd that he didn't know before her phone call that she had been in touch with Kelvin Southwest. Surely such information would be passed on to someone whose job was security officer? But she let it pass, and asked, 'Do you make regular inspections of the beach huts?'

'Yes, of course. Every morning and evening, just to check there hasn't been any vandalism or breach of regulations.'

'What sort of breach of regulations?'

'Could be lots of things. Because the beach huts come under the control of Fether District Council there's pages of them.'

'But what are you mostly looking out for?'

'People staying in them overnight, I suppose. That's the big no-no. Fether District Council gets very aerated about that. Insufficient sanitation and what have you. They're worried about Smalting degenerating into "a shanty town".' Carole had heard the same fear mentioned in connection with the few beach huts in Fethering.

'Do you do night patrols too, Curt?' she asked.

For some reason he looked at her rather slyly before replying, 'Sometimes, yes.'

'Because I was thinking that nobody would have lit the fire under *Quiet Harbour* in the daylight, would they?'

'Probably not.' He anticipated her next question. 'And no, I didn't see anyone trying to torch the place.

If I had, I would have stopped them. Or if I'd seen the fire burning, I would have put it out. And then I would have told the police about what had happened.' There was a sharpness in his tone.

'There was one thing that struck me as odd about what I discovered in *Quiet Harbour* – well, two things, actually.'

'Oh?' There was residual hostility in the monosyllable.

'The fire that had been lit under it was deliberately put out.'

'So? One drunken vandal thinks burning a beach hut is the perfect end to an evening's drinking. His slightly less drunk mucker thinks it's not such a great idea. Or perhaps the original pyromaniac vandal had a sudden moment of conscience and doused it himself.'

'Hm.' What the security officer was saying made sense, but Carole still thought he seemed on the defensive. 'The other thing that struck me as odd was that the bit of carpet in *Quiet Harbour* had been laid down after the fire had been lit and put out.'

'And what's so significant about that?'

'Well, it might suggest that the fire and the laying of the carpet happened the same night, which was also the night that the human remains were buried under the beach hut.'

'Sorry, I'm not with you.'

Carole took in a deep breath before she embarked on her explanation. 'The carpet must have been laid after the fire had been put out, because there was no

mark of singeing or anything on it. And it's reasonable to assume that the carpet was put down to cover
up the fact that the floorboards had been lifted up so
that the human remains could be buried under them.
Then the boards had been replaced, some nailed back
with new nails.'

'I still don't see why this all has to have happened
on the same night, Carole.'

'It must have done. And I reckon it was probably
the night before I first went to *Quiet Harbour*. Last
Monday night.'

'Why?'

'Because otherwise you would have noticed the
evidence of the fire when you did your inspection on
the Tuesday morning.' As soon as she said the words,
Carole saw a new shiftiness come into the man's eyes.
She pounced immediately. 'You said you inspected the
beach huts every morning and evening.'

'*Most* mornings and evenings. I mean, sometimes
I have other demands on my time.'

'So how long could the evidence of the fire at the
corner of *Quiet Harbour* have been there before you
noticed it?' Curt Holderness looked even shiftier. 'Go
on, how long?'

'Well, I suppose . . .' he shrugged '. . . up to a week.'

Their eyes met and immediately Carole understood exactly what the situation was in regard to Curt
Holderness's job. He regarded it as a sinecure. Reginald Flowers had demanded a security officer for the
Smalting Beach Hut Association and, using his usual
old pals' act system, Kelvin Southwest had appointed

Curt, probably in exchange for some reciprocal favour.
Thereafter Curt had just taken the money, lined his
pockets with a few favours of the folding variety, and
done the minimum he could get away with.

Carole was angry. She'd been getting a timetable
of events at *Quiet Harbour* sorted out in her head, and
Curt Holderness's revealed slackness in the discharge
of his duties had made nonsense of it. With some
venom she asked, 'And do you ever actually do night
patrols? Or do you regard them too as more trouble
than they're worth?'

'I do them,' he replied, stung by her accusation.
'Can't do them every bloody night, but I do them from
time to time. I tell you, since I've been operating as
security officer, there have been a lot less thefts from
the beach huts. I just work my own way, try to avoid
getting into a routine. Villains soon catch on if you
stick to a routine.'

'So have you seen anything unusual during your
recent night patrols?'

'Yes, I may have done.'

'And have you told the police about anything
you've seen?'

The question amused him. His teasing manner
returned as he replied, 'Ooh no, I wouldn't do that. I
was a copper for so long that I know how their minds
work, and the kind of questions they ask. And the
golden rule if you're on the other end of their interrogation is: "If they don't ask, don't tell."'

'Meaning what exactly?'

'Meaning never volunteer any information. If they

ask a specific question to which you can supply an answer, then probably best to tell them. Otherwise keep schtum. What they don't ask about, they don't deserve to know.'

'You don't seem to have a very high opinion of your former employers.'

Curt Holderness shrugged. 'I don't exactly have a great nostalgia for the time I spent with them, no.'

'Is that something to do with the reason why you left early?'

That caught him on the raw. 'No, it bloody isn't!' he snapped. But he still managed to look guilty.

'Didn't the police find it odd that you hadn't reported the fire at *Quiet Harbour*?'

He looked away and took a swig from his nearly empty pint glass. Then he mumbled, 'No. Kelvin told them I had reported it.'

'Ah. Old pals' act working out again.' He shrugged. Carole continued, 'The police might be interested to know the truth about that . . .'

'Are you threatening me?'

'No, just thinking out loud.'

He looked even shiftier and not a little guilty. Though Carole had denied threatening him, that was the effect her words had had. She had him on the back foot, so she pressed home her advantage. 'You said you might have seen something unusual during your recent night patrols . . .'

'Did I?'

'Yes.'

She waited. Curt Holderness seemed to be going

through some decision-making process. 'Look, if I tell you this, will you leave me alone?'

'Depends what it is.'

'And will you also keep quiet to the police about when I noticed the evidence of the fire?'

'Again depends on what you tell me.' Carole knew she was very much in control of the situation, and the feeling gave her a warm glow.

'Well, look, you know the couple who had *Quiet Harbour* before you did?'

'Yes. Philly Rose and Mark Dennis. Philly passed the rental over to me because Mark had walked out on her.'

'Mm, I heard some rumour about that.'

'And he's not been seen since the beginning of May.'

'Oh yeah? Well, one night when I was driving along doing my patrol – just after one a.m. I'd say it was – I saw him.'

'Mark Dennis?'

'Yes.'

'When was this?'

'Monday last week. Well, the small hours of the Tuesday, I suppose.'

The night before Carole had made her first visit to *Quiet Harbour*. The night when, quite possibly, the human remains had been buried there. 'What was Mark doing?'

'When I first saw him he was on the prom, then he walked down to the beach.'

'You didn't say anything to him?'

'Why should I have done?'

'As I said, he's been missing for a long time, since the beginning of May.'

The security officer shrugged. 'Not my problem. So far as I know, he hasn't even been reported missing. If a couple split up, that's their business. One thing you learn pretty quickly in the force is: never get involved in a domestic. So if this guy Mark wants to walk on Smalting Beach in the middle of the night, well, that's up to him, isn't it?'

'Was he doing anything strange? Did you see what he did once he got on the beach?'

He shook his head. 'I was just driving past, I saw him, that's all. But the thing is . . .'

'What?'

'He wasn't alone.'

'Oh?'

'He had a woman with him.'

'Philly Rose?'

'No, it wasn't Philly Rose. It wasn't anyone I'd ever seen before.'

Chapter Fifteen

'We've got to talk to her,' said Jude.

'I suppose so.' Carole was strangely reluctant. Maybe it was because she thought of Philly Rose as Jude's friend rather than hers and feared that Jude might be happier conducting the conversation on her own.

'Look, poor kid. She hasn't seen hide nor hair of the man she was hoping to spend the rest of her life with since the beginning of May. Now we know he was seen in Smalting within the last couple of weeks. Of course we've got to tell her.'

'Mm. I was just thinking it might be better – since you're the one who knows her – if you were to—'

'No. You're the one who's got the information. We go and see her together.'

Not for the first time in their relationship, Carole felt a bit sheepish. She built up such mountains of obstacles for herself. Why couldn't she be direct like Jude? But she knew that her own leopard spots were so deeply ingrained that they couldn't be removed even by sandblasting.

*

Seashell Cottage, Philly Rose's home in Smalting, was beautifully appointed, but just as she had done when she first entered *Quiet Harbour*, Carole couldn't help being struck by how everything in the place had been designed for two. The home's very cosiness seemed to accentuate the absence of Mark Dennis.

But it didn't look as though Philly would be able to afford to live there much longer. That Monday morning the open property section of the *West Sussex Gazette* on her kitchen table told its own story.

The room where they sat had probably once been two, which at some point had been knocked through to make a comfortable kitchen/dining area. Philly offered them coffee and while she was operating the gleaming Italian machine that made it, Jude asked casually, 'How's the work?'

The young woman's small face screwed up in disappointment. 'Very little around. Maybe I'll do better if I move back to London.'

'Is that what you're planning?'

'I don't think I'm capable of *planning* anything at the moment. My life seems to be completely random. Nasty things keep happening to me and I'm just reacting to events. Trying to ride the punches. I can't remember when I last felt in control of my life.'

Probably the day before Mark Dennis left, thought Jude. The poor girl did look very stressed; there were dark half-moons under her brown eyes. She appeared to have just thrown on yesterday's clothes and her ash-blond hair needed brushing.

Carole noticed a couple of watercolours on the

wall whose style looked familiar. Both were of Smalting Beach and she realized they were very similar to the ones she had seen in The Crab Inn. 'Are those by someone local?' she asked.

Philly Rose grimaced. 'Yes. Smalting's very own artist and *enfant terrible*, Gray Czesky.'

'Ah. We saw him in The Crab Inn when we were having lunch there yesterday.'

'I'm surprised he was allowed in. I thought he'd been barred.'

'Yes, that was pointed out to him. He made a bit of a scene.'

'Wouldn't be the first time that's happened.'

'He's one of Smalting's "characters", is he?'

'Self-appointed "characters", yes. We saw quite a lot of him when we first moved down here.'

'But not now, you imply?'

'Right. Well, Gray's an artist and, you know, Mark had come down here to paint, so naturally they got together. The theory was they were talking about art. In fact, they were just drinking. Gray is something of a professional in that area.'

'I got that impression in The Crab,' said Carole.

'There was a woman who came in and sort of rescued him,' Jude remembered.

'His wife Helga.' Philly sighed with exasperation. 'What she puts up with from Gray you wouldn't believe. Helga Czesky is the kind of woman who sets back the cause of feminism by about a century. Seems actually to get a charge from spending her life as a doormat.'

Carole looked at the watercolour more closely. 'He's not a bad painter, is he, if you like that sort of thing.'

'Yes, maybe. I myself don't particularly like that sort of thing. Too bland for my taste. Mark ended up buying that one at the end of a long drinking session with Gray.' A new thought struck her. 'I wonder if I could sell it?'

'Worth trying,' said Jude. 'Are Gray Czesky watercolours popular?'

'He seems to sell quite a few. Mostly through that place on the prom, the Zentner Gallery.'

Carole salted away the information. It might be useful at some point.

'If they were friends,' said Jude, 'have you asked whether Gray's had any contact from Mark since you last heard from him?'

'No,' came the terse reply. 'It wasn't a friendship I encouraged.'

'Oh?'

'Mark used to have a drink problem. A lot of City high-flyers do – their way of coping with the stress. And he could turn quite nasty when he'd had a few. But since we moved to Smalting and out of that City environment, Mark'd really got back in control of the drinking. Except when he met up with Gray Czesky. One evening with Gray could undo all the good of the previous month. It was one of the few things Mark and I used to argue about.'

'Did you have a row about his drinking just before he left?' asked Carole. 'I mean, was that perhaps the reason why—?'

'No.' Philly spoke firmly, closing down that particular topic of conversation, and brought the coffee over to them. She and Carole had black. Jude took milk. Seeming to assume that the question about her work and the discussion of Gray Czesky had just been small talk, Philly Rose got straight down to business. 'Jude, you said on the phone you had some information for me.'

'Yes. It's something Carole was told.'

She looked across at her neighbour, who began by recapping, 'It was the beginning of May when Mark walked out?'

'May the third.' Philly had thought about the date so often that there was a dull ritual quality to her words.

'And you haven't seen him since?'

'No. I told you.'

'Or had any contact from him?'

'No.'

There was in her answer a hint of hesitation, on to which Carole pounced. 'Is that true, Philly?' A silence. 'Look, I'm sorry, I'm not badgering you – or at least I'm not meaning to – but the significance of what I was told does depend on whether you were telling the truth about having no contact with Mark.'

This prompted an even longer silence before Philly Rose admitted, 'We have exchanged a few texts.'

'But you haven't seen him?' The young woman shook her head. 'And you have no idea where he is or what he's doing?' The head shake this time was not so definite. 'Are you sure about that?'

'Look, what is this?' Philly demanded petulantly. 'You say you want to see me because you've got some information, so you come here and then start giving me the third degree.'

Jude was instantly in there, good cop to her neighbour's bad cop. 'Philly, it's all right. Carole just wanted to know the background because what she has to tell you concerns Mark.'

'Really?' The girl looked frightened now. It was with a sense of foreboding that she turned to Carole and asked, 'Have you seen him? Do you know where he is?'

'I haven't seen him myself, but he has been seen. Here in Smalting.'

'Oh my God.' The words came out quiet and dead. 'When?'

'About one o'clock last Tuesday morning. The day before I found out there'd been a fire at *Quiet Harbour*.'

Philly Rose's pallor increased. 'Who saw him?'

Carole passed on what she had been told by Curt Holderness. The shock when Philly heard that Mark had been in the company of a woman made her gasp and start to tremble uncontrollably. Jude was instantly at her side, cradling the girl, stroking her shoulders.

It took some minutes for the hysterics to subside. Carole drank her coffee, feeling rather guilty for precipitating this reaction. But Philly had wanted the information.

When she was calmer, Jude said, 'There's clearly quite a lot you're not telling us, isn't there, Philly?' This prompted a feeble nod. 'And if you don't want to tell us any more, that's fine. But what you know is clearly troubling you, and if you think sharing it might help . . . ?'

The suggestion dangled in the air for what seemed like a long time before Philly tore off a sheet of kitchen roll and wiped her nose firmly before saying, 'All right, I'll tell you. It'll be useful practice for me, because no doubt I'll have to repeat it all for the police sometime soon.'

Chapter Sixteen

Neither woman responded, unwilling to break the confessional atmosphere. Philly took a deep breath and started. 'Mark's life has always been complicated. Basically he's married. He was married when we first met – and he didn't make any secret of the fact. He wasn't one of those men who passes himself off as a bachelor and only reveals his real status when the woman's too involved to back out. No, he told me early on that he was married, but he told me things had been difficult with his wife for a long time. She's Irish, very temperamental, called Nuala. Drank a lot, and encouraged him to drink a lot too. Very much part of that City drinking culture. Obviously I was only hearing Mark's side of things, but she did sound an absolute nightmare, a real emotional vampire.

'So when we first started seeing each other, he was having a terrible time. He kept telling her he was leaving and every time she'd overreact.'

'In what way?' asked Jude.

'She'd get ill – or pretend to get ill.'

'Any suicide attempts?'

'Yes, but those were no more real than the illnesses.

She'd take enough pills to make her woozy, but not enough to do any permanent harm. She'd announce on the phone to Mark that she'd slashed her wrists, but when it came to it, she just got a little scratch, something that would heal up without even leaving a scar.'

'Was she ever hospitalised after these attempts?'

'No way. She didn't want a doctor to see how far she'd been from doing herself any real damage. It was all just for Mark's benefit.'

'And did he respond to these "cries for help"?' asked Carole.

'He did at first, yes. After a while, he came to recognize them for what they were – just straightforward emotional blackmail. And then things got better.'

'How?'

'Two things. One, Mark settled some money on her.'

'Bought her off?'

'You could call it that. Anyway, Mark could afford it. He'd saved a lot from his bonuses while he'd been in the City and he'd made what seemed at the time to be some pretty shrewd investments. So Nuala got a monthly payment for keeping out of his hair, and she seemed quite happy with that.'

'If she was reconciled to the ending of their relationship, why didn't they get a divorce?' asked Carole.

'Nuala refused that. She said it was because of her Catholic upbringing, though she had no faith at all. I think it was just a way of keeping an element of control for the moment when she might need it.'

'You said there were two things that improved the situation,' Jude reminded her.

'Yes. The money was the first. The second even better. Nuala met someone else. She got into a new relationship. Suddenly she didn't care anything about Mark . . . though actually I don't reckon she ever did. Anyway, it left him and me free to make our move down here. Everything seemed fine.'

'So what went wrong?' asked Carole.

Philly's face screwed up into an expression of wry despair. 'What didn't? The company in which Mark had most of his investments suddenly went belly up. You know how volatile the stock market's been recently and his were pretty high-risk companies. He lost a packet. Keeping our lifestyle going down here *and* making the payments to Nuala . . . well, there just wasn't enough money in the bank. And then to add to the problems, Nuala's new relationship broke up. Her bloke found out – just as Mark had done – what she was really like, and he got out as quickly as he could. So suddenly Mark's not only getting financial demands from Nuala, she's also back on the emotional blackmail routine.'

'Illness, suicide attempts?'

'All that, Jude. And Mark . . . well, he's a decent bloke. She could still get to him. I kept saying he should ignore her. Call her bluff. Let the spoilt bitch go ahead with one of her threats. I knew she'd never really top herself. But Mark didn't see it that way.'

'And is that why he walked out?' Jude asked gently.

'Yes. He was under so much pressure – from the money, from everything else – that he said he just needed a bit of time to sort things out.'

'So do you actually know where he is?' Carole's question was less delicately put than Jude's.

Philly shook her head. 'If I did, I'd go and find him, tell him he doesn't owe that crazy bitch anything. Tell him that he should be with me, not with her.' The tears, which she had been controlling very well, threatened once again to break through.

'You're suggesting,' Jude observed, 'that Mark has gone back to Nuala.'

'Well, what else am I meant to think? He says he's going away to sort himself out, for about a week I get regular texts from him, then suddenly nothing. Nuala's got her talons into him again.'

'Was that the first explanation you thought of?' asked Carole. 'You didn't worry that he might have had an accident or something?'

'I did at first. But after a while I thought if he had – even if he was dead – I would probably have heard about it, from the police, from the media, from somewhere. People don't just suddenly vanish from off the face of the earth.'

'It happens more often than you might think,' said Jude.

'Well, that wasn't my reading of the situation. I reckoned he'd probably gone back to Nuala. Back to the vicious spiral of drinking and emotional blackmail and . . . The alternative was that he'd gone abroad, just cut loose from everything and arranged a disappearing act. Either way, I wasn't ever going to see him again.' The thought was so painful that again tears welled at her eyelids.

'Well, at least now you know that he's alive,' said Carole. 'If he was seen down here only last week.'

'Yes. But that's not much comfort. Particularly if he was down here with another woman. I'd put money on the fact that that was Nuala.'

'Do you know what she looks like?'

'I've never met her, if that's what you mean. But from what Mark said, I gather she was very tall. Taller than him, nearly six foot. Very slim, and with long black hair. And those blue eyes Irish girls have.'

Carole made a mental note to check out that description with Curt Holderness if she got the opportunity.

'But why would they come down here?' asked Jude. 'Do you think they wanted to meet up with you, actually talk through the situation?'

'No, I wouldn't have thought that was why they came. I bet Nuala made him come down here, just so that she could crow over me. "So here's the nice little seaside idyll you set up with Philly, is it? Well, it was never going to last, was it, because you're back with me now, Mark." I can just hear her saying it.' And indeed for Nuala's imagined words Philly had taken on a hint of an Irish accent.

'That would be very cruel,' said Carole. 'Would coming here and crowing about your unhappiness be in character for Mark as you knew him?'

'Not for Mark as I knew him, no. But when he's

with Nuala he's not Mark as I knew him. She poisons his mind. She's a vile malevolent bitch.'

'I thought you said you hadn't met her?' Jude pointed out mildly.

'I don't need to meet her. I know from the effect she had on Mark what kind of woman she is.'

As she tried to make sense of her boyfriend's actions, the pain that Philly Rose had suffered for the past few weeks had clearly now been curdled with paranoia. And deep hatred of the Irishwoman she had never met.

'Just suppose,' said Carole very calmly and judiciously, 'just suppose that Mark's motive in coming down to Smalting was not just to crow over you.'

'What do you mean?'

'When he was seen by Curt Holderness, Mark and the woman were walking down from the promenade on to the beach.'

'Yes?'

'And when we talked before you said you reckoned he probably still had a key to *Quiet Harbour*.'

'Well, I'm not sure . . .'

'You said you hadn't found it among his things.'

'No, but—'

Carole cut through the interruption. 'You said when Mark left, he told you he "needed a bit of time to sort things out"?'

'Yes. Something like that.'

'Do you remember the exact words he used?'

Philly Rose's brow wrinkled as she tried to remember. 'He promised that he would come back to me, but he said there were things he had to sort out before he did. He said the main thing he had to sort out was Nuala.'

'And a few days after Mark, who had a key to *Quiet Harbour*, was seen at night-time going down to Smalting Beach in the company of a woman, human remains were discovered under the beach hut.'

Philly Rose's hands shot up to clasp her face, as she took in the full implication of Carole's words.

Chapter Seventeen

Philly had clearly wanted them to leave. She needed to be alone to assess the full import of the new suspicion that Carole and Jude had planted in her mind, and they reckoned they would do more harm than good by staying with her.

It was around twelve when they emerged from Seashell Cottage. 'Lunch?' suggested Jude hopefully.

Carole's face disapproved. 'It's a bit early,' she said, 'and I've got the remains of a chicken in the fridge back at High Tor.'

'Oh, go on,' said Jude.

'No.' Carole was very firm. 'There's something else I want to do first.' And she led her friend along the Smalting promenade to a small former bakery, over whose shop windows was a silver-lettered sign reading 'Zentner Gallery'.

As she pushed the door open a bell tinkled, but the room they entered was empty. Its small space was inventively used. By the counter stood rotating stands of postcards and greetings cards. On the wall behind it hung framed prints of the predictably popular – Van Gogh's *Starry Night*, Jack Vettriano's *Singing*

Butler, Warhol's *Marilyns,* and so on. Sample posters and standard-sized frames were stacked upright
in boxes to be riffled through. On the counter itself
were grouped a selection of bookmarks, paperweights,
decorative pencils and other knick-knacks. These
items presumably kept the tills ticking over and were
bought mostly by browsers who'd come into the shop
with no intention of buying any original artwork.

But there was quite a lot of that on display in
the rest of the gallery. On a central table stood
bronze sculptures, mostly hares running and salmon
leaping. Some colourful abstracts decorated the back
wall, out of reach of the sun. On the side opposite
the counter was a display of works by three artists.
Nearest the window were some predominantly blue
fantasy scenes – long-haired blue maidens peering
through blue ferns at blue Arthurian boats on blue
lakes with brooding blue Tolkien mountains in the
background. Further back were a selection of splashy
pictures of racehorses, all looking exactly the same,
except presumably to their owners. And between the
two was an array of Gray Czesky's bland seascapes
and South Downs-scapes. Carole moved forward to
look at them.

'Can I help you?' A small woman in her early fifties with short black hair appeared from the back of
the shop, rubbing her hands on a J-cloth. 'Sorry, just
been doing some framing. The glue gets all over the
place.'

'Good morning,' said Carole. 'I was interested in
these.'

'They're by Gray Czesky.'

'From the subject matter it looks like he's a local.'

'Could hardly be more local. Lives just four houses along from here. By the way, I'm Sonja Zentner.'

'Carole Seddon.'

'And I'm Jude. So you own the gallery?'

'Yes. Fulfilling a long-held dream. I spent twenty years teaching art to uninterested teenagers, and always promised myself I'd retire early and do this.'

'Good. And how's it going?'

Sonja Zentner twiddled her hands in a 'so-so' gesture. 'Comes and goes. Better in the summer, obviously. And the framing keeps things ticking over. Anyway, Carole, you like the Gray Czeskys, do you?'

'Yes,' Carole lied.

'But how much do you like them?' Sonja Zentner grinned. 'Enough to want to buy one? Here are the prices.' She handed across a printed sheet.

Carole's immediate reaction was that Gray Czesky's watercolours seemed very expensive. The cheapest was five hundred pounds and the prices ranged up to over a thousand. 'Oh well, I don't think—'

'Does he take commissions?' Jude interrupted.

The gallery owner laughed. 'Show me the artist who doesn't take commissions. Of course he does.'

'Because you see, we live in Fethering and Carole was only saying the other day that she'd really like a decent watercolour of Fethering Beach to hang in her sitting room.' Jude carefully avoided the look of suppressed fury in her neighbour's eyes. 'And she'd really like to talk to Gray Czesky about it.'

'No problem. I can call him now, if you like. He's usually at home. He might well see you straight away.'

While Sonja Zentner made the call Jude looked demurely out of the window at Smalting Beach, confident that Carole wouldn't make a fuss until they were alone together.

The gallery owner put the phone down. 'Yes, that's perfect. Gray's there and would be delighted to talk to you about a potential commission. As I say, he's just four doors along. The house is called "Sanditon".'

'Thank you, that's so kind,' said Jude graciously. Then looking down towards the white tent surrounding *Quiet Harbour*, she continued, 'Terrible, that business over there, wasn't it?'

'Oh yes. And, needless to say in a place like Smalting, all kinds of theories are being put forward about what actually happened.'

'Any theories that sound believable?'

'Most of them are pretty fanciful, to be quite honest. And I think they'll stay that way until we get a bit more information. The police haven't said anything more about what was actually found under the beach hut. Just "human remains". Once we know the age and gender of the poor unfortunate, I think that'll put paid to some of the sillier conjectures.'

'So what's the latest you've heard, Sonja?'

'There was someone in only this morning who was convinced she knew who'd hidden the remains under the hut.'

'Oh?'

'Yes, she reads rather a lot of crime fiction, I'm

afraid, and she said that the police frequently ignore the most obvious solution. She said the first suspect should always be the person who discovers the body.'

'But in this case that was the Fether District Council-approved contractor who was about to repair the fire damage.'

'Oh no, Jude, she didn't mean him. She meant the one who discovered the fire damage. She was convinced that the murderer must be the woman who took over the hut rental from Philly Rose.'

'Oh, was she?' said a very tight-lipped Carole.

'Jude, will you stop giggling!' They were walking along the promenade towards Sanditon. 'It is not funny. It is not funny that I've just been identified as a murderer. And it's even less funny that you have set up a meeting with an artist who's expecting me to commission him to paint a watercolour of Fethering Beach.'

'It's an introduction. How else were we going to get to talk to Gray Czesky?'

'But I don't want to commission a watercolour from him. Certainly not at those prices. Anyway, I loathe watercolours. I just find them so insipid.'

'Look, you're only discussing the possibility of commissioning the painting. Obviously you don't go through with it.'

'But I can't raise this man's expectations about—'

'Carole, it's a commercial transaction. He's offering a service that you can accept or refuse. You're just checking out the possibilities. It's quite plausible that you could subsequently find another artist prepared to do you a watercolour of Fethering Beach at a much more reasonable price.'

'But I don't want a watercolour of Fethering Beach!' wailed Carole.

'It'll be fine.'

'It won't. Jude, you've put me in a very difficult position. I have to lie to this man about wanting a painting painted, and then I'll have to lie to him again about not wanting a painting painted.'

'As I say, it'll be fine. Trust me.'

'Huh,' Carole snorted.

Gray Czesky's studio was on the first floor of Sanditon, a large front bedroom commandeered for the cause of art. Carole and Jude could see why he had chosen it. A bay of huge picture windows meant that the light was excellent. The scene it illuminated, however, was one of total chaos.

Though the rest of the house, the hall into which the artist's wife Helga admitted them, the staircase and landing they were led through, was almost excessively neat, the studio was grotesquely untidy. Its bare boards and walls were deeply encrusted with spilled paint, the floor was a refuse dump of paint pots, broken brushes and soiled rags.

So total was the disarray that there was an air of parody about it, as though the artist had modelled his working space on images of Francis Bacon's studio. But here were no visceral canvases of tortured

139

souls and twisted bodies. Instead, Gray Czesky's neat chocolate-box watercolours struck a discordant note in the surrounding squalor.

The artist himself also seemed a parody. His long, greying hair and paint-spattered clothing presented an image of someone who didn't care about his appearance, but a lot of effort had gone into creating that effect. It was in marked contrast to his wife's *hausfrau* look, her neat blue skirt and a pink blouse fussy with ruffles.

'If you'd like coffee – or a drink maybe – Helga'll get you some.'

Carole and Jude both refused the offer and Helga left the room, her husband hardly having acknowledged her presence. He reached for a whisky bottle fingerprinted with paint, and poured a good measure into a filthy glass. After a long swig, he gestured to a spattered sofa on to which Carole and Jude sat gingerly. Gray Czesky perched on a tall paint-covered stool.

'Alcohol is a good antidote to thought,' he observed lackadaisically. 'I find I often need to curb my thoughts. Otherwise they overpower me. My mind is so ceaselessly active. I suppose that is one of the penalties of the artistic temperament.'

To Carole's mind instantly came a quotation from G.K. Chesterton that one of her former colleagues at the Home Office had been fond of: 'The artistic temperament is a disease that affects amateurs.' But she didn't say anything, just let the self-appointed genius maunder on.

'There's a common misconception that, if one has

a talent to produce work quickly, that must mean that it comes easily. But no, art is never easy. Art is a very hard taskmaster – or taskmistress is perhaps more accurate.' He gestured across the explosion in a paint factory to his own tidy little creations. 'Each one of those watercolours is torn from my soul, you know.'

This time Carole felt she had to say something. 'Well, they look very nice.'

'"Nice"? "Nice"!' Gray Czesky flung a hand up to clutch at his forehead. '"Nice" is the accolade of the bourgeoisie. And of course the aim of the artist is to *épater le bourgeois.* Call my work anything you wish – challenging, controversial, incompetent even – but never condemn it to the mediocrity of *"nice"*!'

'All right, I won't say it again,' said Carole through tightened lips.

Wishing to move the conversation into less hazardous waters, Jude observed that the studio had a splendid view.

'Yes. Though of course I never look at it. An artist does not look outside himself. The art is inside. The art has to be quarried out from within, like a rich seam of ore.'

'But surely,' said Jude, reasonably enough, 'when you're painting a landscape you have to look at it, don't you?'

'I don't look while I'm painting. I look before I paint. I memorize, I store the image within my mental gallery. For me the act of composition is always an act of recollection.'

Carole hadn't liked the lie that had brought them

into Gray Czesky's studio, but she reckoned it was time to play along with the subterfuge. 'So have you ever memorized Fethering Beach?'

'No. Why should I have done?'

'Oh, of course Sonja Zentner didn't mention the subject of the commission I'm thinking of. I'm looking for someone to do me a watercolour of Fethering Beach.'

'Ah. Well, no, I haven't memorized Fethering Beach, but it would be a matter of moments for me to do so. I could go along with my camera any day.'

'Oh, so you take photographs of the views you're going to paint and work from them? Is that what you mean by "memorizing"?' asked Jude.

This did rather dilute the magic of the creative process that the artist had described, and Gray Czesky seemed to acknowledge that he'd lost ground as he mumbled a yes.

'Well, I've seen examples of your work, which I like a lot,' Carole lied, 'so the question really is: how much would I have to pay to commission you?'

Now it came to money, Gray Czesky was suddenly a lot less airy-fairy. He reeled out a list of prices which seemed to vary according to the size of the picture required. And the smallest option would cost over two thousand pounds.

Carole disguised her real feelings – that if she had a spare two thousand pounds she could think of many things she'd rather spend it on – and said she'd have to mull over her next move. 'I will be checking out the rates of some other artists.'

'Other artists? Other *so-called* artists, I think you mean. I know the work of most of the so-called artists in the area, and there are few who aspire to being above competent draughtsmen. If you are looking for a mere wallcovering, you would do better to buy a poster or a reproduction than one of their efforts. If you want your wall to have a work of art hanging on it, then you need to commission Gray Czesky.'

Jude saw an opportunity to move the conversation in the direction of their investigation. 'You say you know all the local artists. Do you know Mark Dennis?'

'Yes, of course I do. Good bloke, Mark. Not much talent as an artist, I'm afraid, but still a good bloke. He didn't buy into all the bourgeois crap you get in a place like Smalting any more than I do.'

'I gather he's left Smalting,' said Carole.

An expression of crafty caution came into Gray Czesky's face as he responded, 'Yes, I'd heard that.'

'We know Philly, his girlfriend,' said Jude. 'She's terribly cut up about Mark leaving.'

The artist shrugged. 'Man's gotta do what a man's gotta do. Can't be tied down by bourgeois morality if you're an artist.'

Carole bit back her instinctive response to that remark, instead asking, 'I don't suppose you have any idea where he went?'

Gray Czesky grinned roguishly. 'There is a kind of freemasonry among men, you know. We support our mates, but we don't get involved in their love lives. If a bloke splits up with a girlfriend, not our problem. Doesn't matter whether we like the girl or not, we know where our duty lies. We'll support him, go out for a few drinks, help him forget, but we won't offer advice or comment. He's done what he wants to do, he no doubt had good reasons for doing it, it's his business.'

'You're saying you don't know why Mark walked out on Philly?'

Another shrug. 'Presumably he didn't want to stay with her any more.'

'You don't know if he'd met someone else . . . or gone back to someone?' asked Jude.

'No. And if I did know I wouldn't tell you. As I say, there's a freemasonry among blokes about that kind of thing. We leave the Mills and Boon stuff to the gentler sex. Me and Mark were just good drinking mates. We got healthily smashed from time to time and we didn't talk about *relationships*.' He put a heavy, doom-laden emphasis on the word.

'And you haven't seen Mark Dennis since he left Smalting?'

'That's another of those things where if I had I wouldn't tell you.'

It didn't seem as though their information gathering was going to progress much further. Carole rose to her feet and said, 'Thank you very much for your time, Mr Czesky. I'll make my decision about the commission very soon and get back to you either way. Do you have a card with your phone number on it?'

'Helga's got some downstairs.'

'I'll ask her as we go out.'

'Don't worry, I'll see you down. Don't feel ready to go straight back to the coalface of my art.' This was so melodramatically pronounced that Jude looked to see if Gray Czesky was actually sending himself up. But there was no gleam of humour in his eye. When it came to the subject of himself, he was a man incapable of irony.

He led the two women out on to the landing, and once again they were struck by the contrast between the manufactured squalor of the artist's workplace and the middle-class neatness of the rest of the house. Just as Jude started down the stairs, Carole suddenly said, 'Oh, will you excuse me? I just want to have one more look at one of the watercolours – to help me make up my mind,' and slipped back into the studio.

Gray Czesky shrugged and followed Jude down to the hall. He called to his wife as though she were a servant, asking her to bring one of his cards. Moments later Carole joined them.

'Thank you again, Mr Czesky.' She smiled at Helga. 'And Mrs Czesky.'

'No point in thanking her,' said the woman's gracious husband. 'She didn't do anything. Never do much, do you, Hel? Except get under my feet and stop me concentrating on my art.'

Carole and Jude waited for the explosion they reckoned those words must have detonated in any twenty-first-century woman, but none came. Instead, Helga Czesky giggled. And then her husband giggled too. Clearly his insulting of her was some kind of love ritual that seemed to turn them both on.

Helga was the first to recover her powers of speech. She grinned mischievously at the two women and said, 'I am very lucky, aren't I, to be married to a genius – no?'

No, thought Carole and Jude in unison.

Outside Sanditon, Carole became very mysterious, hurrying back to where she had parked the Renault. Jude kept asking what was happening, but she got no reply till they were both inside the car.

Then, milking the drama from her revelation, Carole announced, 'When I went back into the studio just now, it wasn't to take another look at the water-colours.'

'Oh?'

'It was to pick up this.'

'What?' asked Jude, playing along with her neighbour's narrative style.

Carole unclasped the handbag on her lap and produced from it a paint-spattered scrap of cloth. Jude's close inspection revealed it to be a strip of an old tea towel with a design of ponies on it.

'This,' Carole declared, 'is an exact match to one of the pieces of cloth that was used to set fire to *Quiet Harbour*.'

Chapter Eighteen

'So where do you reckon we stand now?' asked Jude. They had got a takeaway baguette lunch from The Copper Kettle and were sitting outside *Fowey* eating it. Although gathering clouds suggested that they'd had the best of the day, Jude had nonetheless stripped down to her bikini. Gulliver lay panting on the sand, having accepted there was no point in complaining further about being chained to a beach hut.

'I'm not quite sure,' Carole replied. 'But although he wouldn't tell us, I did get the strong impression that Gray Czesky had seen Mark quite recently.'

'As recently as the early hours of last Tuesday morning?'

'Hm, it'd be nice if we could prove that, wouldn't it? Be nice also if we could confirm that the woman with Mark was his wife Nuala.'

'Well, from what Philly said she sounds quite easy to recognize.'

'Yes, I'll try to get a description from Curt Holderness of the woman he saw that night. Give him a call when I get home.'

'Haven't you got your mobile with you?'

'Yes, I have, but . . .' Carole blushed.

'What?'

'I don't really approve of mobile phones being used on beaches.'

Jude's eyes shot heavenwards. Her neighbour always retained the capacity to surprise her with a new prohibition or neurosis. But she made no comment and asked, 'You know what Philly thought, don't you?'

'That Mark had done away with his wife, and that they were her remains under *Quiet Harbour*?'

'Yes. Does it work for you?'

Carole screwed up her face as she evaluated the proposition. 'I don't think it does really. "Human remains" . . . it all comes back to the definition of "human remains". To me that implies that they're from someone who's been dead quite a while. Wouldn't the media talk about "a dead body" if it was from a recent killing? And I'm sure they'd give the gender. "The body of a woman was discovered under a beach hut at Smalting," that's what they'd say. Not "human remains".'

'Maybe not.'

'I must say the police are being very slow to give out any more information, aren't they?'

'Presumably the remains are undergoing forensic investigation. When they've identified who the remains belong to then they'll announce it in a press conference.'

'Well, I wish they'd get a move on,' said Carole testily. 'It's been nearly a week.'

'They just don't think about the necessities of amateur sleuths, do they?'

'No, they don't.'

Though the sun was now hidden behind banks of clouds, Jude lay in her lounger as if sunbathing and it took Carole a little while to realize that her neighbour was asleep.

Quietly Carole detached Gulliver's lead from the hook on *Fowey* and set out along the shingle with him, following the curve of the beach huts. He gave her only a token look of reproach, recognizing that a walk on a lead was better than no walk at all.

Shrimphaven was still locked up. Whatever it was that the girl did in there on her laptop, she wasn't doing it that Monday afternoon.

Outside *Mistral*, as ever, Lionel Oliver, still apparently dressed for the office, lay back on his deckchair, his suit jacket hanging over its back. There was no sign of his wife but, as Carole approached, he waved down to the shoreline and she saw Joyce walking along with her bare feet in the water.

'Loves paddling,' the old man observed. 'The wife's always loved paddling. Even now she's whatever age she is.'

'Well, there's nothing like the feeling of the sand between one's toes,' said Carole, more expansive than usual. The fact that she would do anything to avoid the feeling of the sand between her toes was not relevant. Making conversation with people on Smalting Beach was now part of an ongoing enquiry, and Carole had always been more at ease doing things for a work purpose rather than just in her own persona.

She was surprised how affable Lionel Oliver appeared. When she'd seen him before, he'd looked detached, 'in a world of his own' as Joyce had put it. But now he seemed ready to talk, and it wasn't an opening that Carole was about to waste. Any of the regular beach hut users were potential witnesses to what had really happened on Smalting Beach.

She told Lionel her name and he gave her his. Though they had been aware of each other on the beach, this was the first time they had actually spoken. Then Carole moved into investigative mode.

'Terrible business, wasn't it?' She nodded over towards *Quiet Harbour*.

'What's that?'

She spelled it out. 'What was found under the beach hut there.'

'Oh yes,' he said. 'Most beaches have had their tragedies. Funny how everyone thinks of a beach as a friendly place and you look out from somewhere like here and the tide goes out so far and you think of the sea as a warm, friendly thing. But it has great power. Even here it has power to wash people away, power to drown them.'

Carole wasn't quite sure what kind of conversation she'd been expecting from Lionel Oliver, but it hadn't been a disquisition on the qualities of the sea. She didn't make any comment, though. He hadn't finished yet.

'I worked as an undertaker,' he went on. 'And I

suppose in that line of business we do get closer to human tragedy than people in other walks of life. We see people at their most disturbed, and we see the consequences of carelessness and folly . . . and misery.'

'Well, most people are bound to be miserable when they lose someone,' suggested Carole.

But that wasn't what he'd meant. 'I mean sometimes it's misery that makes someone do something that requires an undertaker's services. It's very sad, that. I mean, if you're dealing with bodies every day, you get a kind of immunity to the sort of shock most people'd feel. Because most people, what, they see a dead body once, twice in their lives perhaps? But we . . . we never get to the point of forgetting that the bodies we deal with are human beings – at least I hope we don't. I hope I never did. But we get so's we can deal with bodies without emotions getting in the way.

'And most of the bodies we dealt with . . . well, it's clearly a blessing that they come to the end. Bodies that have been worn away by disease and decay and pain . . . that cliché "a merciful release" . . . it's true for many of them. But when there's a body there's nothing wrong with, that's when it gets to you.'

'"Nothing wrong with"? But they're dead, aren't they?'

'I'm talking about the ones who needn't be dead, who've made the decision to die.'

'Suicides?'

The old man nodded. He looked out over the placid grey-green sea as he continued, 'There one did it here, you know.'

'Oh?'

'Ten years back, maybe not that long. I didn't see it, not when it happened. But obviously I saw the body. They'd got him out of the water quite quickly, so there wasn't a mark on him. Wearing a suit he was, he'd come straight down to the beach from his office. He worked in one of the Smalting estate agents. And the reason he'd done it, well, it wasn't a good enough reason. I'm not sure that anything's ever a good enough reason, not for that. Some girl he was in love with had dumped him, that was all. I mean, all right, I can see you might get upset over something like that, it might take you a few months, even a few years to get over it, but's not a reason to top yourself, is it? Not enough reason.'

He was silent for a moment, but Carole was confident he'd continue.

'What he'd done, how he did it . . . he'd just filled his pockets with stones, hardly stones, really. There are not many big stones on the beach here, mostly just shingle. And he'd put the shingle in the pockets of his jacket and his trousers, and he'd just walked straight out into the sea.

'It was low tide, I heard, so it took him a long time before the water got up to his knees, a long time till it got up to his waist, a long time till it got up to his neck. So he had plenty of time to think about what he was doing, plenty of time to change his mind. But he didn't.

'There were quite a lot of people on the beach, apparently, but no one did anything. I don't think any of them realized what he was doing. Yes, perhaps they thought it odd, a man dressed in a suit walking straight into the sea, but maybe they thought it was some stunt, that he'd done it for a bet or something. And by the time they'd realized that he'd disappeared under the sea and someone had phoned the coast-guard . . . well, it was too late.

'And when they brought the body to my parlour, there was, like I say, not a mark on him. He must have worked out in a gym, he was well toned. Could have lasted another fifty years. It was when I had to bury ones like that that it upset me. That and the children too. You never quite get used to burying the children.'

The old man shrugged, shook his head and re-lapsed into silence.

After a few moments, Carole said softly, 'And now there's another dead body on Smalting Beach.'

'Mm?' He came out of his reverie and looked puzzled.

'I was meaning the body under *Quiet Harbour*.'

'Oh yes.' He spoke without much interest in the subject.

'You haven't heard any thoughts from anyone as to who it might have been . . . ?'

'No,' he said, almost sharply. 'Well, that is to say I've heard lots of thoughts from lots of people – all rubbish. I'm sure when the police have identified the remains, they will make an announcement as to who it is.' Again he spoke as if the subject was rather tiresome, not something that impinged on his own life.

Carole didn't think she would have found out much more from Lionel Oliver, but was in fact prevented from asking further questions by the return of his wife from her paddle. 'Lionel been keeping you amused, has he?'

'He's been very interesting.'

'Oh yes? That probably means he's been talking to you about undertaking. It's a subject that was never very interesting while he was doing the job, and hasn't got any more interesting since he's retired.' But Joyce Oliver spoke with affection and no rancour.

After his surprisingly personal monologue, her husband seemed to have dropped back into a kind of torpor. Maybe he was only talkative when his wife was absent.

Joyce got back into her chair and picked up one of her wordsearch books.

'I must be on my way. Nice to see you,' said Carole. 'Come on, Gulliver.'

Chapter Nineteen

Carole moved on to *Seagull's Nest*, the hut directly next to the still-cocooned *Quiet Harbour*. Outside it sat the matriarch who, thanks to Reginald Flowers, she now knew to be called Deborah Wrigley. Dressed in a designer towelling beach-robe, the widow had on her head another wide straw hat tied with a scarf and on her feet golden rubber sandals. She wore sunglasses with elaborate gold rims and an accumulation of rings sparkled on her bony brown fingers.

There was no sign of her son or daughter-in-law, but nearby her grandchildren Tristram and Hermione were deeply involved in patting crumbling sandcastles out of plastic buckets.

Carole did the Smalting equivalent of the 'Fethering nod', a slight inclination of the head to acknowledge someone one knew by sight but did not necessarily want to engage in conversation with.

Deborah Wrigley smiled graciously back. 'We've had the best of the day, I fear,' she observed.

'Yes, be rain before the evening's out,' said Carole, wondering what kind of Pavlovian reaction it was that prompted her at such moments into talking like a Central Casting Sussex fisherman. She nodded towards *Quiet Harbour*. 'Nasty business, what they found there, wasn't it?'

'Oh yes. I have to be very careful with the grandchildren, making sure they don't overhear people on the beach talking about it.'

'Mm. Are their parents not around? Last time I saw you here they were with them.'

'No, my son and daughter-in-law have gone back to London. I always insist on having a couple of days' quality time with the grandchildren when they come down here. I think it's good for them. Their parents indulge the little ones so much, you know, and so they get tantrums and what have you. But Tristram and Hermione behave very well when they're with me. They don't play up at all.'

They wouldn't *dare*, thought Carole. Recognizing the opportunity for a little investigation, she gestured again towards *Quiet Harbour* and said, 'I don't suppose you've heard any more than the rest of us about what was actually found in there?'

'"Human remains", that's all I've heard.' But Deborah Wrigley was the kind of woman who always liked to have some exclusive information, so she couldn't stop herself from saying, 'Of course I knew the young couple who rented it before you.'

'What, you mean you met them down here on the beach?'

'I met the girl down here for the first time. But I did actually know the young man from some time back.'

Carole was instantly alert. 'Oh?'

'He used to work with my husband at NMB.'

'NMB? I'm sorry, the initials sound familiar, but I'm not sure I . . .'

'Neuchâtel Mutual Bank. My husband Ronald ran the London end of that.'

'Oh, did he?'

'And Mark Dennis – that's the name of the young man who had the beach hut when—'

'Yes, I'd heard it.'

'Well, he joined NMB straight out of university. Very bright boy. Ronald had a lot of time for him. And I used to meet Mark from time to time at business functions.'

'Ah.'

A sly look came into Deborah Wrigley's face. 'They're not married, you know.'

'Mark and Philly? No, I know that.'

The older woman looked a little peeved at Carole having information about the couple for which she had not been the source. 'He used to be married, you know. Tall, beautiful girl, worked in another bank. Goodness knows why Mark let that go wrong.'

'Did you meet her?'

'Yes, some odd Irish name.'

'Nuala.'

'That's right.' Again Deborah Wrigley seemed peeved that Carole knew more than she did. 'Yes, I met her a few times. At functions, you know. Very attractive couple. Very successful couple. They had a bit of motivation. So few young people seem to these days. Like my son. He was a severe disappointment to Ronald.' Even *in absentia* Gavin Wrigley was not protected from his mother's sideswipes.

'Have you seen Nuala Dennis recently?'

'No, no reason why I should. I no longer moved in City circles after Ronald died. Anyway, their marriage broke up. Then I heard through mutual friends that Mark had given up his extremely promising career to become a painter or something equally fatuous. Next thing I know he appears down here with this new girl in tow.'

'Did you see him here at the beach hut?'

'Yes. The keen hutters tend to start using them at Easter. I always invite Gavin and the children down for a week at Easter.'

Invite? I bet it's a three-line whip, thought Carole. And she noticed that Deborah Wrigley's daughter-in-law Nell didn't even merit a mention.

'Anyway, I think Mark must've had some kind of breakdown – or mid-life crisis do they call it these days? The generation who lived through the war didn't have time for mid-life crises. He must have been potty, though, because he chucks a perfectly good job, leaves a delightful and beautiful wife and sets up with some young floozy. I've met her. Called Gillie or something.'

'Philly.'

'Whatever. Insipid little thing, I thought. Not like Nuala. At least Nuala had something about her.'

Deborah Wrigley's words made Carole think. First, the idea that Mark Dennis might have had some kind of breakdown. It hadn't occurred to her before, but maybe it wasn't such a silly idea. He'd certainly been under a lot of pressure at the time of his disappearance. Maybe he had cracked up and been hospitalized. That would explain the lack of contact Philly had had from him.

The other realization that Deborah Wrigley had prompted was that the only version of Nuala Dennis that Carole and Jude had heard about had been Mark's views passed on by Philly. And people from broken relationships don't always provide the most balanced assessments of their ex-partners' characters. Maybe Nuala wasn't the complete villainess that she had been painted.

All this went through Carole's mind in a flash before she asked, 'Do you know if Nuala still works in the City?'

'I assume so. She and Mark didn't have children, I know that. Whether there was some problem, or whether she just put her career first I've no idea. When I last had contact with her she was working for PWC.' In response to Carole's interrogative eyebrow, she spelled out, 'PricewaterhouseCoopers. But we're talking some years ago. Goodness knows if she's still there. These City high-flyers tend to move around a lot these days. Different in Ronald's time. He was at NMB most of his career. Climbed his way up the management ladder. But then that's how things worked in those days. People had a sense of loyalty to their employers. Whereas today's young people don't even seem to understand what the word "loyalty" means.'

'So you don't have any other means of contacting Nuala Dennis?'

The expression on Deborah Wrigley's face told Carole how odd her question must have sounded. 'No,' came the reply. 'We are talking about someone I only met a few times through my husband's work. And I can't imagine any reason why you might want to contact her.'

'No, I'm sorry. I just . . . well, I've met Philly Rose . . .'

'Have you?' The words were not enthusiastic.

'Yes. And I know how cut up she is about Mark's leaving, and I thought if he had gone back to his wife, then contacting her might be a way of—'

'I'm sure if Mark Dennis has gone back to his wife – which I very much hope he has – the last thing the two of them would wish for would be a call from his former floozy.'

'You're probably right. Well, Gulliver and I had better be on our way.'

'Yes, perhaps you had.' Deborah Wrigley's smile of dismissal had all the warmth of a low-energy light bulb.

When Carole got back to High Tor she rang Curt Holderness's mobile. Prompted to leave a message, she asked if he could phone her back, though without great confidence that he would. When they had parted on the Sunday in the Crown and Anchor, the security officer hadn't shown much enthusiasm for the idea of their ever speaking again.

Since it was not yet five o'clock, Carole – again

without much optimism – thought she might try PricewaterhouseCoopers to get a contact number for Nuala. Using her laptop to check the number on their website, she rang through to the main London office near Charing Cross. No, they did not have a Nuala Dennis working for them. And no, they couldn't divulge details of former employees.

As she put the phone down, it struck Carole that a City go-getter like the Nuala Deborah Wrigley had described would quite probably have worked under her maiden rather than her married name. And trying to guess that would be a hopeless task. She wondered whether Philly Rose might know. It didn't seem very likely. Few women are interested in their lovers' wives' maiden names.

Later that evening, as they shared a bottle of Chilean Chardonnay in her cluttered sitting room, Jude agreed that it was worth trying to get a bit more information from Philly and rang through to Seashell Cottage. But no, the girl had no idea what Nuala had been called before she married Mark.

'So you don't have any means of contacting her?'

'Why should I have?'

'That wasn't really the question I was asking, Philly.'

'No.' There was a silence from the Smalting end. Then, 'I do actually have a mobile number for her.'

'Oh?'

'I copied it from Mark's phone once when he was out. I don't know why. I think perhaps I'd always been aware of the risk Nuala represented. But then when he left, I didn't dare ring the number. I kept wanting to, but something stopped me.'

'The thought that Mark might actually be with her?' Jude suggested intuitively.

'Yes, just that. It was what I was afraid might have happened, and I suppose I was equally afraid of having my fears confirmed.'

'I could ring her,' Jude proposed gently.

'But why should you?'

'For the same reason you would – to find out if Mark's with her.'

'Yes, but how would you explain why you were doing it?'

'I'd be trying to contact Mark and say I'd been given that number.'

'And who would you claim to be – someone trying to sell him double glazing?'

'If I can't think of anything better, yes.'

'Okay, you try. And make sure you let me know if you find out anything about where he is.'

'Of course I will. Could you give me the number?'

After Philly had done so, she said, 'And of course if you call you might also find out whether anything's happened to Nuala.'

Clearly Philly's anxiety of that morning had not gone away. She was still worried that Mark Dennis might have done away with his inconvenient ex-wife.

Chapter Twenty

'No time like the present,' said Jude, and instantly she was keying in the number that Philly Rose had given her.

It was answered almost immediately, but the voice was male. 'Hello?'

'Good evening. I was trying to contact Nuala Dennis.'

'Oh, were you?' The name didn't seem to prompt happy memories.

'I'm sorry. I was given this number as Nuala Dennis's mobile phone.'

'Well, it used to be hers. Now I reckon it's mine.'

'Oh. Erm, who am I speaking to?'

'My name's Cyrus Maxton. Who are you?'

'Jude.'

'A friend of Nuala's?'

'More an acquaintance, really.'

'And what do you want with her?'

It was one of those moments when the truth might be as effective as any falsehood. 'I'm trying to track down her husband Mark.'

'They've separated.'

'Yes, I know that, but—'

'Listen, I know nothing about Nuala's bloody husband! All I know is that Nuala and I were in a relationship for about three months and then the cow walked out on me, having managed to take quite a lot of my money with her. So you might understand that I don't welcome calls from her friends or acquaintances and I'm damned if I'm going to—'

'Why have you got her mobile phone?'

'She left it here when she stormed out. I was about to upgrade mine, so I thought I'd use hers. Get something out of three wasted months! And so far she still seems to be paying the bill – which suits me fine!'

'Have you had any contact with Nuala since?'

'Texts. I've tried ringing her, but she won't talk.'

'So you do have a current mobile number for her?'

'What if I do?'

'If you could give me that number, I—'

'Why should I? After the way the bitch treated me, I don't feel particularly inclined to help her maintain her social life with her girlfriends.'

'I'm not one of her girlfriends.' That was true, though what Jude said next wasn't. 'She stung me for a lot of money too. That's why I'm trying to contact her.'

Cyrus Maxton's manner changed immediately. Now that he appeared to be talking to someone keen to make Nuala Dennis's life difficult, he was all co-operation. He gave Jude the new mobile number. 'But I should warn you, you may not get through.'

'Oh?'

'I've been texting her regularly trying to get

back some of the stuff she nicked from my flat and I haven't been getting any replies.'

'Well, presumably when she recognizes your number she just doesn't text back.'

'Sure. But recently when I've tried I get a different response. Like the phone's switched off. Or run out of juice.'

'You mean she hasn't been recharging it?'

'That's what I've been beginning to think. Okay, not taking my calls, not responding to my texts, I can understand that. But switching the thing off? Nuala's mobile is like an extra appendage of her body. She never switched it off – or at least not for as long as this.'

'You said "recently". When was the last time you texted her phone when it was switched on?'

'Weekend before last. I tried again . . . when? Let's think . . . Today's Monday . . . it would have been last Tuesday. Didn't get any response then and the phone's been switched off since.'

Last Tuesday. The day in whose small hours Mark Dennis and a mystery woman were seen by Curt Holderness walking down on to Smalting Beach. The day since Nuala Dennis had perhaps not been able to recharge her mobile phone.

After she'd finished her call to Cyrus Maxton, Jude tried the new number he had given her for Nuala. She was sent straight to voicemail. The phone was switched off . . . or out of charge.

Chapter Twenty-One

Carole Seddon woke the next morning feeling pressured by time. It was Tuesday and in five days Gaby and Lily would be coming to stay in High Tor. Was it possible that she and Jude could have found a solution to the mystery of the human remains under *Quiet Harbour* by then? At their current rate of progress the prospects were not promising.

But when she joined Jude later for coffee at Woodside Cottage, they did have a small breakthrough on the case. Without much optimism, Jude once again tried the number Cyrus Maxton had given her. And this time it was answered.

'Hello?' The voice was hard, businesslike and unwelcoming, but there was a little trace of Irish in it.

'Good morning. Is that Nuala Dennis?'

'My name's Nuala Cullan.'

'But is your married name Nuala Dennis?'

'I never use my married name.'

'But your married name is Nuala Dennis?'

'It was once.' Jude felt a little flutter of relief. At least she'd be able to reassure Philly that Mark's wife was still alive, that he hadn't done away with her.

'Who is this calling?' asked Nuala, even less welcoming.

'My name's Jude.'

'Jude who?'

The question was ignored. 'I'm calling about your husband, Mark Dennis.'

'Look, if it's some financial trouble Mark's got himself into, you're calling the wrong person. I have no responsibility for what he's done. We're separated. And you are calling me at work and I do have a very busy day ahead of me, so—'

'I'm interested in Mark's whereabouts.'

'So am I.'

'You mean you don't know where he is?'

'No. Why, do you?' For the first time there was a flicker of interest in the Irishwoman's voice.

'I might do,' Jude lied.

'Tell me what you know.'

'I'd rather we met up and talked about it.'

'Look, who are you? Are you Mark's latest woman? I heard he'd left his little girl at the seaside. Is he shacked up with you now?'

'No. I can assure you he isn't.'

'Then what's your interest in this?'

'I'll tell you when we meet.'

'*If* we meet.'

'You want to find out where Mark is, don't you?'

There was a silence from the other end. Then a reluctant, 'Yes. The bastard owes me money, apart from anything else.'

'Well, when could we meet?'

'I've got a hell of a schedule today, but I could probably finish early and meet you round seven.'

Seven? Finishing early? Jude realized she was definitely dealing with someone from the City.

'That'd be fine. Where do you work?'

'NMB.'

'Neuchâtel Mutual Bank. Where Mark used to work?'

'Yes. Not many people have heard of it.' There was a hint of grudging respect in Nuala's voice.

'Okay. Seven o'clock. At NMB?'

'No, better somewhere else.' Whether this was because Nuala feared eavesdroppers at work, Jude could only guess. 'There's a wine bar called Sec. Just off Milk Street.'

'We'll find it.'

'"We"?'

'Yes, I'll have a friend with me.'

'Look, I'm not sure that I—'

'You do want to find out where Mark is, don't you?' Jude interrupted forcibly.

Nuala conceded that she did.

'Right, we'll be at Sec at seven o'clock this evening.'

'How will I recognize you?'

'I'm blond and plump, my friend Carole is thin and grey-haired with glasses. You'll recognize us. We'll rather stand out in a City wine bar. We're in our fifties.'

To their surprise, Carole and Jude did not stand out in Sec as much as they had expected to. The time of year and its relative proximity to St Paul's, the Bank of England and other London sights, meant that the wine bar had more than its fair share of tourists that June evening. And though there were a few young, lean besuited slickers quaffing champagne, there were at least as many men and women of ample American proportions. And in fact Carole and Jude identified Nuala Cullan, rather than the other way round.

It wasn't difficult. They remembered Philly Rose's description and when, shortly after seven, a tall slender woman in a pinstriped trouser suit and pointy black shoes entered, they knew it had to be her. She was beautifully groomed, and the long black hair contrasted with the piercing blue of her eyes. But for the sharpness of her features and a slight discontent in her expression, Nuala Cullan would have been beautiful.

Jude crossed the bar and introduced herself, asking what Nuala would like to drink. She and Carole, straying from their usual Chilean Chardonnay, were on the Sauvignon Blanc.

'I'll just have a mineral water, thank you.' So much for the hard-drinking image that Philly had put across. 'I'm on antibiotics,' continued Nuala, explaining her abstinence.

'This is my friend Carole.'

'Oh?' Nuala Cullan stretched out a long cool hand and shook Carole's.

'Grab a seat and I'll get your drink.'

Nuala subsided elegantly into a chair and gave the woman opposite her a hard, appraising look. 'So you know Mark too, do you?'

Carole was flustered. She wished she and Jude had discussed a cover story to answer such a question, but her neighbour was never very keen on preparation for this kind of encounter. She always felt confident the right words would come when required. Well, they might, to Jude. Carole couldn't think of anything very convincing to say.

'I haven't actually met him, but I've heard a lot about him from Philly.'

'Ah, so you've only had her version. In which he no doubt appears like a cross between Mother Theresa and the Angel Gabriel.'

'Well—'

'Do you know where he is at this minute? Do you have an address for him?'

'Well . . .'

Carole's discomfiture was fortunately then reprieved by a bleep from Nuala Cullan's handbag. She pulled out an iPhone and deftly answered a text message. By the time she had finished Jude was back from the bar with Nuala's mineral water.

'Right, what is all this?' Nuala asked peremptorily.

'Have the police been in touch with you?' asked Jude.

'What the hell should the police be in touch with me about?'

'You heard about the discovery of human remains on Smalting Beach?'

'There was something in the news, yes, and I remember thinking, "Well, there you go – Mark's moved out of the wicked City and into his seaside love nest and suddenly it's down there that all the crimes are happening."'

'But the police haven't been in touch with you about it?'

'No.' She looked faintly nauseated by the idea. 'Why on earth should they be?'

'The beach hut under which the remains were found was rented by Mark and Philly.'

'Was it?' This seemed to amuse her. 'Sounds like their life was even further away from the perfect country idyll.'

'And,' Jude went on, 'we were wondering whether the police might have been in touch with you as they tried to track down Mark.'

'Well, I suppose they might have been.' She shrugged. 'But they haven't. So it seems like everyone's looking for Mark, doesn't it?' A sudden thought shocked her. 'You're not suggesting the remains are of Mark, are you?'

'No, no, there's no suggestion of that,' replied Carole. 'When did you last see him, Nuala?'

'I don't know. Some time in May, I suppose.'

'After he'd walked out on Philly?'

'What?' Nuala's fine brow wrinkled in puzzlement. 'He's walked out on her?'

'Didn't you know?'

'Of course I didn't.' But as she took in the idea she started to chuckle. 'So domestic bliss in Smalting didn't work out, did it?'

Jude looked at the cool, self-possessed executive in front of her and wondered for a moment whether this could also be the vengeful hysteric, the emotional black-mailer whom Philly had described. And her knowledge of human nature told her that it all too easily could.

'Mark walked out on Philly at the beginning of May,' said Carole, 'and she hasn't seen him since.'

'Oh, well, I have the advantage of Little Miss Perfect then, don't I?'

'Philly thought he might have moved back in with you.'

'Did she?' This seemed to Nuala another funny idea. She laughed openly as she said, 'I'm not sure that I could cope with that.'

'I believe,' Carole went on, 'that Mark had made some kind of financial arrangement with you . . . that he paid you a monthly amount to let him get on with his life?'

'Well, don't make it sound so shabby. I am his wife, you know, still his wife. And that does give me some rights. Bloody Mark can't just abandon me and start spending all his money on some other woman.'

'I understand he hasn't got much money now.'

'That's not my problem, is it? Look, if my husband wants to act like he's divorced, then I ought to get something from him, something like I would get if we were actually divorced.'

'Do you want a divorce?'

Nuala Cullan smiled slyly. 'I might think about it. But I am a Catholic, you know, and however lax I have been in observing Catholic rules of behaviour, my Church still does not approve of divorce. So I'm in no hurry to make Mark's life any easier for him.'

Carole and Jude both now realized exactly how manipulative the woman in front of them could be. She would never let Mark Dennis go, never let him find real freedom. Nuala Cullan was trouble. They could understand how readily Philly Rose had entertained the idea that Mark might have murdered her. And from the way he spoke on the phone, Cyrus Maxton sounded as if he wouldn't have minded topping her as well.

'Have you had any money from Mark recently?'

'No.' She pouted with annoyance. 'That's why I want to find out where the bastard is. Last payment I had from him was in May. When I do track him down, he's going to be paying interest on those arrears.'

'So when exactly did you last see him?' asked Carole.

'May. I said.'

'When in May?'

Her forehead wrinkled as she tried to remember. The tracery of lines on her face showed through the expert make-up. She wasn't as young as she had first appeared. Well over forty. Getting to an age when she might not be able to rely on her looks quite as much as she used to, to get what she wanted. Getting to an age when she might well be wanting to safeguard her future.

'I think it was the eighth,' Nuala replied eventually. 'Mark said he wanted to meet up and talk. He took me to the Oxo Tower, one of our regular haunts . . . in happier times.'

'And he didn't mention that he'd left Philly?'

'I've told you, this evening is the first I've heard of it. He just told me that he couldn't afford to continue paying anything to me.'

'He told you this at the Oxo Tower?'

'I'd booked the venue.' She smiled at the memory of another small triumph over her husband. 'And I told him, no way, José. I told him he could take the idea of stopping payments to me and put it where the sun don't shine.'

'But surely,' said Carole, 'if he chose to stop paying you, there was nothing you could have done about it.'

'I could have sued him.'

'You mean it was more than a verbal agreement?'

'You bet it was. I'm not stupid. I got a schedule of payments drawn up by my lawyer.'

'And Mark signed it?'

'Of course he did. All neatly tied up with pink ribbon it was. So when I said he owed me arrears, I meant just that. He is legally in default of those payments.'

'But why did he sign it?' asked Jude.

'I don't know.' Nuala smiled a smile of mock innocence. 'Maybe he thought I was capable of causing a lot of trouble in his relationship with Little Miss Perfect. Though why he should think that,' she continued, maintaining the wide-eyed pose, 'I cannot imagine.'

Jude exchanged a momentary look with Carole. They were beginning to realize just how destructive Nuala could be if she set her mind to it.

'How did he seem that evening at the Oxo Tower?' asked Jude. 'Just like you remember him?'

Nuala Cullan shook her head. 'No, there was something strange about him. Mark seemed distracted . . . almost as if he was frightened of something.'

'Had you seen him in that state before? During your marriage?'

Another shake of the head. 'Mark was always very confident, even brash at times. But that night at the Oxo Tower he was very jumpy. Nervous. Stressed.'

'He didn't say why?'

'Didn't need to. The details he told me about his financial situation were enough to make anyone stressed.' Suddenly Nuala Cullan seemed to lose patience. 'Look, what is this all about? You got in touch with me because you said you knew something about Mark's whereabouts. I don't have the whole evening to waste. Tell me where he is.'

It was Carole who answered. 'He was seen down in Smalting in the small hours of last Tuesday morning.'

'Oh? So he's back with Little Miss Perfect, is he?'

'Philly Rose said she hadn't seen him since May.'

'Has it occurred to you she might be lying?'

'I don't think she would,' said Jude.

'Oh, I see. So you've been fooled by her wide-eyed innocent look, have you?'

More than I have by yours, thought Jude. But all she said was, 'I thought you hadn't met her.'

'I don't need to meet her. I know the kind of woman Mark would be a sucker for.'

'But he was a sucker for you at one point. I wouldn't have thought "wide-eyed innocent" was a very accurate description of you,' said Carole with some asperity.

'No, you're right. It isn't.' Nuala Cullan smiled a feline, controlling smile. 'Our relationship was very powerful, passionate, but also potentially toxic. Mark couldn't always keep up with me. I am strong liquor, the hard stuff, you see. And Mark's basically a coward. Which is why he opted instead for milky afternoon tea in Smalting.'

'Anyway,' said Carole, who had had quite enough of this preening, 'when Mark was seen down there last Tuesday morning, there was a woman with him.'

'So?'

'Philly's first thought when she heard was that the woman must be you.'

'Why?'

'Because she thought you and Mark were back together.'

'Well, I've told you, we're not.' Nuala Cullan looked at the small Rolex on her slender wrist. 'And is that all you've come to tell me? That he's been seen? Or can you actually tell me where I can contact the bastard?'

'No,' said Carole rather feebly. 'We just wanted to tell you he's been seen down in Smalting.'

'Well, thank you very much,' came the sarcastic reply.

'We thought you'd want to know.'

'Why?'

'At least it proves he's still alive,' said Jude.

'And why shouldn't he be alive?' Nuala looked sardonically thoughtful. 'Though if he were dead, it would in a way solve all my problems, wouldn't it?'

'How?'

'I'm still his wife. I would inherit everything.'

'Though it doesn't seem there'd be that much to inherit.'

'Don't you believe it. Someone as canny as Mark's always going to have something stashed away.' There was a gleam of pure greed in her eyes as she spoke.

Repelled by this, Jude said, 'Well, he's not dead, so the issue doesn't really arise, does it?'

'No.' Nuala Cullan took another look at her watch and picked up her handbag. 'I won't say thank you, because so far as I'm concerned our meeting has been a total waste of time. But if you do find out where Mark is, let me know. You have my mobile number.' She stood up.

'And there wasn't any other contact Mark gave you?' asked Jude, desperate to retrieve something from the situation.

The tall woman stood undecided for a moment. Her desire to be uncooperative conflicted with her interest in tracking down her absent husband. She still wanted to leech more money out of him.

She made up her mind. 'There was a number he gave me, some acquaintance down in Smalting where he said I could leave a message. I tried it a few times, but my messages never got a response from Mark, so I stopped bothering.'

'Did you speak to this acquaintance of his?'

'No, the phone was always on voicemail.'

'Would you mind giving us the number?' asked Jude.

The area code was 01903, which covered Worthing,

Littlehampton, Fethering and Smalting. Jude wrote it down, and Nuala Cullan walked out of Sec without a word of farewell.

The two women decided to have another glass of Sauvignon Blanc to bolster them for the slow train journey back to Fethering. And they both knew exactly why Mark Dennis had wanted to get away from his wife.

Chapter Twenty-Two

They were back home too late to do anything else that evening. And on the Wednesday morning Jude had to go and visit one of her Fethering clients who was immobilized with what the patient thought to be a slipped disc, but the healer knew to be anxiety about her daughter's forthcoming wedding.

It was after her neighbour had gone – and therefore too late – when Carole realized that Jude had got the piece of paper with the phone number Nuala Cullan had given them. That was annoying. She'd been hoping that contact might offer some breakthrough on the intractable mystery that confronted them.

But even as she felt the frustration building within her, Carole received a phone call that brought her new information. It was from Curt Holderness.

She was surprised that he had rung back. The message had been left on his mobile without much optimism. But the fact that he had got back to her and his manner when he spoke gave Carole a lift. He was clearly still worried that she might draw the attention of the authorities to his lax approach to his job. Which gave her a position of power over him.

'You rang me, Carole. What can I do for you?' Curt Holderness's opening words were breezy enough, but there was an encouraging undercurrent of anxiety in his voice.

'Oh, thank you so much for getting back to me. Yes, there was something I wanted to follow up with you, further to our previous conversation . . .'

She let the silence dangle for a moment and was rewarded by a nervous 'What?' from the other end of the line.

'Oh, it was about that night, you know, when you saw Mark Dennis going on to Smalting Beach.'

'Yes.' He sounded relieved now he knew the subject of her enquiry. She wasn't raising issues of low-grade local council corruption.

'You said that he was with a woman . . .'

'Yes.'

'. . . but you didn't recognize her.'

'Right.'

'So could you give me a description of her?'

'Shortish.' If Nuala Cullan hadn't already ruled herself out that would have done it. 'I don't know, it was fairly dark that night. Shortish, as I say, and maybe on the chubby side.'

'What age?'

His manner implied a shrug as he replied, 'I don't know. I mean, she wasn't the kind of woman who made much impression, if you know what I mean. Just like plenty of women you see in the street, nothing remarkable about them.'

'Hair colour?'

'Blond, possibly.' He didn't sound very sure.

'And how was Mark Dennis behaving with her?'

'What do you mean?'

'Well, were they holding hands, arm in arm?'

'Oh no, nothing like that.'

'Were they just ambling along or were they looking furtive? Were they hurrying?'

'Yes, I'd say they were hurrying. The man might even have been swaying about a bit.'

'You mean – as if he was drunk?'

'Possibly.'

'And you couldn't tell exactly where they were going?'

'I was just driving past,' he protested. 'I only saw them for a couple of seconds.'

'You're absolutely certain the man was Mark Dennis?'

'Absolutely certain,' said Curt Holderness.

A silence stretched out between them. Then suddenly a new thought came into Carole's head, a recollection of something the security officer had mentioned when they'd first spoken. It was a long chance that the question would lead anywhere, but anything was worth a try. 'There's another thing I want to ask you,' said Carole.

'Oh?' He was once again wary.

'When we first spoke on the phone, Mr Holderness, you assumed – wrongly –that I'd contacted you because there was some rule about use of the beach hut on Smalting Beach that I wanted you to bend for me.'

There was an uncomfortable silence from the other end of the line, so Carole pressed on. 'You also gave examples of rules that you had managed to bend, of people having small generators in their huts, or staying overnight in them . . .'

'So? Are you planning to report me for it?' There was a new menace in his question. Carole visualized the thickset security officer and was in no doubt that he would be quite capable of physical violence.

'I don't think that'll be necessary, ' she said, more calmly than she felt, 'if you were to tell me which of the current owners of Smalting Beach beach huts you have allowed to stay there overnight.'

'Well, in the past there's been the odd adulterous couple who use the place for their assignations . . .'

'Any of that going on at the moment?'

'No. Last one of those broke up just before Christmas. The woman's husband found out and surprised them at it in the beach hut. Very messy and violent.'

'How violent?'

'Nobody was killed, if that's what you mean. But a heavy beating was administered to the wife and her lover.'

'Was it reported to the police?'

'Of course not. Not in any of their interests to make the thing public, was it? Mind you, we had to get professional cleaners in to get the blood off the walls.'

Carole winced. 'And currently?'

'How do you mean?'

'Is there anyone staying overnight in any of the huts to whom you're currently turning a blind eye?'

'Look, if I tell you this, will you get off my back?'

'Oh yes,' said Carole glibly. But she had no intention of doing so. She knew she had a powerful hold over Curt Holderness, and if there was further information she thought she could get from him, she wouldn't hesitate to put further pressure on him.

'All right,' he said grudgingly. 'There's just the one. Girl in *Shrimphaven*.'

'The one next to *Fowey*, which I'm using at the moment.'

'That's right. Kel Southwest put the girl on to me and we . . . sorted out an arrangement.'

'Of the folding variety?'

'Maybe.'

'What's her name?' asked Carole.

'Katie Brunswick.'

Carole smiled to herself. Her hunch had been right. Now she had a potential witness to night-time goings-on on Smalting Beach. She decided another trip to *Fowey* might be in order.

The day was nondescript. Warm enough, but with no sun showing through the clogged clouds. When – and if – they blew away, the afternoon might be quite pleasant.

Carole had the decency to take Gulliver for a walk along Smalting Beach before subjecting him to the ignominy of being chained up. She had brought a bottle of water with her to fill his bowl and after a couple of thirsty slurps from it he lay down in the shade, apparently reconciled to his fate.

183

Carole's preparations had not only included the water. She had brought with her her customary smokescreen of *The Times* crossword and also a bag of chocolate brownies that she had made that morning. This was most unusual behaviour. Carole Seddon didn't have a sweet tooth and she rarely baked anything. She also, from her childhood onward, had Calvinistically resisted the wicked crime of *eating between meals*. But the chocolate brownies had been made with two purposes in mind. One was the imminent arrival of Gaby and Lily on the Sunday. Both her daughter-in-law and granddaughter were suckers for anything containing chocolate.

And the second purpose of the brownies was to act as an ice-breaker to the young woman in *Shrimphaven*. After erecting a base camp on *The Times* crossword by filling in a couple of clues, Carole picked up her bag of goodies and steeled herself to the challenge of being affably sociable. It was something that she knew Jude would do more naturally – and better.

She had noticed that the doors of *Shrimphaven* were open when she'd walked Gulliver back. And she'd even directed a kind of 'Fethering nod' to its interior, though she couldn't say whether any response had emerged from the shadows. But she had definitely seen the outline of the girl she now knew to be called Katie Brunswick, hunched as ever over her laptop.

Carole took a deep breath and stepped across to block the daylight from *Shrimphaven*'s doors. Inevitably Katie Brunswick had to look up at her.

'Good morning,' said Carole in her best attempt

at affable sociability. 'Since we're kind of beach hut neighbours I thought I'd say hello. My name's Carole Seddon and I was about to have one of these chocolate brownies I've just made. And then I thought maybe you would like one?'

She was now close enough to get her first proper view of Katie Brunswick, seated on the bench at the back of what was an otherwise very empty beach hut. Probably in her thirties, the girl had large round glasses and black curly hair pulled back untidily into a scrunchy. Her slight figure was dressed in a plain white T-shirt, jeans and flip-flops.

She didn't exactly look pleased to be interrupted, but was too well brought up to be positively rude. 'That's very kind of you,' she said in a voice that had also been well brought up.

Carole stepped into *Shrimphaven* and proffered her paper bag. With something like reluctance, Katie Brunswick shifted her laptop on to the table by her side and accepted a brownie. Carole also took one out and bit into it, an indication that she was going to stay until the cake was finished. Katie was again too well brought up not to gesture Carole to sit on the bench beside her. There were no other chairs in the hut.

'Would you like some coffee?' she asked, gesturing to a large thermos on a white table through whose paint little aureoles of rust had worked through like acne.

'No, thank you. I've just had some.'

The girl seemed relieved at this response, perhaps because it suggested Carole's visit was going to be eating-a-brownie length rather than eating-a-brownie-and-drinking-a-cup-of-coffee length. Or maybe she'd carefully calculated the contents of the thermos as her coffee supply for the day.

'I'm sorry, I don't know your name,' Carole lied. Katie Brunswick identified herself. 'You're rather a woman of mystery on Smalting Beach.'

'Am I? Why?'

'Everyone's intrigued by what you do here all day.'

'Oh?'

'Do you know Reginald Flowers?' The young woman shook her head. 'He's the President of the Smalting Beach Hut Association.'

'I haven't joined that.'

'Anyway, he's worried that you might be running a business from here.'

'Hardly. Is he the man with the beard and the beach hut that's full of naval stuff?'

'Yes.'

'Oh, I remember him coming to ask what I was doing, but I was embarrassed to tell him. He did actually ask if I was running a business.'

'Well, you do seem to spend all day on your laptop.'

'That's not running a business. I wish it were.'

'Oh?'

'I hope ultimately to make money from what I'm doing, but I think that's still a long way off.' Carole hoped that silence would prompt more revelation, and was rewarded when Katie Brunswick went on, 'I'm writing something.'

'Oh?'

'A book.'

'Ah. Is it going to be published?'

'I hope so. I've got the interest of an agent.'

'That's a good thing for a writer to have, isn't it? I'm sorry, publishing is not a world I'm very familiar with.'

'Yes, if you're a writer it's good to have an agent.'

'So at least you've got one of those.'

'Well, I haven't exactly got one. I've got the *interest* of one. I met her at the Truro Literary Festival. And she said she'd read anything I sent her.'

'That sounds good. She must have liked your work.'

'No, she hadn't actually read any of my work.'

'Ah. Anyway, what kind of book is it you're writing? I mean, don't tell me if you don't want to. I've heard that some writers are superstitious when it comes to talking about "work in progress".'

'No, I don't mind talking about it. I always welcome feedback. You can get very isolated when you're writing.'

'I'm sure you can. But at least here you're surrounded by people.'

'Still isolated, though.' She sounded almost proud of the fact. 'You're often at your loneliest when you're with people.'

'So you use this beach hut as your writing room?'

'Why not? Where else round here are you going to get an office for six hundred quid a year?'

'That's true.'

'So I've got a "room of my own".'

'I'm sorry? I don't get the reference.'

'Virginia Woolf said: "A woman must have money and a room of her own if she is to write fiction."'

'Ah.'

'So I've got the room.'

'How about the money?'

'I've got two years' worth.' Carole looked at her curiously. 'I'd saved enough for me to survive for two years when I gave up my job.'

'You gave up your job to write this book?' To Carole that seemed a very odd thing to do.

'Oh no. I'd already written it. In my spare time.'

This was becoming increasingly confusing. 'So why did you take the two years off?'

'I wanted to make it better.'

'The book better?'

'Yes. On a course I went on I was told that the most important part of writing was rewriting.'

'Oh.' Carole supposed in a way she could see the sense in that. While she was at the Home Office she had prided herself in the accuracy with which she marshalled facts in memoranda. And that had involved a certain amount of redrafting. 'This was a writing course you're talking about?'

'Yes.'

'But I thought writing was something one either could do or couldn't do. It can't be taught, surely? I don't quite see how a course could help.'

'Oh, they do. There's lots you can learn. I mean, obviously you have to want to write, have an innate aptitude for it. Joseph Joubert said: "A fluent writer always seems more talented than he is. To write well, one needs a natural facility and an acquired difficulty."'

'Who was Joseph Joubert?'

'I don't know. I heard the quote on another writing course I went on.'

'Do you go on a lot of them?'

'At least two a year.'

'So, Katie . . . if it's not a rude question . . . have you ever had anything published?'

'No.'

'But have you written other, unpublished books before this one?'

'No. I've really just been working on this one.'

'For how long?'

'Well, I suppose in this form for about twelve years.'

'Ah.'

'I mean it came from an idea I had for a short story. And then I started writing it in a different way. And then I submitted the first chapter in a First Chapter Competition for the Godalming Arts Festival and it got commended.'

'That must have been encouraging.'

'Yes. But of course the first chapter now has changed quite a lot from the first chapter as it was then.'

'Right.'

'Apart from anything else it was a first person narrative and I've changed it to third person.'

'Ah. So this is all improving the book?'

'I hope so, yes. There are some friends I get to read it, and some people in my Writers' Circle, and a lot of them think it's getting better.'

'And when do you think you'll finish it? I mean, this draft?'

Katie Brunswick jutted forward a dubious lower lip. 'Ooh, hard to say. I mean it's seven months since I gave up my job, that was just before Christmas, so I've still got, what . . . seventeen months to go.'

'So that's your deadline?'

The girl still looked doubtful. 'I don't know that I'll have finished it by then.'

'Look, I'm sorry,' said Carole, 'I know I don't know anything about writing, but I can't see why this book's going to take so long.'

'Well, I want to get it right . . .'

'Mm. Yes, well, I can see that would be a good idea.'

'And every time I go on a course, I learn new ideas.'

'I see.'

'And I want to apply them, you know, to the book.'

'So you start rewriting the book again, to accommodate these new ideas?'

'Yes, that's what I do exactly, more or less.'

The girl was silent. Carole didn't think it was the moment to comment that Katie Brunswick's way of writing a book seemed a rather odd approach to any enterprise, so she moved on to the real purpose of her chocolate-brownie subterfuge. 'I was speaking to Curt Holderness this morning.'

'Oh?' Katie was alert, alarmed even.

'He was offering me various ways in which he could bend the rules with regard to these beach huts.'

'Was he?' she asked cautiously.

'He did actually tell me that he's made an arrangement with you . . .'

'Mm?'

'. . . allowing you to stay here overnight when you want to.'

'Yes, well, I went on this course where one of the tutors told me two important things about being a writer. He said that you had to have a dedicated room of your own to work in – just like Virginia Woolf said. A space with the minimum of distractions in it.'

'Which you've got here.'

'Yes.'

'And he also said a writer never knows when inspiration is going to strike, and you must never ignore its summons. As soon as you have an idea you must leap to pen and paper, or the keyboard or whatever else you use.'

'I see. So sometimes you need to stay here overnight when inspiration strikes you?'

'Yes. Or when inspiration *might* strike me.'

'Ah.'

'Curt Holderness only charged me a hundred quid for the concession. It still makes this a jolly cheap office, doesn't it?'

'Yes. Well, I hope inspiration didn't strike much in the last few days.'

'What do you mean?'

'The most recent couple of times I've been here, this place was locked up.'

'Yes.' Katie Brunswick looked a little embarrassed. 'The fact was, when the police started investigating here on the beach, well, I didn't particularly want to be around.'

'Squeamishness?'

'No, I just didn't want to be questioned . . . you know, in case the fact that I was sometimes staying here overnight came up.'

'Ah. I understand.' Carole looked beadily at her. 'So when was the last time you spent the night here?'

Katie Brunswick screwed up her eyes as she tried to remember. 'Last Monday. I mean, not the Monday just gone, the one before.'

A little charge of excitement ran through Carole. 'And did you see anything that night?'

'What sort of thing?' came the cautious response.

'Any people on the beach?'

'I did see some actually.'

'Oh?'

'Normally if I stay overnight I close the doors, so that it's not so obvious that I'm in here. But it had been a hot day and was still pretty warm in the small hours. It was very stuffy in here, so I reckoned I could risk leaving the doors open.'

'So who did you see?' asked Carole, her throat tense with excitement.

'I saw that painter guy who lives on the prom.'

'Gray Czesky?'

'Yes. He was very drunk. He wandered down on to the beach and staggered off behind the beach huts over there.'

'What? Near *Quiet Harbour*? Near the one the police are investigating?'

'Yes.'

'Was he carrying anything?'

'Perhaps. I can't remember. I think perhaps he had a plastic carrier bag with him.'

'What time would this have been, Katie?'

'I don't know. I was quite caught up with what I was writing. Early hours, I suppose. One or two in the morning.'

'Did you see him leave the beach?' A shake of the head. 'Did you see anyone else?'

'Yes. A bit later . . . I don't know how much later because I was caught up in the book, but I heard voices whispering. A man and a woman.'

'Could you hear what they were saying?'

'No. But I looked out and I saw them both going the same way Gray Czesky had gone.'

'Towards *Quiet Harbour*?'

'Yes.'

'Who were they, Katie?'

'One was the guy who used to be in *Quiet Harbour* with his girlfriend.'

'Mark Dennis?'

'I don't know his name, but he's got that small girl-friend with almost white-blond hair. Actually, come to think of it, I haven't seen them down here on the beach much recently.'

'And did you see the woman he was with?' asked Carole.

'Yes. She doesn't go out much, seems to spend most of her time in the house. But I have seen her a couple of times with Gray Czesky. It was his wife, Helga.'

Jude was back at Woodside Cottage when Carole returned to Fethering. They stood tensely together in Jude's sitting room while Carole dialled the number Nuala Cullan had given them.

A machine answered. It requested anyone who wanted to leave a message for Gray or Helga Czesky to speak after the tone.

Chapter Twenty-Three

Carole switched off the phone, then consulted Jude who advised her to leave a message. 'We need to see them, don't we?'

'What should I say? Maintain the pretence that I want Gray to do me a watercolour of Fethering Beach?'

'No, I think we've gone beyond that. Take the direct approach. Say you want to talk about the fire that was started under *Quiet Harbour*.'

'Strange that they don't answer. I got the impression that they were both in the house most of the time. Katie Brunswick said Helga don't go out much.'

'Maybe they're the sort who always leave the answering machine on. So that they can screen incoming calls.'

So it proved. Carole left a terse message ending with Jude's number, and it was a matter of moments before the phone rang. Jude answered. It was Helga. She sounded cautious and a little distressed.

'Please, who am I talking to?' Over the phone her German accent was thicker.

'My name's Jude.'

'It was not your voice which left the message.'

'No. That was my friend Carole. We did meet on Monday. We were the ones who came to your house to discuss a commission with your husband.'

'Ah.' Helga didn't take issue with them about the subterfuge. She had more pressing priorities. 'You said you knew something about the fire at *Quiet Harbour* . . . ?'

'Yes. We know who lit it,' said Jude, making what was little more than a conjecture sound like a certainty.

'I see.' Helga was silent for a moment. 'Yes, we must meet,' she said finally, in a voice of long suffering.

They had agreed to come round to Woodside Cottage. Gray Czesky had been tidied up, presumably on his wife's insistence. He was out of his paint-spattered work clothes, and in grey trousers and a blue blazer looked somehow like a large naughty schoolboy waiting for a dressing-down from the headmaster.

It was evident that in the current situation his wife represented that kind of authority figure at least as much as Carole and Jude did. Once the couple had sat down and refused offers of tea and coffee, Helga announced, 'Gray has something he wishes to confess to you.'

He was shamefaced, but still had a bit of his old bravado left. 'It's hell,' he began, 'having an artistic temperament. Nobody really understands, nobody knows what goes on inside my brain.'

None of the three women said anything, leaving him to dig himself out of his own hole. 'I don't really always have control of myself. My emotions are so volatile, I don't know what I'm going to feel from one moment to the next. It's as if I'm being blown all over the place by an unidentifiable power that is stronger than I am.'

'An unidentifiable power like drink?' Carole suggested rather meanly.

'Well, yes,' he conceded, 'I suppose drink is part of it. But that's more a symptom than a cause. I sometimes have to drink to subdue the agonizing thoughts that come unbidden into my mind.'

'Oh yes?'

'And then sometimes I admit that I do things under the influence of drink that I might not do in my more sober moments.'

'Not that you have many of those,' said Helga.

There was an expression of pure shock, almost as though Gray Czesky had been slapped in the face, at this surprising and sudden disloyalty from his wife. Carole and Jude wondered whether they were witnessing the moment of a worm turning, of the final straw being placed upon the overladen camel's back.

'Well, yes, I agree, the drinking does sometimes get out of hand. But I need it. I have some of my best inspirations when I'm drunk.'

Carole and Jude exchanged looks. Both were wondering how much inspiration it took to paint mimsy-pimsy little watercolours of local beaches and the South Downs.

'I think, Gray,' said Helga, 'you had better tell them what happened last week. That evening when Mark came down to see you.'

Her husband nodded his head ruefully.

'Would this have been the Monday?'

'Yes,' said Helga. 'Go on, Gray.'

There was a truculent silence before he obeyed. 'Okay, I'd had a call from Mark that day.'

'Had you been in touch with him ever since he left Smalting?' asked Jude.

'No, it was a long time since I'd last heard from him. When he left Philly, whenever that was . . .'

'Beginning of May,' his wife supplied.

'Yes. At the time he asked if I minded him using our phone number for people who wanted to contact him.'

'And did many people want to contact him?'

A shake of the head. 'Hardly anyone. He gave me a mobile number and—'

'If he'd got a mobile,' Carole objected, 'why did he need to have your number for messages?'

The painter shrugged. 'I don't know. Maybe he wanted to keep people at a distance. Maybe it was a new mobile and he didn't want people to know the number. Anyway, after the first few days he never answered it when I called him. Until suddenly he rang out of the blue last week.'

'What did he say?'

'Just that he was coming down to Smalting, and did I mind if he dropped in. I said fine.'

'He didn't say whether he was coming down to see Philly?'

'No.'

'And how did he seem when you saw him?' asked Carole.

'How do you mean?'

'Did he seem exactly the same as he had when you last saw him?'

Gray Czesky shrugged. 'Pretty much, I guess.'

'No,' said Helga firmly. 'That is not true. He had put on a lot of weight. He seemed to have lost his confidence. Very . . . what's the word? Jittery. No, he was in an extremely strange state when he arrived.'

'Was he?'

'Yes, Gray. Though you were pretty soon too drunk to notice.'

Her husband chuckled with a schoolboy boastfulness. 'True, we did get well stuck into the sauce that night.'

'Which of course led to you doing something rather stupid, didn't it?' Helga prompted implacably.

'Yes.' His face took on a hangdog expression, which, if it was meant to curry sympathy for him, did not have the desired effect with the three women. 'Okay, well . . . Mark and I got into a kind of argument . . . not really an argument, more a sort of . . .'

'Drunken shouting match,' suggested Helga.

'All right. Anyway, I was telling him that artists have to be free and that bourgeois values were a trap to prevent artists from a true expression of themselves, and he was defending the smug middle-class life, saying all he wanted was to live like what he called "a normal human being" – by which he meant an inhibited, tight-arsed wage-slave with a bloody pension and life insurance and a nice neat little beach hut in Smalting. And I said that going down that route was the surest way to stifling artistic talent and nobody who gave a stuff about a beach hut could possibly be any kind of artist, and so I went out and . . .'

He shrugged again, as Carole completed the sentence for him. 'Set fire to the beach hut that Mark and Philly used to use.'

There was a long silence before Gray Czesky admitted that yes, that was exactly what he had done. 'As I say, I was pretty well plastered,' he added, as though that might be some kind of mitigation.

His wife took up the narrative. 'And Gray comes back home and he is boasting about what he has done, so Mark and I rush back to the beach hut to put out the fire.'

Carole looked at Jude, who gave a little nod. Yes, that must have been when the two of them were seen by Curt Holderness. Odd, though, that Curt hadn't noticed that the beach hut was burning. Or perhaps not so odd, given how laxly the man interpreted his duties as a security officer.

'And you did put out the fire, Helga?'

'Yes. Fortunately it had not got much of a hold on the hut. Only one corner was burnt. If we had not got there so quickly I hate to think what would have happened.'

Gray Czesky, now his folly had been exposed, looked sheepishly defiant. 'As I said,' he pleaded to deaf ears, 'it's not easy having an artistic temperament.'

'Well,' said Carole, 'we're very grateful to you for telling us all of this.'

'I felt we had to,' Helga responded. 'I was suspicious of you when you came round on Monday.'

'Oh?'

'Yes, I did not think you were really wanting to commission a painting from Gray.' Carole felt herself blushing to know how transparent their ruse had been. 'It was when you rang again today that my suspicion was confirmed.'

'Really?'

'I knew then that you were plain-clothes police officers.' Carole and Jude tried to avoid catching each other's eyes. Instinctively, Carole was about to say that Helga had got the wrong end of the stick, but a moment's thought made her realize that there was no harm in the woman continuing with her misapprehension. And their mistaken identities could actually be rather useful in advancing their investigation.

'The question is now,' Helga continued, 'what you do about what we have just told you.'

Jude took note of the pleading in the woman's eyes as she said judiciously, 'Well, setting fire to the beach hut was obviously very stupid behaviour on your husband's part . . .'

'Yes?'

'. . . but at its worst it was nothing more than a drunken prank.'

'No,' Helga agreed, her hopes rekindled.

'And it wouldn't have become so important had it

not been for subsequent events at the beach hut; the discovery of the human remains there. But . . .' she extended the pause, aware of the tension in the sorry couple in front of her '. . . now we know that the two discoveries are unrelated to each other . . .' she looked across to her neighbour, as if for confirmation of what she was about to say, '. . . I don't really think it'll be necessary for any further action to be taken.'

The relief in the sitting room of Woodside Cottage was almost palpable. Both the Czeskys sank back into their chairs, as Carole picked up the conversational baton. 'Though of course,' she said sternly, 'we might take a different view were you not to co-operate fully with us.'

'Of course we will,' said Helga earnestly. 'In what way do you wish us to co-operate?'

'We will require you to inform us . . .' Where had that 'require' come from? Carole realized she was dropping into 'police-speak'. 'We will require you to inform us of anything else you may know that might be of relevance to our investigation into the discoveries on Smalting Beach.'

She chose her words with care. With her background in the Home Office, Carole Seddon was well aware how serious a crime impersonating a police officer could be. So she deliberately hadn't confirmed Helga's assumption that their enquiries were official ones. As she walked her casuist's tightrope, Carole curbed her natural instinct towards guilt.

'Oh, of course,' said Helga. 'If there's anything we know that's relevant, of course we will tell you.'

Jude nodded with satisfaction. 'Right. Good. Well, the first thing we want to know is: where is Mark Dennis? Do you have a way of contacting him?'

Chapter Twenty-Four

It turned out to be remarkably simple. Gray provided Carole and Jude with a new mobile number for Mark Dennis. The moment the Czeskys had left Woodside Cottage, Jude, trembling with excitement, keyed it into her phone.

A brief ringing tone was quickly replaced by a message informing her that the phone she was calling was switched off. She tried again. With exactly the same result.

Neither Carole nor Jude could disguise their disappointment. To have come so close to making contact with Mark Dennis and then to . . .

'I'll keep trying it,' said Jude defiantly.

'Yes, of course. He'll answer it soon.'

But neither of them really believed the optimism in Carole's words.

Smalting was the lead story on the television news that evening. The human remains that had been found buried under a beach hut there had been identified by the police. They had belonged to a small boy called Robin Cutter.

Chapter Twenty-Five

The name was familiar, but in front of their separate televisions Carole and Jude both needed reminding where they had heard it before. The news bulletin supplied all the promptings their memories required.

The story of Robin Cutter was a sad and painful one. He had been five at the time of his disappearance, and nothing had been seen of him in the intervening eight years. At the time, relatively soon after the high-profile abduction and murder of a local schoolgirl, there had been a huge uproar in West Sussex about the case. It aroused all the country's latent visceral horror of paedophilia.

Though it was nearly ten-thirty at night, Jude went straight round to knock on the door of High Tor. The evening air was quite cool, reminding the denizens of Fethering that they were still only in June, not yet August.

Carole and Jude stayed watching television after the main bulletin, because the disappearance of Robin Cutter had happened in the area and there remained a very distant possibility that more information might be available on the local news.

Of course there wasn't. The local news reported the story with characteristic ineptitude, but added nothing to what had been seen on the national bulletin. They showed the same shot of a smiling Robin Cutter, wearing a very new blue uniform, in one of those school photographs taken against a backdrop of cloud effects. They showed the same library footage of the boy's distraught parents – Rory and Miranda – banked by police at a press conference, begging anyone who knew anything to come forward, and sending hopeless love to their son. The woman was slender with long bottle-blond hair, the husband chunky and bewildered. They faltered and were so overcome with emotion that one of the policemen had to finish reading their prepared statement.

'The mother looks vaguely familiar,' said Jude. 'Who is she?'

'I don't know. It'll come to me.'

They switched off the television. At the time Robin Cutter disappeared, Jude had not yet moved to Fethering and had only been aware of the national reaction to the case. That had been strong, but as nothing compared to the frenzy in West Sussex. Carole could vividly recall the local furore and hysteria about what was assumed to be another paedophile atrocity. 'We must find out more about it,' she announced.

'What, now?'

'Yes, Jude. I'm sure there'll be lots more on the internet.'

'You're right. Will you bring your laptop down?'

Carole was given a moment's pause by this novel

idea. Though, after a slow and sceptical start, she had now embraced computer technology with considerable enthusiasm, she still somehow had not accepted the concept of her laptop's portability. It never moved from the spare bedroom, which she used as a kind of study. 'No, I think we'd better go upstairs,' she said.

Jude converted an incipient giggle into a sigh and followed her neighbour.

Carole's view that there would be 'lots more on the internet' proved to be an understatement. There were literally hundreds of thousands of references to Robin Cutter, ranging from the straight facts of his disappearance on Wikipedia, newspaper and BBC websites, to the homicidal ravings of anti-paedophile fanatics. Though at the time of his supposed abduction bloggers had hardly existed, the contemporary ones still included his names in their lists of victims. As ever, the internet offered opportunities to the kind of people who used to write letters in block capitals with lots of underlining. It had become the soap box of the unhinged bigot.

'God, it's nasty,' said Jude, as they both looked at one of the wilder polemics. 'I suppose paedophiles are about the only minority left that everyone feels justified in denouncing.'

'I'm sorry? I don't know what you mean.'

'Well, it's no longer politically acceptable to discriminate against women or foreigners or lesbians or gays. About the only targets left to criticize are paedophiles.'

Carole was appalled. 'Jude, are you saying you support what they do?'

'Of course I'm not. I'm just saying it must be terrible to grow up with those kind of impulses.'

'What, you think they can't help themselves?'

'Possibly not.'

Carole Seddon was so shocked to the core of her being that she could hardly get her words out. 'But the things they do! You're not going to try to defend those on the grounds that the poor paedophiles can't help themselves?'

'No, no. I'm just saying that it must be very difficult to grow up discovering that the only way you can get sexual satisfaction is by committing an act that society reckons to be the ultimate taboo.'

Carole shuddered. 'I am sorry. There are times when I just don't understand you, Jude.' Which was true. There were many subjects on which the two of them were never going to think alike. Which perhaps made their friendship all the more remarkable. And strong.

'What I'm saying is that people lose all sense of proportion when paedophilia is mentioned. And there's a lot of ignorance about the subject. I mean, do you remember that case of the paediatrician who had graffiti scrawled over her house?'

'Jude, paedophilia remains a horrible and unforgivable crime.'

'Yes, Carole, but . . .' Jude decided it wasn't the moment to pursue her argument. She was as appalled as anyone by the crimes perpetrated by paedophiles, but her healer's instinct was always to look inside personalities, to try to understand what triggered their behaviour. But explaining what she meant to Carole would not have been an easy task, so she turned her attention back to the laptop. 'Anyway, let's just see how much basic information we can get about the case.'

'Very well,' said Carole, still looking at her neighbour in a rather old-fashioned way.

They returned to Wikipedia. 'With that name I'm surprised they haven't been attacked too,' Jude observed.

The basic information was quite simple, almost banal in its simplicity. Robin Cutter had been spending a day with his grandparents near Fedborough while his mother and father had gone to London to see a matinee of *Les Miserables*. In the morning his grandfather had driven the boy down to Smalting Beach. After they'd parked the car, Robin had asked for an ice cream. While his grandfather went into the shop, the boy had asked to stay outside and watch the windsurfers. When his grandfather came out of the shop, Robin Cutter had disappeared. And he had never been seen again.

But it was the name of the grandfather that made Carole and Jude gasp.

Lionel Oliver.

Chapter Twenty-Six

The identity of the victim whose bones had been discovered under *Quiet Harbour* led to a predictable media frenzy. The Robin Cutter story was again on the front pages of many of the Thursday morning's national newspapers. The red tops didn't need any encouragement to go into anti-paedophile overdrive, and even Carole's more sedate *Times* gave wide coverage to the revelation. As ever in such instances, much was made of previous cases of similar atrocities, turning knives in the wounds of other families who had already suffered enough.

Carole and Jude watched the lunchtime television news in Woodside Cottage. There had been little development overnight, so they found out little more than they had been told in the Wednesday evening bulletin. The last part of the report, however, was an interview with the dead boy's mother.

Miranda Cutter had changed considerably in the years since her son's disappearance. The slender blond had morphed into a plump woman with dyed red curls. And her surname had changed to Browning.

In the interview she said what all bereaved parents say in such situations, that at least now she finally knew Robin was dead, that now he could have a proper funeral, and she could try to move forward with her life. Miranda Browning didn't say anything about her son's killer and the need for him to be brought to justice. She didn't need to. Every newspaper in the country was doing the job for her.

As soon as the interview had finished Carole looked across at Jude and saw a strange expression on her neighbour's face. 'What is it?'

'I know her. Miranda Browning. She's one of my clients.'

'Oh?'

'Yes. Someone referred her to me last year because she'd been getting these terrible headaches. I managed to alleviate the symptoms, but I knew what was really causing them was some deep inner tension, some powerful emotion she was holding in. She wouldn't tell me what it was. Now I know, though.'

'When you say she's a client, Jude . . .'

'Hm?'

'. . . do you mean she's a friend too?'

'I don't know her that well.'

'Well enough to ring her with condolences, you know, about what's happened?'

'I wouldn't want to trouble her at a time like this.'

'A time when she probably needs your healing services more than ever,' Carole suggested. 'If our investigation's going to get any further . . .'

'What do you mean?'

'If we find out who killed her son, then we'll help

her get that psychological thing Americans go on about so much.'

'Closure?'

'Yes. Look, she probably knows more about the case than anyone else, and you've got a direct line to her.'

Jude felt uneasy. When it came to client confidentiality, she had strict boundaries. To contact Miranda Browning at a time like this simply to find out more about her son's disappearance would definitely be a step too far. On the other hand, if her intervention as a healer could help ease the woman's suffering . . .

'What do you say, Jude?'

'I say that at times you can be surprisingly unsentimental.'

Carole Seddon smiled. She took what her friend had just said as a compliment.

On the following morning, the Friday, the phone rang in High Tor. It was a very flustered-sounding Reginald Flowers. 'Carole, I'm ringing about the quiz night tonight.'

'Oh yes?' She had forgotten all about the event, but quickly prepared a battery of excuses as to why she couldn't attend. Then she had a moment of uncertainty. The Smalting Beach Hut Association quiz night would quite possibly gather together many of the principals who might have information about the grisly discovery under *Quiet Harbour*. Maybe if she and Jude were to attend, they might advance the course of their investigation.

But this thought became immediately irrelevant, as Reginald Flowers went on, 'Anyway, I'm afraid I'm going to have to cancel it.'

'The quiz? Oh dear. Is that out of respect?'

'I'm sorry? What do you mean?'

'Out of respect for Robin Cutter, you know, now he's been identified as—'

'For heaven's sake, it's nothing to do with Robin Cutter,' he responded testily. 'I wouldn't change my plans because of something like that. I thought all that was safely dead and buried – in every sense. If some silly child chooses to put himself in danger's way . . .' This was a novel reaction to the tragedy, one that Carole certainly hadn't heard before. 'No, the reason the quiz night is going to have to be cancelled is that I have once again been guilty of assuming that other people are as efficient in the basic, simple things of life as I am myself. The SBHA has a secretary – or at least someone who has the title of secretary—'

'Yes, I met her with you on Smalting Beach the other day. Dora Pinchbeck.'

'Dora Pinchbeck, exactly. Dora, who, as I say has the title of secretary of the Smalting Beach Hut Association, but who turns out to be totally incompetent. She undertook to make the booking for tonight's quiz night at St Mary's Church Hall, but when I rang the caretaker there this morning to check some details, it turns out she hadn't done it. Not a difficult task to undertake, you might think, but clearly beyond the capacity of our secretary Dora. "Oh, I'm sorry, I forgot," she said when I rang her about it this morning.

213

Forgot! And, needless to say, there's now something else booked into St Mary's Hall for tonight. A meeting of the Smalting Local History Society, would you believe? I am, needless to say, extremely angry. It's the old thing, isn't it – if you want a job done properly, do it yourself. Dora, my so-called secretary, offered to ring round all the members of the SBHA, but I said, "No, thank you, Dora. I want to ensure that everyone gets the message, so I'll do it myself." Which is why I'm calling you, Carole,' he concluded, on a note of affronted martyrdom.

'So all we lack for this evening's quiz night is a venue?'

'You say "all we lack", Carole, but it is a rather major lack. There's nowhere else suitable in Smalting, except for one of the rooms at The Crab Inn and, as I may have said, the prices there are now quite extortionate . . .' Belatedly he seemed to catch on to something in her intonation. 'Why, you're not suggesting that you might know of a suitable alternative venue?'

'There's somewhere I could try. I'll ring you back if I have any luck. Well, I'll let you know either away.'

She rang straight through to the Crown and Anchor. Ted Crisp was initially grouchy at her suggestion, but then it was a point of honour with him to be initially grouchy to most suggestions. And his attitude quickly softened. Though Carole Seddon didn't have the natural charm of her neighbour, in her background was the unlikely fact that she and Ted Crisp had once had a brief affair, and he was still more indulgent to her than he might have been to other supplicants.

Within three minutes he had agreed that the Smalting Beach Hut Association could use his function room that evening at no charge, 'so long as they all drink lots of booze'.

Carole immediately rang back Reginald Flowers to pass on the good news.

Jude was still tussling with her moral dilemma. Part of her wanted to ring Miranda Browning, to offer condolences and, if required, some healing treatment. But another part accused her of shabby opportunism for even thinking of the idea. Was it born out of compassion or, as Carole had baldly suggested, to help them advance on their investigation? Jude couldn't decide.

While she was going through this uncharacteristic agonizing, her phone rang. The woman at the other end identified herself as Miranda Browning.

'I was desperately sorry to hear the news,' said Jude. 'I hadn't realized that you were the poor boy's mother, you know, when I met you before under that name.'

'Browning's the name of my second husband.' The woman's voice was strong. Though there was tension in her tone, there was no self-pity. She wasn't about to give way to tears.

'So you are Lionel and Joyce Oliver's daughter and you first married someone called Cutter?'

'No, Cutter's my maiden name. His father's Rory Oliver.'

'But why was Robin's surname not Oliver?'

'Rory and I weren't married when Robin was born.

We weren't together at the time. I didn't think it likely we ever would be again, so I registered Robin under my surname. All his documentation was as "Cutter", when he started at play school he was 'Robin Cutter'. By the time Rory and I had got back together and married, the name had stuck. I'm sure in time we would have changed it, but . . .' Her voice wavered for the first time, '. . . we weren't given that opportunity.'

'No.' Jude spoke softly, already in therapist mode. 'As I say, I'm desperately sorry . . . about what happened eight years ago . . . and about what's happened now.'

'Thank you,' said Miranda Browning, with considerable grace. 'Obviously this has brought it all back, and, inevitably perhaps, the headaches have started again. I could hardly get out of bed or stand up this morning. And I can't imagine the stress is going to get any less over the next few weeks, so I just wondered . . . the treatment you gave me last time worked so well . . . if you've got a spare appointment you could slot me into?'

'I'm free this afternoon,' said Jude.

They fixed a time. As she put the phone down Jude beamed, unsurprised by what had happened. But she wouldn't tell her neighbour whether she had made the call to Miranda Browning or Miranda had called her. Unlike Jude, Carole Seddon didn't believe in synchronicity.

Chapter Twenty-Seven

Miranda Browning arrived at the gate of Woodside Cottage in a taxi. In spite of the June heat, she had a scarf tied over her hair and wore dark glasses. She looked anxiously from side to side as she paid the cabbie and was still casting nervous glances back to the road when Jude opened the door to her.

After welcoming her client and leading her into the sitting room, Jude gestured to the glasses and asked, 'For the headaches?'

'Not really,' replied Miranda Browning, taking them off. 'More so's I'm not recognized. It's all started again. Bloody press camped outside my front door. They're quite capable of following me here and door-stepping you as well.'

'So how did you get away?'

'Practice,' came the wry response. 'I've got a cab firm I trust completely. They pick me up in the alley at the back of my garden. So far the press pack haven't caught on to that yet. Early days, though, this time round.'

Again Jude was aware of the lack of self-pity in Miranda Browning's tone. The woman had had to develop a stoicism, a survivor's instinct. Whatever she was feeling inside, she was damned if she was going to expose her emotions to the world. Which was probably why her deep, suppressed pain manifested itself in physical symptoms, like headaches.

Jude uncovered her treatment bench, another draped shape in her sitting room of swathed furniture. The windows were all open, letting in a light breeze that set her bamboo wind chimes tinkling. She pulled out paper sheeting from a roll at the end of the bench and laid it over the plastic surface. Then she set down a pillow shaped like a fat horseshoe. 'Take off as much as you feel comfortable with, Miranda. And then lie on your front.'

The woman stripped down to bra and pants. Though she had put on weight in the eight years since she'd appeared on television after her son's disappearance, her skin was still firm and her muscles well toned.

'Just lie still, relax as far as you can and I'll check where the trouble's originating from.' Jude's eyes fixed in an expression of intense concentration as she ran her hands up and down the woman's body, not quite touching, sensitive to the variations of temperature she could feel. The hands lingered a while over the small of the back, then moved up and hovered around the shoulders. Jude's fingers tensed. Although they still made no contact, they seemed to be pressing against some resistance.

'We both now know what's been causing the headaches, don't we, Miranda? The problem is convincing

your body of what's really going on. Stop it from expressing your grief in this physical way.'

'I don't know that it is grief now, Jude. Oh, I've
had my share of grieving, but that's been kind of sub-
sumed. Since the remains were identified as Robin's
I haven't cried at all.'

'Maybe it'd be better if you did?'

'I don't know. I've certainly served my time on
the crying front. But now . . . there's a kind of deadness in me. Not the wild mood swings I used to have
after it first happened. I think, except for the bloody
headaches, I feel better now I know there's no hope.
I suppose, so long as there was a possibility that
somewhere in the world a thirteen-year-old Robin was
walking around, so long as there was this vague, vague
chance that I might one day see him again . . .'

Miranda's words were heavy with the deadness of
which she had spoken. Jude didn't say anything, but
she began to feel less guilty about the possible pruri-
ence of her interest in the woman's tragedy. Talking,
she knew, would be part of the healing process for
Miranda Browning. And if what the woman said
helped Carole and Jude in their investigation, well,
that was just a bonus. But she wasn't going to prompt,
just let Miranda Browning talk if she wanted to.

And evidently she did want to. 'Now I know, you
see. I am a woman whose child died. A mother whose
son died. It's not a nice thing to know, but it's now
a fact. Soon we'll have to have a funeral and all that
entails. And presumably that'll involve Rory and his
parents . . . it won't be easy.

'Some women who've lost children say it helps having the physical remains to mourn and a grave to visit. Mothers of boys killed in war, that kind of thing. I don't know whether that'll make much difference for me. I'm certainly not expecting ever to feel . . . closure,' she said, echoing Carole. 'I don't think I'll ever achieve closure. The loss of a child is like an open wound. It'll never heal properly, but perhaps it can be dressed in such a way that you are not in constant pain.'

Jude moved her hands to touch the sides of the woman's neck. 'I'm just going to do a bit of ordinary massage. The muscles here are very knotted. And then we'll try the proper healing.'

Miranda Browning submitted meekly as the fingers and thumbs probed into the taut flesh. 'Yes, I can feel that releasing something,' she said.

Jude feared that her interruption might have stemmed the woman's flow, but it hadn't. 'What I hope will change is the amount of blaming I've done over the last eight years. Blaming my ex-husband, blaming his parents, most of all blaming myself. I must say I can't see that ever going away.'

'Why do you blame your husband's parents?' asked Jude, feigning a little more ignorance than she actually had.

'Oh, don't you know the circumstances of Robin's disappearance? Sorry, there was so much media coverage down here at the time I thought everyone knew every last detail.'

'I wasn't living in Fethering when it happened.'

'Ah. Well, I've told it so many times, another telling won't hurt. I can almost do it without getting upset now, so I suppose that's progress. Right . . .' And Miranda Browning reiterated the information that Carole and Jude had found on Wikipedia.

But she did add a few details that hadn't been available online. Yes, she and Rory had gone to London to see a matinee of *Les Miserables*, leaving Robin in the care of her husband's parents.

'Joyce and I never really got on. If she'd been in charge when Robin was abducted I don't think I'd ever have forgiven her. With Lionel, well, it was a terrible thing, but I liked him and he really adored Robin. No amount of blame from me could equal the way he blamed himself for what happened. I don't think it'd be overstating it to say that his life really stopped at that moment. He's been kind of going through the motions ever since.'

'And what about Joyce?'

Miranda Browning shrugged. 'I don't think it made a lot of difference to her. She only ever thinks about herself.'

Jude wondered whether this was just traditional daughter-in-law/mother-in-law antipathy. It didn't fit in with what she had heard from Carole, though. Granted, her neighbour hadn't spent much time with Joyce Oliver, but the comfortable woman she had spoken of seemed to be at odds with Miranda's description.

'And it was on Smalting Beach that the abduction happened?'

'Well, on the prom. On June the fifteenth. Just a little over eight years ago. I don't know why anniversaries have such significance, but I'm afraid they do.' For the first time the woman's emotions threatened to overwhelm her. Her voice wobbled for a moment, but she was quick to reassert control. 'Smalting Beach was quite crowded. And Robin loved boats of all kinds, windsurfers in particular. I can understand why Lionel let him stay outside the shop while he bought the ice cream. I'm sure I would have done the same.'

'But if the beach was crowded, why didn't anyone witness the abduction?'

Jude's massaging fingers felt the shaking of Miranda's head. 'I thought that was strange at first. But I think the fact that it was so crowded was the reason why nobody noticed. Robin was a very trusting little boy – too trusting probably. If a stranger had started talking to him, he wouldn't have been shy about replying.'

'Presumably the police talked to your father-in-law about what had happened?'

'Endlessly. And he had to suffer the agony of being a suspect, all kinds of probing into his private life, having his car forensically examined. It was very tough for him. But he never changed a single detail of his story. Which shows it must have been true – not that Lionel is capable of lying, anyway. He's a rather splendid man, I think – certainly given what he's had to put up with from Joyce.'

Again the apparently disproportionate animus against her mother-in-law. Jude would have liked to have found out more about the reasons for that, but it wasn't the moment to divert the course of Miranda's narrative.

'No, that's one of my great sadnesses about the whole thing – the estrangement from Lionel. There are terribly destructive aftershocks from an event like what happened to Robin.'

'Presumably it was that that broke up your marriage?'

'Yes. It had always been an on-off sort of relationship. But once he came back to me and we got married, I'd hoped . . . Then Robin disappeared. There were a lot of other things too. Small fault lines in the relationship that might, I suppose, in other circumstances, have been papered over. But with Robin gone they became huge great rifts. I don't really blame Rory. I just can't imagine any marriage surviving something like that. All the time you spend together there's this one huge subject looming over you. The elephant in the room. If you talk about it, it's painful. If you don't talk about it, it's equally painful. Eventually you just don't want to be together, you don't want to have the constant reminder of your shared pain.

'And, of course, had circumstances been different, I suppose we might have had another child. Been a proper little family. Still, it's too late to think about that now.' She allowed herself a small sigh of frustration.

'I hope your second marriage has been happier.'

Jude's words were greeted by a grunt of cynicism.

'No, that one didn't last either. Less than a year. I was stupid to think it would work. I'm afraid I'm not marriage material at the moment. I'm still just an emotional minefield.'

There was a silence. Then Jude removed her hands from Miranda's neck and shoulders. 'Does that feel easier? Just move your head from side to side. See if it's less tight.'

The client did as she was told. 'Yes, it is much better.'

'That's only alleviated the symptoms. Now I'll see if I can heal what's causing it.'

'Good luck,' said Miranda Browning, with a hint of bitterness. 'Sadly I don't think healing can change history.'

'No, I agree. But it maybe can change the way you react to history.'

'Diminish how much I blame myself?'

'Maybe a bit. If you turn over and lie on your front, Miranda.'

An expression of intense concentration came into Jude's brown eyes as she ran her hands along the contours of the woman's body. Once again there was no contact made, but the effort was more intense and exhausting than it had been for the actual massage.

'Did it actually help last time I did this?' Jude asked.

'Yes, it did for a few days. In fact I have felt generally better since then. That is . . . until recent events.'

'Yes, it must be ghastly having it all brought back to you.'

'Still, maybe I will be able to find a workable *modus vivendi*, now there's no longer any uncertainty.' But she didn't sound over-optimistic about the prospect.

'Presumably . . .' Jude chose her words with sensitivity '. . . now the police actually have a body, there's a stronger chance they may be able to track down the perpetrator, you know, the person who actually abducted Robin?'

'Maybe. They certainly seem in no hurry to release the body. So presumably every kind of forensic test is being . . .' The images this prompted were too graphic for her to finish the sentence.

'Were there suspects at the time?'

'The usual ones. Everyone vaguely local who featured on the Sex Offenders Register. They couldn't pin it on anyone, though. Lack of evidence.'

'Did you have any suspicions of anyone?'

Miranda Browning shook her head. 'It never occurred to me for a moment that it might be anyone I had met.'

'No.' Jude didn't raise the fact that in a lot of such cases the perpetrator was someone known to the family.

'Do you think it'll be a comfort to you when the culprit is found?'

'I really don't know. Whoever he is, I have hated him very deeply at times. At times I know I have wanted him dead. How I'll react now, I've no idea. I didn't know how I'd react to Robin's body being found. And through all the pain I think there may eventually be a positive side to that. Maybe it'll be the same when they arrest his murderer. As I say, at the moment I just don't know.'

The healing session, as ever, left Jude wrung out like a damp rag. Miranda Browning was very grateful, saying that it had left her feeling more relaxed. But both women knew that the residue of pain inside her was something that could never be fully healed.

Chapter Twenty-Eight

'Which tennis player was in every final of the Men's US Open Championship from 1982 to 1989?'

Carole and Jude looked at each other, both with wrinkled brows. 'Was it Jimmy Connors?' Carole suggested without much conviction. 'Or would he have been earlier than that?'

'What's the name of that boring one?' asked Jude.

'Pete Sampras?'

'No, the other boring one. Czech, never won Wimbledon.'

'Ivan something . . .'

'Lendl!'

'Yes, that's right. Ivan Lendl!'

'Shall I write it down, Carole?' asked Jude.

'Yes, I'm sure it's right.'

Whether the gruesome discovery of Robin Cutter's remains had anything to do with it or not, there was a very good turn-out for the SBHA quiz night in the function room of the Crown and Anchor in Fethering. Reginald Flowers was, needless to say, the quizmaster, smart in a blazer and tie, which looked vaguely naval (but probably wasn't). Needless to say, he had his own neat little portable amplifier and a microphone to talk into.

Beside him at his table sat Dora Pinchbeck, with a pile of forms to fill in and tick off. Her crushed expression suggested that she hadn't been allowed to forget her lapse over the booking of St Mary's Church Hall.

Many of the Smalting Beach regulars were there, but there were also quite a lot of faces Carole didn't recognize. Twenty-two people including Reginald, dividing up into four table teams of four and one of five. Carole and Jude were sitting with a married couple; enthusiastic hutters they hadn't met before. The husband plumed himself on being Captain of the Smalting Golf Club, and it was a mercy when the start of the quiz stopped him talking about the fact. His wife spoke little, only nodding in admiration at his every pronouncement.

Deborah Wrigley was there, somewhat to Carole's surprise. She would have thought a quiz night was too common an entertainment for the self-styled *grande dame* of the Shorelands Estate. But maybe curiosity about the Robin Cutter case had persuaded Deborah to slum a little. She had her son Gavin and his unfortunate wife Nell with her, so at least she was not without people to patronize. Carole reckoned the young couple were probably back on the South Coast to rescue Tristram and Hermione from their grandmother's rigid tutelage. 'Quality time' with Deborah Wrigley somehow seemed unlikely also to be fun time.

Carole hadn't expected to see Katie Brunswick in the function room either. Again she wouldn't have thought quizzes were the obsessive rewriter's kind of thing either. But there she was, sitting rather incongruously at a table with Kelvin Southwest, Curt Holderness and an unfamiliar third man who made up the team.

'I didn't expect to see you here,' Carole whispered to the girl as she passed.

'Very important to get local colour,' Katie whispered back. 'I was told that at a writing course I went to once in the Dordogne.'

Earlier in the evening Carole had been rather surprised when she and Jude had met Kelvin Southwest in the Crown and Anchor's main bar. Gone was all his smarm, all his creepy compliments about 'lovely ladies'. He had almost cut the pair of them dead, immediately turning away to seek out the company of Curt Holderness and some other men Carole hadn't recognized. At the time she and Jude had exchanged looks of the 'What's got into him?' variety.

The members of the Smalting Beach Hut Association conspicuous by their absence at the quiz night were Lionel and Joyce Oliver. Given the news they had recently received, there was no surprise about that, but Carole and Jude couldn't help feeling a slight disappointment. Persuading herself that it was not a breach of client confidentiality, Jude had passed on to her neighbour what she had heard from Miranda Browning, and they were both aware that, if they were to advance in their investigation, they would probably have to talk to the Olivers at some point. It was not, however, destined to be that evening.

Another absentee was Philly Rose. But then that was hardly a surprise. Since she'd passed *Quiet Harbour* over to Carole, she was no longer really a member of the hutters' community.

'Have you all put down your answers to the question?' asked Reginald Flowers.

'Well, we've put down *an* answer,' said Kelvin Southwest, who, after his earlier frostiness, now seemed determined to be the life and soul of the party. 'Whether or not it's the right answer is another matter.' And he and Curt Holderness guffawed. Even if she hadn't known what she did about the two men, Carole might still have felt there was something slightly sinister in their complicity.

'Have you ticked that one off, Dora?' Reginald Flowers spoke to 'his' secretary as one might to a small child with learning difficulties.

'I have,' she replied humbly.

'Very well, next question . . .' The quizmaster cleared his throat into the microphone and coughed. 'I'm sorry. I think my bronchitis is coming on.' And his voice certainly did have a dry, husky quality. 'Right, this is the last question before we have a twenty-minute break when you can go and refill your glasses.'

Good, thought Carole, mindful of Ted Crisp's demand that the participants in the quiz night should 'drink lots of booze'.

Reginald Flowers again cleared his clogged throat and asked, 'Of which creatures is the collective noun a "parliament"?'

'MPs!' shouted Kelvin Southwest raucously. 'That wasn't too tricky, Reg.'

'No, no, I said "creatures", not human beings.'

'MPs are not human beings!' riposted Kelvin, proud of his rapier wit.

'The question is, "Of which *creatures* is the collective noun a 'parliament'?" And it's a *creature*, not a human being,' Reginald Flowers repeated, clearly put out at what he saw as a challenge to his authority. He made himself feel better by having another go at Dora. 'Make a note of that, please. That question may need rephrasing to deal with the nit-picking fraternity.' The note was duly made, and the quizmaster was siezed by a bout of coughing.

Jude looked blankly at her teammates. 'Haven't a clue.'

'I know it,' whispered Carole. And she mouthed 'Owls' at them.

'How on earth do you know that?' asked Jude.

'It came up in a *Times* crossword clue,' said Carole smugly.

'So how are you two lovely ladies?' asked a leering Kelvin Southwest, more outgoing to them now as he queued at the bar with Curt Holderness. The Crown and Anchor would have been busy that night, even without the sudden influx of the quiz night crowd from the function room. Ted Crisp, Zosia and her girls were kept hard at it.

'We're very well, thank you,' Carole replied primly. 'Curt, this is my neighbour Jude.'

'Very nice to meet you,' said the security officer, with a lazy look of appreciation at Jude's ample curves.

'Things have developed a bit since we last met,' Carole observed.

'Things?'

'I was referring to the discovery on Smalting Beach.'

'Yes.' A guarded look came into Curt Holderness's eyes. 'Nasty business.'

'Presumably the police have talked to you about it?' asked Carole, possibly pushing her luck.

'Why should they?' came the tart reply.

'Well, I was thinking, since you're the security officer, they would automatically want to know if you'd seen any disturbance or anything unusual happening.'

'Yes,' he conceded, apparently relieved. Carole wondered what he had thought she was going to ask him about. 'I did talk to them, yes. Not that I could be much help. I didn't see anything odd happening.'

'You didn't volunteer any information to them, did you, Curt? Because I seem to remember when we last met you were very against the idea of telling the police anything that—'

'Excuse me,' he said, having just attracted Zosia's attention. But he wasn't about to give the order. He turned to his friend. 'Here, Kel, get the drinks in. Mine's a pint of Stella.' True to the Curt Holderness principle of never buying a drink for himself. Kelvin Southwest looked slightly sour at being landed with the round, but he didn't demur. Clearly the Crown and

Anchor was not one of the local places that owed the Fether District Council official a favour and wouldn't charge him.

Carole was intrigued by the relationship between the two men. They clearly knew each other well, yet there didn't seem to be much affection between them. And Curt Holderness appeared to hold the balance of power. She wondered what favours they had done each other in the past.

Saddled with buying the drinks, Kelvin Southwest all of a sudden became elaborately chivalrous and asked if he could treat 'the lovely ladies' as well. To Carole's surprise, Jude responded quite sharply that they were fine, 'thank you very much'.

When they eventually got their Chilean Chardonnays and were walking back to the function room, Carole asked her neighbour why she had bitten off Kelvin Southwest's head. 'It's unlike you, Jude.'

'Yes. There's just something I find rather creepy about him'.

'I agree. All that smarm about "lovely ladies".'

'And from someone who really loathes women.'

'What?'

'Kelvin Southwest is not attracted to women.'

'But all his going on about "lovely ladies" . . .'

'It's a front.Women don't turn him on sexually.'

'How do you know, Jude?'

'I just know.'

Carole didn't argue. She knew there were certain areas of life in which Jude's instincts were much more accurate than her own. So maybe the fact that Kelvin

Southwest appeared to fancy her more than he fancied Jude wasn't such great news after all. 'Then what do you think does turn him on sexually?'

'I don't know,' replied Jude. And she shuddered.

Chapter Twenty-Nine

'Now you've all heard of scuba diving but the next question is: what do the letters "S – C – U – B – A" stand for?'

At the tables around Reginald Flowers and his microphone, discussions erupted and a few confident contenders started writing down answers. Jude puffed out her cheeks in an expression of ignorance and looked around at her teammates. 'Sea Coast . . . Underwater . . . Breath Aid . . . ?' she hazarded.

'Not bad,' said the Captain of Smalting Golf Club. 'But not right, I'm afraid. In fact, the correct answer is: "Self-Contained Underwater Breathing Apparatus".'

'How do you know that?' asked Jude. 'Have you ever done it?'

'Oh yes,' he assured her. 'I used to do a lot of other sports before golf took over my life. I don't know if I happened to mention it, but I am currently Captain of Smalting Golf Club.'

'Yes, you did mention it,' said Carole testily. 'Quite a few times.'

The golf captain and his wife looked at her open-mouthed, as Carole, who had been appointed team scribe, wrote the answer down. There were still a distressing number of blanks on the form. She had hoped, with her crossword expertise, to be doing rather better on the quiz. But then she hadn't really been anticipating questions on the names of the Arsenal team who won the 1994 European Cup Winners' Cup. And German aircraft of the Second World War could hardly be described as her specialist subject. Nor indeed could the hits of Beyoncé.

Though slightly soured by the fact that she knew so few answers, Carole was grudgingly impressed by the range of questions. It was fair enough, she supposed, that the subject matter covered should be broad. That ensured that no one – including, unfortunately, her – had any special advantage.

She wondered whether Reginald Flowers had taken his list from a book or the internet, or whether he'd done his own research. From her assessment of the man's character, she thought the latter was probably the answer.

Reginald coughed again into his microphone. 'Right, you've all had enough time on that one. Let's move on. The next question is a literary one.' There was groaning from some of the tables, which encouraged Carole. She reckoned here was a subject on which she was in with a chance. 'What is the name of the terrible school run by Wackford Squeers in Charles Dickens's novel *Nicholas Nickleby?*'

As she smugly wrote down the answer, Carole was cheered by the sound of more groans. Through which sounded a raucous shout from Curt Holderness. 'Was it maybe Edgington Manor School? I heard some well dodgy things went on there.'

Few of the quiz contestants took any notice of what he'd said. It was lost in the general badinage of disappointment about having another literary question. But the effect of the security officer's words on the quizmaster was astonishing. Reginald Flowers's face went suddenly red and he reached up to loosen his naval-looking tie. For a moment he looked as if he was about to throw up. Dora Pinchbeck stared at him with a mixture of alarm and compassion. When Reginald next spoke there was a distinct wobble in his husky voice.

'Right, have you all got that one? The school in *Nicholas Nickleby*? And we'll move on. Next question: what is the name of the guitarist brother of the Kinks' main songwriter, who co-wrote and took the vocal on *Death of a Clown?*'

Carole raised her eyes to heaven. How could any normal human being be expected to answer that?

Jude nudged her and whispered, 'Dave Davies.' Carole wrote it down. But then she'd never thought of Jude as being quite a *normal* person.

They hadn't won. In fact, when the answers were read out, the combined intellects of Carole, Jude, the Captain of Smalting Golf Club and his silent wife had only managed to beat one other table. Carole left the Crown and Anchor feeling a little disgruntled. Of course, the quiz had been just for fun. It didn't matter who won. But she had rather prided herself on her general knowledge and was disappointed not to have done better. Though she hid it well, Carole Seddon did have a surprisingly competitive instinct.

She and Jude were in the car park on their way home when Carole suddenly remembered she'd left her cardigan in the function room. She went back to fetch it, annoyed at having forgotten it and equally annoyed at having brought it in the first place. Sometimes the instinctive caution in her own nature infuriated Carole. Nobody else had taken a cardigan. Everyone else had trusted the warmth of the June evening, without worries about the fact 'that it might get a bit nippy later'. Sometimes just being Carole Seddon was an extraordinarily exhausting experience.

The lights were off in the function room, but enough illumination came from outside for her to see the way to her table and pick up the offending cardigan from the back of the chair. As she moved towards the main pub she was stopped by the sound of voices she recognized.

Between the function room and the bar ran a narrow corridor that led to the toilets. Carole shrank back into the shadows to listen. The two men, she reckoned, must have just been using the facilities, and fortunately the first words she heard from Kelvin Southwest were exactly the question she would have wished to put to Curt Holderness.

'What was all that about the school? You know, what you shouted out to old Reg?'

'You get a lot of useful information when you work

for the police, Kel. Some of it information that people would rather never became public knowledge.'

'Are you saying you've got something on Reg Flowers?'

'You bet I have.'

'Something he'd pay for you to keep quiet about?'

'He's already made one payment, yes. But now he's not quite so forthcoming. So I think I need to have another chat with Mr Flowers rather soon. See if we can sort out some . . . more regular arrangement. I don't think he'll argue. Did you see how he reacted when I mentioned the name of the school?'

'Mm. I'd heard he was a teacher. That where he used to work?'

'Edgington Manor School, yes.'

'I haven't heard of it. Is it local?'

'Oh no. Up in the Midlands. But someone I knew on the force worked up there before he was transferred to West Sussex. And I met the bloke at someone's retirement do, and I told him I'd got this security officer job for the beach huts, and I was telling him about the set-up with the SBHA and what have you, and when by chance I mentioned the name of Reginald Flowers . . . well, he pounced on it and gave me chapter and verse.'

'Yeah? So what had old Reg been up to?'

'Well, let's just say he didn't get to full retirement age at Edgington Manor School. In fact, not to put too fine a point on it, he left the place under something of a cloud.'

Chapter Thirty

On the way back from the Crown and Anchor to their respective homes, Carole told Jude what she had just overheard.

'So you reckon Curt Holderness is blackmailing Reginald Flowers?'

'I can't put any other interpretation on what he said.'

'But you didn't hear exactly what had happened? Why he'd left the school under a cloud?'

'No, I didn't,' said Carole, before adding darkly, 'but I could make an educated guess. I think we should try to talk to Reginald as soon as possible. Are you free tomorrow morning?'

'Certainly am.'

Carole had reckoned that Reginald Flowers would be an early bird on Smalting Beach. Goodness only knew where he lived, where he spent his nights, but *The Bridge* was clearly the centre of his daily life. So Carole had decided to get there at half-past seven on the Saturday and give Gulliver his morning walk on Smalting rather than Fethering Beach. Jude, whose body clock favoured a more leisurely getting-up routine, was silent and, by her usually sunny standards, almost grumpy.

Still, both women had the sense that their investigation might finally be getting somewhere. Curt Holderness's admission the night before that he was blackmailing Reginald Flowers offered intriguing revelations.

But nothing, as it turned out, was going to be revealed that morning. The bar and padlocks on the front of *The Bridge* were locked in place, and there was no sign of the hut's owner.

'Staying in bed with his bronchitis,' Jude suggested. 'He did sound fairly ropey last night.'

'Yes,' Carole agreed glumly.

They took Gulliver for a long walk along Smalting Beach, as far as the headland that separated it from Fethering. But when they returned to the crescent of beach huts, there was still no sign of Reginald Flowers.

Disconsolately, they returned to the Renault, wondering who they knew who might have an address for the chairman of the SBHA.

As soon as she got back to High Tor, Carole checked her copy of *The Hut Parade*. There was a landline number for Reginald Flowers, but each time she tried it, the phone just rang and rang. Not even an answering machine message.

Carole Seddon took out her frustration by cleaning High Tor to within an inch of its life.

*

Next door at Woodside Cottage, Jude was equally restless. She tried to read the manuscript of a friend's book about the origins of acupuncture, but interesting though she found the subject, she found her mind kept slipping away from the text.

Till they contacted Reginald Flowers, there was nothing they could do on the Robin Cutter case.

It was early afternoon before she realized that there was still something she could try doing on the Mark Dennis case. She retrieved the phone number Gray Czesky had written down two days earlier, and keyed it into her mobile.

To her astonishment it was answered. By Mark Dennis.

He sounded subdued, but not adversarial. Jude didn't try any subterfuge, no pretence that she was a member of the police force. She just said that she was a friend of Philly's and she remembered meeting him with her. She said that she and her friend Carole would really like to meet up with him. Without demur, Mark suggested a rendezvous at six that evening in the Boatswain's Arms in Littlehampton.

'How did he sound?' asked Carole when Jude came rushing round to High Tor with the news.

'A bit sort of tentative. Vague maybe.'

'But not frightened?' She was remembering Nuala Cullan's description of the last time she saw her husband.

'No, I wouldn't have said frightened.'

*

Mark Dennis was not there when they got to the Boatswain's Arms. It was a roughish pub, the opposite end of the spectrum from The Crab Inn at Smalting. Littlehampton was like that. Although undergoing selective gentrification by expensive new developments of flats near the sea and the trendy modernity of the East Beach Café, parts of the town remained resolutely tacky. When Carole and Jude asked for Chilean Chardonnay at the counter, the Boatswain's Arms barman only offered them 'White Wine'. It was rather too sweet for either of their tastes. Lachrymose country and western music whined away in the background.

They sat down at a sticky round table and were aware of the scrutiny of the pub's other, silent customers. The atmosphere wasn't exactly hostile, but it wasn't welcoming either. Carole and Jude realized at the same time that they were the only women there. The chalkboard ads for Sky Sports suggested the Boatswain's Arms was a male haven, a place where lugubrious men dropped in after work to sink a silent pint or two, while they put off returning to their wives and other responsibilities.

Carole and Jude were both very excited at the prospect of meeting Mark Dennis. Finally, it seemed, at least one part of their investigation was making headway. Though neither of them could imagine that Mark himself had anything to do with the placing of Robin Cutter's remains under *Quiet Harbour*, they were still convinced he had important information to give them.

But as the minutes after their six o'clock agreed

meeting time passed, the two women started to worry that he wasn't going to turn up. In her head Jude tried to analyse exactly how he had sounded on the phone. Not frightened, no, but certainly nervous. Maybe he'd agreed to their meeting on the spur of the moment, and then thought better of the idea as its reality approached. Jude wished she'd asked Gray Czesky for an address as well as a phone number for Mark. Though the painter might well not have known one.

It was nearly six-thirty when the two women exchanged looks. Both were thinking the same thing: it was time to give their proposed meeting up as a bad job. But at that moment Mark Dennis came in through the door.

Had she not been expecting him, had they just passed in the street, Jude would not have recognized the young man. When she'd last seen Mark Dennis, probably in the April, he had been slender and gym-toned. With his sharp features, outdoor tan and straw-coloured hair, he and Philly Rose had made a singularly attractive couple.

But in the intervening months Mark Dennis had put on a lot of weight. The sideways spread of his face had made his eyes, nose and chin look too close together. And the weight gain seemed to have taken him by surprise. He hadn't yet adjusted his wardrobe to cope with it. The buttons down the front of his short-sleeved shirt strained against their buttonholes, and his thighs were very tight against his jeans.

His expression also was of someone taken by surprise, someone bewildered by what life had done to him. Recognizing Jude, he gazed rather blearily at the two women as she introduced him to Carole.

Asked what he'd like to drink, Mark Dennis opted for mineral water and Carole went to the bar to order it. She wondered for a moment whether the Boatswain's Arms would stock something as girlie as mineral water, but fortunately they did.

When she rejoined them, Carole found Mark already deep in conversation with Jude, apparently with no inhibitions about discussing his missing months. 'It was very odd. I was just out of it.'

'How do you mean "out of it"?' asked Jude.

'Not here. On another planet.' His voice still carried the vagueness that she had noticed on the phone.

'Take us back to the beginning of May,' she said. 'When you left Philly.' He winced at the reminder. 'Tell us what happened, that is, if you don't mind?'

'No, I don't mind. I've been trying to make sense of it myself for some time. It might help to talk about it.'

'Why haven't you talked about it to Philly?' asked Carole, possibly in too sharp a tone.

But Mark Dennis was unfazed by her question. 'I'll come to that. I'll explain it. Well, the main thing is, back in May I was in a pretty strange state, when all that happened. Not behaving very rationally.' He looked at Jude, almost pleadingly. 'I don't know if Philly told you anything about our circumstances . . .'

'A bit. I gather you had money problems.'

'And how. Yes, we'd moved out of London and down to Smalting in January. And then everything was fine. I'd got quite a lot of savings from various bonuses and what have you, then we made a bit of profit from selling our two London places and buying Seashell Cottage. Anyway, I invested all we'd got in various directions. Do you understand derivatives?'

Both women shook their heads.

'Neither, as it turned out, did I. I thought I understood them, but some freak activities in the world markets meant . . . well, effectively I'd lost the lot. Our little seaside idyll was looking very shaky, very much under threat.'

'So why didn't you talk to Philly about it?' asked Carole. 'Why did you just walk out on her?'

Again he didn't react to the aggression in her questions. 'I didn't mean to just walk out on her. I meant to . . . sort things out. In fact, I don't know if you know, but there were other complications in my life. I'm still technically married.'

'We know that,' said Jude.

'Yes,' Carole added. 'We have actually met Nuala.'

'Have you?' Mark Dennis grimaced. 'Something I must do again soon at some point. Not an encounter I look forward to.'

'We gathered from Nuala,' said Jude, 'that she was pressing you for money too.'

'Mm. We had this odd arrangement. I wanted to get divorced. The marriage had been over in everything but name for quite a long time. But Nuala wasn't keen on the idea of divorce.'

Carole nodded. 'We've heard her views on the subject.'

'Anyway, to keep her out of the scene and to let me get on with my life with Philly, I made this arrangement to . . . I don't know what you'd say . . .'

'Buy her off?' suggested Carole.

'Yes, that's what it effectively was – buying her off. And she insisted that it was done properly, with a legal agreement, which may give a pointer to the kind of character she is. But at least it got her out of my hair. Anyway, that was all fine, so long as I had this big income, but when things started to go pear-shaped on the money front, oh God, I couldn't keep Philly in our Smalting lifestyle and I couldn't pay what I'd agreed with Nuala, and . . . I was very stressed.'

Mark Dennis was silent for a moment. Neither Carole nor Jude said anything, giving him time to gather his thoughts.

'Well,' he said eventually, 'I still thought I could sort things out. I thought I could do it on my own. And I didn't think it would take long. I only intended to leave Philly for a few days. Go up to London, borrow some money from various City friends to dig me out of my financial hole, then meet up with Nuala, somehow get her off my back . . .'

'And what happened?'

He shook his head wryly. 'Should have known, really. Most of my City mates were feeling the squeeze as much as I was. Some of them actually asked to borrow money from me before I could put in my own request. Then I met up with Nuala . . .'

'At the Oxo Tower.'

'Yes, Carole. At the Oxo Tower. Typical of bloody Nuala, that. She knows I haven't got two penny pieces to rub together, so she books in at one of the most expensive bloody restaurants in London.'

'How did you pay for it?'

'Oh, credit cards.' He let out a bitter little laugh. 'Same way I'd been paying for everything else for the previous few months.'

'So there was quite a big debt built up there too, was there?' asked Jude.

'I'll say. And of course I'd been a very high earner, so I had no problem getting new cards or increasing my credit limit, which meant the debts just spiralled upwards and upwards.' He sighed. 'And the pressure on me was getting more and more intense . . .'

Carole broke the silence that followed this. 'What happened?'

Mark Dennis shook his head in bewilderment. 'I don't know.'

'What do you mean – you don't know?'

He sighed. 'I literally don't know. I had . . . I suppose you'd have to call it some kind of breakdown. I mean, when I left Philly, I can remember that happening. And I can remember having dinner with Nuala at the Oxo Tower – that was on the eighth of May – but . . .' He shook his head again, unable to fill in the gaps in his recollection.

'So where have you been for the last few weeks?' asked Jude gently.

'I've been in a psychiatric hospital for most of it. Only came out a couple of weeks ago.'

'How did you get in there? Did you go in voluntarily?'

'No, I was sent there. Look, I can't actually remember a lot of this stuff myself, but from what the doctors and nurses have told me, I've kind of pieced together what happened. As I say, the last thing I can clearly remember was having that dinner with Nuala at the Oxo Tower on the eighth of May. What I did for the next few days I have no idea, but I was found on Dover Beach on the morning of the eleventh. I had been in the sea, was drenched through and was only wearing a pair of boxer shorts. What was more, I couldn't speak.'

'And you have no recollection of how you got there?'

'None at all. And only hazy recollections of the following weeks. Because of the location, because I had apparently come out of the sea, and because I couldn't – or perhaps wouldn't – speak English, the fairly reasonable assumption was made that I must be an illegal immigrant, who had been shipwrecked, or perhaps dumped in the English Channel by some unscrupulous trafficker. So I was handed over to the police, who apparently questioned me for some time.'

'Do you remember any of that?'

'Only vague sort of impressions – and not very pleasant ones at that. I think the police thought I was holding out on them, that I actually could speak but was just pretending to be traumatized to conceal my identity. So they didn't exactly treat me with kid gloves.'

'Are you saying they beat you up?' asked Carole,

whose Home Office background made her particularly
sensitive about criticisms of the police.

'No, I'm not saying that. I don't think there was
any violence involved, just a lot of suspicion. And my
recollections are so hazy that I don't know which bits
really happened and which I've invented. Anyway,
after a few days the police must have decided that I
was suffering from some genuine psychological condition – amnesia at the very least, and possibly some
other arcanely named syndromes. So I was then sent
to this secure psychiatric hospital in Lewes. Which is
where I've been until a fortnight ago.'

'But clearly your memory's come back. You know
who you are now, don't you?'

'Yes, Jude, I do. The process was gradual. The psychiatrists who worked with me were very good. And I
had a lot of medication too.' He gestured to his flabby
body. 'I think that's probably why I put on so much
weight. The medication and lack of exercise.'

'Did the psychiatrists have any explanation for
what had happened to you?'

'Conjectures, nothing concrete. They reckon
that I'd just got to a point of stress where my system
couldn't cope, so everything kind of shut down. I
couldn't deal with the world around me and so my
body reacted by excluding me from that world, shutting me off from it.'

The two women exchanged looks. Something in
Jude's expression prevented Carole from expressing
the scepticism Mark Dennis's words had engendered
in her.

He shrugged. 'Anyway, that was what the psychiatrists reckoned. Whether it's true I've no idea, but I suppose it sounds like a kind of explanation.'

'When you went down to Dover Beach,' asked Carole, 'do you think it was with the intention of drowning yourself, of escaping your problems that way?'

Mark Dennis pursed his lips. 'To be honest I don't know. I don't think so. During the last few months I've never contemplated suicide, however bad things have been. And before that, when I was normal, if that's the right word . . . well, the idea of me topping myself would have been laughable. I've never suffered from depression. I've always been told I'm a rather annoyingly positive person.'

Jude nodded. 'Yes, but depression can lie low in someone for a very long time. And your lifestyle had always been pretty pressured, hadn't it?'

'That's exactly what one of the psychiatrists said to me. Almost word for word. Do you have special expertise in that area, Jude?'

'I do a bit of healing.'

'Ah.' He looked at her appreciatively. 'I would imagine you're very good at it.'

'Thank you.'

'What I can't understand,' said Carole, 'is when you did finally begin to remember who you were, why you didn't make contact with anyone?'

'I hadn't got many people to make contact with. My parents are both dead. There was no way I wanted to see Nuala again until I was sure I was firing on all cylinders.'

'But what about Philly?'

'Yes.' Mark Dennis looked sad and confused. 'Yes, I know I should have got in touch with Philly as soon as I could, but . . . it's complicated. I guess it's something to do with our relationship. Philly . . . she's . . . well, she hasn't got a lot of confidence. She doesn't show it, she always seems bright and bouncy, but her self-esteem is actually very low.'

Jude, who knew this all too well, didn't say anything, as he went on, 'And the previous men in her life haven't done much good for her. From what I can gather, they were mostly inadequates, needy emotional vampires who monopolized all of her energy with their problems rather than her giving any time to her own.

'But when we met, it was different. I was used to being in charge, I was full – perhaps over-full – of confidence, and I loved her. And the fact that someone like me loved her, that gave *her* a lot of confidence. And the fact that I enjoyed being in charge, and that I sort of protected her, she liked that too. Then of course I'm that much older, so a bit of a father figure maybe. I was like her rock. She knew that, whatever happened, she could rely on me.'

Carole and Jude guessed more or less what he was about to say, but they did not break the silence. 'Well, when our finances started to go belly up, I wasn't so much of a rock, was I? No more Mr Reliable.'

'But Philly didn't take it out on you for what had happened?' asked Carole.

'Good Lord, no. It's not in her nature to do that. No, she was very understanding and supportive. And very practical. She said we'd have to sell Seashell Cottage, and I knew how much she loved the place, but she didn't put any pressure on me. Philly is entirely incapable of emotional blackmail.'

'Which, after Nuala,' Carole suggested tartly, 'must have been quite a relief for you.'

'God, you can say that again.'

'So, when you got your memory back, the reason you didn't contact Philly,' said Jude perceptively, 'was because you were afraid you had become needy, like all her previous men.'

'Exactly that. I wanted to wait till my own confidence had built up a bit, till I could once again be the person she needs. But I'm afraid getting to that situation promises to be a horribly slow process.'

'You could at least have just given Philly a call, though.' There was a note of reproach in Carole's voice. 'Assured her you were still alive. She's been worried sick about you.'

Mark Dennis looked shamefacedly down at the sticky table top. 'I know. I should have done it. But I didn't want her to see me . . . damaged.'

'You did, however, come down to Smalting last week, didn't you?' continued Carole in the same tone. 'Why didn't you see her then?'

'Ah.' His naughty schoolboy expression was just the same as Gray Czesky's in similar circumstances. 'I didn't know anyone had seen me down here.'

'You must've lived in a country village long enough to know that nothing – absolutely nothing – you do in a place like that is unseen.'

'Yes, I suppose you're right.'

Jude's approach was, as ever, less confrontational than her neighbour's. 'So why didn't you contact Philly?' she asked gently.

'That was what I meant to do. I'd been out of the Lewes hospital for over a week, I'd sorted out the rather dingy room I've got here in Littlehampton, and I felt ready to at least try and see Philly. So I took a cab to Smalting that Monday evening.'

'Without ringing Philly to tell her you were coming?'

'Yes, without doing that. And I think I know why. If I'm brutally honest with myself, I didn't ring her because that meant I could still duck out of the meeting if I wanted to. You know, if when I got to Smalting I lost my nerve.'

'And I assume you did lose your nerve. That was why you didn't go to see her.'

'Well, it wasn't exactly losing my nerve, though I suppose it was in a way. I got to Smalting and rather than going straight to Seashell Cottage, I . . . well, I thought I might drop in on Gray Czesky, just to see if he'd heard anything about Philly, to see if he knew whether she was actually still in Smalting and . . . Yes, I suppose I did lose my nerve.'

'And you also, I assume, knew,' said Carole, 'that going to see Gray Czesky would inevitably lead to another drinking session with him.'

Jude continued the chain of thought. 'And you wouldn't want Philly to see you in a drunken state, because that is one of the few things you argued about. So the moment you decided to go and see Gray was the moment you decided you weren't going to see Philly that evening.'

Mark Dennis's nod confirmed that she'd got it right. 'And I did get very drunk, I'm afraid. I'd been off the booze since I'd had the breakdown. No bars in psychiatric hospitals – at least not that kind of bar. So the stuff I drank at Gray's went straight to my head. And I don't think it mixed very well with the medication I was on. Am still on, actually.' He gestured to his mineral water. 'That's why I'm drinking this. Anyway, that night I was certainly in no condition for a heart-warming, violins-in-the-background reunion with Philly.'

'And then, of course,' Carole observed acidly, 'Gray Czesky chose that evening for another of his anti-bourgeois exploits, didn't he?'

'Setting fire to the beach hut,' Mark agreed glumly. 'Yes, he's a madman when he gets a few drinks inside him.'

'What exactly happened?'

'Oh, he got into one of his tirades about how no one understands artists, and the rest of the world has a down on them and only cares about middle-class consumerism.'

'Great from someone whose lifestyle is funded by a rich wife.'

'I know, I know. Anyway, Gray suddenly gets into this great rant about beach huts symbolizing everything that's wrong with the bourgeoisie, and then he disappears. Helga and I thought he'd just gone for a pee, but ten minutes later he's back proclaiming that he's set fire to one of the beach huts.'

'Do you think he deliberately chose *Quiet Harbour?*' asked Carole. 'Did he know that you and Philly had rented it?'

'Who knows? Perhaps he did. Quite possibly he was getting at me because he reckoned I was too bourgeois to be what he defined as a proper artist.'

'So you and Helga,' suggested Jude, 'immediately rushed down to the beach to put the fire out?'

'Yes.' The two women exchanged looks. Curt Holderness's sighting had been confirmed. 'Fortunately the fire hadn't taken much hold. We were able to extinguish it quite easily.'

'So what did you do then? Go back to Sanditon?'

'No, I was feeling so shitty with the booze, all I wanted to do was get to bed. I called a cab, just managed to avoid throwing up over its upholstery, and went to bed the minute I got back to my room here in Littlehampton. The next morning I woke up with the worst hangover of my life.'

'So that again wasn't the perfect day for your reconciliation with Philly?'

'Too right, Jude.'

'But that was over a week ago,' said Carole. 'Why didn't you get in touch with her once you'd recovered from the hangover?'

'I kept putting off calling her. I was worried about how she'd react to me, whether she'd be furious, whether I'd ruined everything. But finally by the Friday I'd convinced myself I had to take the risk.

Call Philly, accept whatever consequences that action might trigger.'

'I don't think they'd be bad consequences,' said Jude gently.

Mark Dennis appeared not to hear her, as he went on, 'Then of course on the Thursday morning I hear on the news that human remains have been found under a beach hut at Smalting. Well, I knew that meant the place was going to be swarming with police and, though my recollections of what had happened to me after I was found on Dover Beach were vague, there was no way I was ever voluntarily going to put myself in touch with the police again, so . . .' His words trickled away to silence.

'Have you heard about the identification of the remains that were found?' asked Carole.

'Yes. It keeps being on the news. You can't escape it.'

'And do you know anything about Robin Cutter?'

'Only what I've heard in the last few days.' From the way he spoke there was no doubt that Mark Dennis was telling the truth.

He shook his head in puzzlement. 'So that's where I am. Still totally confused.' He looked earnestly at Jude and asked, 'What do you think I should do?'

She held out her mobile phone towards him. 'Ring Philly.'

Chapter Thirty-One

Mark Dennis was afraid – tremblingly, shudderingly afraid. They had driven straight from the pub to Seashell Cottage. When the Renault drew up outside, he asked the two women to come to the front door with him. Then he changed his mind and asked Jude to go on her own and check whether Philly Rose really wanted to see him.

As they waited in the car, Carole was aware of his body convulsing with bone-deep sobs. She was embarrassed and couldn't think of anything to say.

Their wait felt long, but it was only a couple of minutes. Then Jude came out on to the street and said through the Renault's open window, 'She wants to see you, Mark.'

Reassured but still scared, he again asked them to come into the cottage with him. The two women felt a little strange as they escorted Mark through the front door, which Philly held open, but such was the emotional tension between the two young people, they could recognize the need for some kind of catalyst for this first explosive contact.

Awkwardness filled the tiny hall while Philly

closed the door. Wordlessly, she ushered her three guests into the kitchen/dining area. The uneasy silence continued until their hostess offered tea.

'Yes,' said Mark very formally. 'Yes, thank you, Philly. I'd like a cup of tea.'

Carole and Jude refused the offer. 'We should really be on our way,' said Jude.

'No, don't go!' The plea from Mark Dennis was instinctive, and still frightened.

'I think we should.' Jude looked at the two of them, facing each other, frozen, their eyes avoiding engagement. 'Come on, Carole. We'll see ourselves out.'

In the Renault on the way back to Fethering, Carole asked, 'What do you reckon? The minute we left, they fell into each other's arms and love's young dream was re-established?'

'I hope so,' said Jude. But she didn't sound sure.

'Well, at least that's one mystery solved,' Carole observed, 'but I can't believe Mark had anything to do with Robin Cutter.'

'No.' Jude was thoughtful, abstracted.

'So I suppose it's another visit tomorrow morning to Smalting Beach. Hope that Reginald Flowers's bronchitis has cleared up, assuming that that's why he wasn't there today.'

'Hm.'

'Are you up for a return visit?'

Shaking herself out of her reverie, Jude said, 'What? Tomorrow? Saturday? No, sorry, I'm committed to a Past Life Regression Workshop in Brighton.'

A lot of knee-jerk responses sprang to Carole's lips,

but she restricted herself to a rather acid, 'Are you? Well,' she continued, 'I'll see if I can get a chance to talk to Reginald Flowers.'

Chapter Thirty-Two

The bronchitis must have cleared up. Carole exactly repeated her timescale of the previous morning: a seven-thirty walk with Gulliver on Smalting Beach. Sure enough, even at that hour, as she and the dog passed, Reginald Flowers was sitting in his bolt-upright chair at the doors of his museum of naval memorabilia.

There was no problem about selecting her opening conversational gambit. 'Very good do the other night. Jude and I really enjoyed the quiz.'

'I'm glad to hear it.'

'Thank you very much. It must have taken a lot of organization.'

'Oh, I'm used to it,' he said in heroic self-deprecation. 'Anyway, I must thank you too. Without your prompt action, Carole, we wouldn't have had a venue, would we?'

'I can always get round Ted Crisp,' she said with uncharacteristic winsomeness.

'He was the one with the beard behind the bar?'

'Yes.'

An expression of irritation crossed Reginald

Flowers's face. 'I always think if a man is going to
have a beard, he should keep it in good order. At
least he had a full beard, rather than one of those
goatees or other forms of contemporary topiary.'
Instinctively his hand stroked his George V number.
'But I can't imagine why anyone would want to go
around looking like a cross between a Viking and
a hippy. It certainly made that landlord look very
surly. Positively forbidding. And he wasn't particularly forthcoming when he opened his mouth either.
Downright rude, if you ask me.'

'That's just his manner. Ted Crisp really does have
a heart of gold.'

'Well, I'll have to take your word for that. Anyway,
many thanks for making the arrangement, Carole.'

'No problem at all.'

Reginald Flowers was silent for a moment, looking
back inside *The Bridge*. Then he said, 'Look, I've got
the kettle on. Was about to make a cup of tea. Would
you care to join me?'

Carole was struck by the nervousness with which
he made this offer, almost as though it were something
much more momentous, like asking her out on a date.
She was also aware again of his deep loneliness. The
Thursday night in the Crown and Anchor she'd recognized it too. Reginald Flowers had been at the centre
of everything, he'd known everyone there, but he
still seemed separate, outside any community spirit
there had been in the function room. The only person
he'd connected with – and that had been at a level of
guilt and reproach – had been Dora Pinchbeck.

'Yes, I'd love a cup of tea,' Carole replied. 'Do you mind if I tie the dog up to that hook?'

'Be my guest.' Reginald Flowers went into his shrine to fetch another chair for her, and then to busy himself with the tea making.

The early morning sun was pleasantly warm and had already burned off any residual mist from the night before. Carole looked out over the sea and found herself recalling the image that Lionel Oliver had told her about – of a young man disappointed in love walking straight out to his death. The scene before her suddenly seemed less idyllic.

She looked across to Gulliver, now amiably reconciled to having his walk truncated and being tied up. He snuffled at the shingle in the shadow of the beach hut, searching out delicious-smelling morsels of seaweed.

'Do you take milk and sugar?' came the call from inside the hut.

'Just milk, thank you.'

Before Reginald Flowers emerged with the cups, Carole forced herself into a moment of intense concentration. Amidst all the pleasantry with the President of the Smalting Beach Hut Association, she mustn't forget her purpose in being in front of *The Bridge* that morning. She had an investigation to pursue.

When they were both seated with their cups of tea, she reverted to the quiz night. 'I was wondering about the range of questions you managed to come up with, Reginald.'

'Please call me "Reg".'

'Very well, Reg. But, as I say, I was impressed by the variety. Did you research all the questions yourself?'

'Some I did. Some I got from other reference sources.'

'I was totally stumped by a lot of them – certainly the sport and pop music ones. I mean, I've just about heard of Beyoncé, but I certainly couldn't name a song by her.'

'Oh, nor me. But I thought, to be fair, I should have questions for a broad age range, for the younger people like . . .' He was hard put to it to come up with any names of younger members of the Smalting Beach Hut Association. 'Anyway, those kind of subjects I got off the internet. There are whole websites devoted to pub quizzes, you know.'

'Really?' Carole was surprised to hear that Reginald Flowers was an internet user. His age, his manner, his old-fashioned way of dictating letters to Dora – and indeed the amateur printing of *The Hut Parade* – had marked him down in her book as someone whose acquaintance with computers was minimal.

What she was thinking must have coloured her response, because Reginald said, 'I use the internet quite a lot, you know.' He gestured back into *The Bridge*. 'For my collection. You'd be surprised how much naval stuff – some of it very good naval stuff – comes up on eBay. Particularly badges, buckles, that kind of thing.'

Looking at the display behind her, Carole observed that he didn't have much room for new additions.

'Oh, this isn't all I have. Only a selection. I change

around what I put on show here. I've got about ten times this amount at home.'

This was the first time he'd mentioned a home, so Carole asked him where it was.

'Littlehampton. Rented flat in Littlehampton,' he grunted. It was clearly not something that he wanted to discuss further. 'And to save you asking, I live on my own.'

There was a waspishness in his reply, so Carole moved on to less controversial ground. 'How long ago did you start the collection?'

'Really started when I was a boy. As I may have mentioned, a good number of my family were in the navy.'

'Yes. Given your interest, it's surprising that you didn't follow in their footsteps.'

'Perhaps.' He looked uncomfortable at the direction the conversation was taking. 'The fact is, I did try to join up. My parents wanted me to train at Dartmouth, but I . . . I didn't get in.'

Alert to the awkwardness in his hesitation, Carole prompted him with an, 'Oh?'

'I was rejected on medical grounds.'

'Ah.' Carole tried to work out the timescale. If, as she assumed, Reginald Flowers was now in his seventies, then it would have been over fifty years ago when he'd applied for Dartmouth. And back then it was quite possible that rejection 'on medical grounds' might well have covered sexual deviancy.

But she was getting ahead of herself. She needed more information before she could form any conclusions about Reginald Flowers's guilt or innocence. 'So you went into teaching, I gather?'

'Yes. It was always second best for me, but I derived some satisfaction from the profession. I was teaching English History, which of course, because we are an island nation, involved a lot of research about the navy. Yes . . .' He smiled without much humour, '. . . the only thing wrong with teaching I found was the wretched pupils.'

'Did you not get on with them?'

'Some I got on with. The ones who had some sense of motivation, the ones who actually saw the point of learning. They were few and far between, though. I'm afraid to say they were not encouraged by the ethos of the place. The school I taught at put much higher value on prowess in the sports field than it did on academic achievement.'

'Ah. And you didn't teach sport as well?'

'Good heavens, no,' he replied peevishly. 'There were plenty of bone-headed former Blues on the staff to do that.'

Carole took a deep breath. She'd been given the cue, and now she had to pick it up, whatever the consequences. 'The place you taught was called Edgington Manor School, wasn't it?'

'Yes.' He looked at her sharply. 'Did you know that before Thursday night?'

'No.'

'I rather hoped no one had noticed the mention of the school in all the shouting and excitement of the quiz.'

'Well, I heard what Curt Holderness said. I also saw the way you reacted to it.'

'Yes. It was a shock. I thought I'd got away from all that. I didn't realize that anyone down here knew of my connection with . . . that place.'

'The school?' He nodded. 'Edgington Manor School. I gather you had to leave there before you'd got to retirement age.'

'I did.' The expression he turned on her was one of disappointed fury. 'So are you one of them too, Carole?'

'One of what?'

'One of the people who's out to blackmail me?'

'No, I'm certainly not!' There was a silence before she continued, 'You asked whether I was one of them *too*. Does that suggest that Curt Holderness and Kelvin Southwest have already been in touch with you?'

'Curt Holderness has been. I haven't heard anything from that little pervert Southwest.'

'And Curt's trying to blackmail you?' She asked only for confirmation of what she had heard the other night.

'Yes. He was first in touch about a month ago. He said he'd found out something about the circumstances under which I had left Edgington Manor School and would I mind if he made it public? Well, of course I minded, so I agreed to pay him some money. I thought he was talking about just a one-off payment, but then a couple of weeks later he asked for more.'

The classic experience of the blackmail victim, thought Carole.

'I said I couldn't afford it – well, I can't, I'm only on a pension. But he said I could afford it if I sold some of my collection.' The horror of the idea spread across his face. 'Well, of course I couldn't do that, could I? So I still haven't paid him. But Thursday night was like a warning to me. Curt Holderness knew nobody at the quiz night would pick up the reference in what he shouted out – nobody except me, of course. He was saying: look, I'm quite capable of talking about this business in public and, if you don't pay up, I'll do it more vocally. Well, I can't risk that, can I? I'll have to somehow find the money and pay him. This time. But I'm afraid this won't be the last time. There's no reason why his demands should ever stop, is there?' he concluded miserably.

'Do you think Curt might go to the police with what he knows?'

'Why should he do that? It's not a police matter. I paid my dues for my crime. I served my sentence. Why on earth should it have anything to do with the police?'

'I meant in the light of . . .' Carole nodded discreetly towards *Quiet Harbour* '. . . recent discoveries.'

Reginald Flowers stared at her in bewilderment. 'What's that got to do with anything?'

'Well, the boy, Robin Cutter, was supposed to be the victim of a paedophile and I—'

'Are you suggesting that I ever had anything to do with paedophilia?' He sounded appalled at the idea.

'Well, you did leave Edgington Manor School under a cloud.'

'Yes, but that wasn't because I was fiddling with

the children. For God's sake, Carole! If you're looking for a pervert on Smalting Beach, you'd do much
better concentrating on Kelvin Southwest. Ask him
about those afternoons when he goes into one of the
empty beach huts with his binoculars and spies on
the nippers changing. And it wouldn't surprise me at
all to hear that that's only the beginning of what he
gets up to. But don't you dare accuse me of anything
like that!'

'Then, if it wasn't for that reason, why did you
leave the school?' asked Carole evenly.

He sighed, shook his head and looked shamefaced.
'I stole something.'

'Stole something? What?'

'Edgington Manor School was founded quite a long
time ago. Late eighteenth century. And one of its first
old boys was an admiral in Nelson's navy. Admiral
Henryson. Not very well known, but like Nelson he
was killed at Trafalgar. And his widow presented his
dress uniform to the school. It stood in a glass case in
the Lower Hall. I passed it half a dozen times a day,
and each time I passed it I was more determined that
it should be mine, that I should add it to my collection.
At first the idea was just an idle fancy, but it became
an obsession.

'So I worked out how I'd steal it. During the school
holidays. Make it look as though vandals had broken
into the school. I'd got it all worked out, all justified
in my own mind. Edgington Manor School had never
done me any favours, the place owed me something.
I was two years off retirement and I was determined

that there was one final favour the place was going to do me.

'Plan all went fine. I had keys to certain doors in the school, I knew how to switch off the burglar alarm. I took Admiral Henryson's uniform. Nobody in the school ever looked at it, none of those sports-obsessed spotty boys gave a damn about the thing. It was right that it should belong to someone who appreciated its full value. I felt no guilt. I still don't feel any guilt.'

'But you didn't get away with it, did you, Reg?'

He shook his head wearily. 'No. I'd been seen breaking into the school by some officious young housemaster. Out in the grounds pushing his bloody infant in a buggy or whatever they call those things. By the time I got out of the building, the police were waiting for me.'

'And you were charged with theft?'

'Yes. Some schools would have hushed it up. They wouldn't have wanted the adverse publicity. But that wasn't the way my sanctimonious bloody headmaster thought. He said Edgington Manor School was trying to make its pupils into honest citizens and they should therefore be made aware of the penalties for dishonesty. We'd always hated each other, and suddenly he saw the perfect opportunity to make an example of me. So yes, I went through the courts, which let me tell you was pretty bloody humiliating. I subsequently spent six months at Her Majesty's pleasure . . . which wasn't much fun either. However many times I told them the truth of what I was in for, the other prisoners assumed . . . schoolteacher, kicked out at my age, must have been for . . .' He shuddered. 'Anyway, somehow I survived that, but obviously when I was released, my career was finished.

'So after a time I moved down here, where I thought, where I hoped, that no one would ever know about that episode in my past. I still don't know how Curt Holderness did find out about it.'

'Through a policeman he'd met who'd worked up near Edgington Manor School.'

'Ah. Right.' Reginald Flowers looked very weary. His long confession had taken its toll.

'One thing I can't quite understand,' Carole began, 'is why it matters so much to you. I mean, you did wrong, but most people would not think that you did anything very seriously wrong. Given all the stuff you've got here in the beach hut, you could almost laugh it off, as an example of the single-mindedness of the obsessive collector. I mean, if Curt Holderness did go public about what you did, who do you think would actually be that worried? You're only successful as a blackmailer if your victim has got a lot to lose. And I don't really see that you have a lot to lose.'

'What!' demanded Reginald Flowers in amazement. 'How can you say that? It'd be a total disaster. Are you suggesting that, if it was known I had a criminal record, I would be allowed to remain as President of the Smalting Beach Hut Association?'

Chapter Thirty-Three

Smalting Beach was considerably busier when Carole left *The Bridge* and continued Gulliver's interrupted walk. They covered half a mile in the Fethering direction, and though the dog would much rather not have been on a lead, he still patently enjoyed himself.

With a slight shock, Carole realized that she was only a day away from the arrival of Gaby and Lily. The mysteries of Mark Dennis and Robin Cutter had been preoccupying her. One of them was solved. She wondered what the chances were of the second being elucidated before she had to go into full-on grandmother mode. The odds weren't promising. She tried to close her mind to the case and concentrate on her imminent visitors. She wasn't successful.

On their way back to *Fowey*, Carole and Gulliver's route took them along the line of the other beach huts, of which more had been opened up during their walk. Outside *Cape of Good Hope* sat Dora Pinchbeck with a piled-high cornet of pistachio ice cream and a *Daily Mail*. In her personal domain, in front of her beach hut, she looked very much more in control of life than on the previous occasions Carole had met her. It seemed that, when she wasn't being diminished and patronized by Reginald Flowers, the woman did actually have an identity of her own.

She greeted Carole warmly and glowed when congratulated on the success of the quiz night. 'Yes, it all seemed to go very well,' she agreed. 'In spite of the snafu over the booking of the venue.'

Carole was surprised at Dora's use of the military slang expression 'snafu'. Easier to imagine it coming from Reginald Flowers's lips. And she wondered whether Dora was actually quoting her 'boss'.

'Oh well, everyone makes mistakes,' she said soothingly.

'I agree. Some of us just don't admit to them, though.' Carole's look asked for an explanation, so Dora nodded towards *The Bridge*. 'Lord High and Mighty over there never admits to having made a mistake.'

'Oh?'

'Did he tell you that I'd screwed up the booking at St Mary's Church Hall?'

'Yes, he did.'

'Typical. That's how control freaks always come unstuck. Incapable of delegating, on the rare occasions when they do make mistakes, they always have to find someone else to blame. And in Reg's case it's nearly always Little Me.'

She spoke with remarkable lack of rancour, given the way her 'boss' treated her. Carole began to wonder if the efficient master/incompetent secretary routine was some kind of game they played, and whether their relationship was in fact rather closer than it appeared on the outside.

'Anyway,' she said, 'good to see you, Dora. Come along, Gulliver.'

She was stopped by a question from Dora that was spoken so softly that she hardly heard it. But it sounded like, 'Any developments on the case?'

She turned back. 'I beg your pardon?'

'The investigation into Robin Cutter's death.'

Oh dear, thought Carole, are Jude and I that transparent? There we are, imagining we're conducting our enquiry secretly and it seems that the whole of Smalting – and quite possibly Fethering too – knows all about our endeavours. She tried to think of some appropriately enigmatic response, but before she could say it, Dora Pinchbeck went on, in a confidential tone, 'I'm a friend of Helga Czesky . . .'

'Oh?'

' . . . and she told me . . . you know, who you really are.'

'Ah.' It took Carole a moment to realize the significance of this. It was only a few days since she and Jude had had the confrontation with Gray and Helga Czesky at Woodside Cottage, but so much had happened since that it felt a lifetime away. Of course, as she recalled with some pleasure, the Czeskys had left that meeting convinced that Carole and Jude were both plain-clothes policewomen. If that was the information that Helga had imparted to Dora Pinchbeck, then Carole was in a situation of which she could take advantage.

She tested it out by saying, 'I'm afraid I'm not allowed to give out any information about the case until there's an official press conference.'

'No, no, of course I can see that.' Dora sounded disappointed but realistic. It had just been a punt. She hadn't really been expecting to be given the inside track on the investigation.

'And in fact,' Carole went on, gaining confidence in her new spurious role, 'I would rather you kept the information that Helga Czesky gave you under wraps. The work we do is kind of undercover, so we don't want everyone in Smalting to know about it.'

'I understand completely.'

Carole fixed Dora Pinchbeck with a beady eye. 'May I ask whether you have told anyone else what Jude and I really do.'

The embarrassed expression on the woman's face told Carole that she had struck gold. 'Well, I'm sorry,' Dora Pinchbeck floundered. 'I shouldn't have, I suppose, but, you know, if you're in conversation with someone, well, it is quite easy to let things slip.'

'Who have you told?' came the implacable question.

There was a long silence, during which Carole suddenly became aware of a moral dilemma. Given her background in the Home Office, she knew full well how serious was the crime of impersonating a member of the police force. That was black and white. But considerably greyer was the ethical position of someone being assumed to be a policewoman and not putting right the person who had made the assumption. Jude, she knew, would have had no worries at all about the situation, regarding it as an instance of serendipity, of some cosmic force displaying generosity, a gift from the gods, which it would be bad manners to turn down, or some other New Age mumbo-jumbo. But Carole Seddon was wary of such casuistry.

Fortunately, her moral meanderings were cut short when Dora Pinchbeck gave her the name of the person she had told about her supposed status as a plain-clothes policewoman. And the minute she heard the name, all qualms vanished.

'Kelvin Southwest.'

'When did you tell him?'

'Thursday night. Just after he arrived at the Crown and Anchor. I was chatting to him and then when you and your friend came in, he said something about the two of you, and I told him what I'd heard from Helga. I'm terribly sorry.'

'Don't worry about it,' said Carole with magisterial generosity.

She couldn't believe her luck. Now she knew why Kelvin Southwest had avoided her at the beginning of the previous evening. And now she had a hold over him. If Kelvin Southwest thought she was a member of the police force, then he wasn't going to refuse to answer her questions about what he got up to in an empty beach hut with binoculars, was he?

Chapter Thirty-Four

There was no 'lovely lady' flirtatiousness from the Fether District Council official when Carole rang his mobile number. The tension in his voice suggested that he had been expecting her call, and he proved to be very biddable. Yes, of course he would meet her whenever she liked. He'd rather not make it at his house, because he didn't want his mother to get upset. On Smalting Beach would be fine. Yes, at *Fowey*. He'd be with her in as long as it took.

Carole Seddon felt a glow of satisfaction as she sat outside the beach hut waiting for him. The odds on her getting a solution to the case seemed suddenly to have shortened considerably. And she relished the prospect of telling her neighbour how she solved it single-handedly while Jude was in Brighton. Past Life Regression Workshop – huh.

She looked along the row of beach huts and felt as if she belonged there. She was almost a hutter, and would be more than competent to welcome Gaby and Lily to *Fowey* the next day. Or would she be able finally to return to her original beach hut?

Carole had noticed earlier that all traces of the

police presence around *Quiet Harbour* had now been removed. Maybe she could reclaim it? Architecturally the two beach huts were absolutely identical, but, in spite of everything that had happened there, Carole did have a sneaking preference for *Quiet Harbour* over *Fowey*. It felt more hers.

Smalting Beach was getting back to normal, though. The doors to *Shrimphaven* were open. Inside no doubt Katie Brunswick was continuing the Sisyphean task of rewriting her novel.

And further along the Olivers had taken up their customary positions: Joyce on her lounger with another wordsearch book, Lionel, as ever dressed for work with his suit jacket over the back of his chair, looking out to sea. Carole could only conjecture what thoughts might be going through their heads, and the extent to which memories of their lost grandson filled them. She felt something approaching a crusading zeal at the prospect of her interview with Kelvin Southwest. At last she might be able to unearth some information that might help the Olivers and Miranda Browning come to terms with their family tragedy.

'Good morning.'

Carole looked up to see that her quarry had arrived. As a concession to the weekend, he was not in his Fether District Council livery, but still dressed in virtually identical style. A green polo shirt and much-pocketed khaki shorts strained over his chubby body. His footwear remained leather sandals over short white socks.

He looked ill at ease, his right hand tugging nervously at his silky goatee.

'Good morning. Do sit down.' Carole gestured to the other director's chair she'd set out for him. Shiftily he did as she suggested, looking anxiously to the beach huts on either side. Both were closed up.

'Nobody will hear what we're saying,' continued Carole, 'but of course if you'd rather go inside the hut or move somewhere more private . . .'

'No, this'll be fine.' Kelvin Southwest perched uncomfortably on the edge of his seat, as though suffering from a bad case of piles. 'Incidentally,' he said, 'we've had the all-clear from the police. They've finished their investigations in *Quiet Harbour*, so you can go back there if you want to.'

'Oh, thank you. I might go back there tomorrow. That's when my daughter-in-law and granddaughter are arriving. Do you have the key?'

He had come prepared and passed it across.

There was a rather awkward silence. Having actually got the man there, Carole was beginning to wish she'd given a bit more thought to how she intended to conduct their interview. But fortunately Kelvin Southwest made it easy for her by saying, 'Look, I haven't done anything that's harmed anyone.'

'No?'

Happily this was sufficient prompt for him to continue, 'Who told you about me using the binoculars? Who shopped me?'

'I don't think it's relevant for me to disclose that information at this point,' said Carole, amazed at how instinctively she had once again dropped into police-speak.

'Look, all right, I'm attracted to kids, but I'd never do anything that'd harm them,' he reiterated.

'I'm not sure that you're necessarily the best judge of that, Mr Southwest.' She was damned if she was going to go back to calling him 'Kel'.

'I can't help the feelings I have,' he said, hoping – unsuccessfully – to engage her sympathy. 'And I have now got much better control over them.'

'Could you explain to me what you mean by that?'

'Listen, all right, a few years ago, yes, I did sometimes take my binoculars into one of the empty beach huts. I actually made spy holes in it, so's I could . . . Look, I'm not proud of what I've done, but back then I couldn't control my urges.' He reverted to another thought that still nagged at him. 'I bet I know who it was who shopped me to you. It'd be that Dora Pinchbeck. I'd put money on it. She's always been a nosy cow.'

'I will neither confirm nor deny your conjectures, Mr Southwest,' Carole pronounced in magnificent police-speak. 'The identity of the person who, as you put it, "shopped" you is not important, and will only become important if that person needs to be called as a witness in court.'

In a less excited mood Carole wouldn't have gone so far. Threatening someone with legal action was taking the crime of impersonating a member of the police force to another level. But she was in no mood for caution. She was determined to get some kind of confession out of Kelvin Southwest.

And the approach did pay off, because he responded, 'Yes, all right, I used to look at kids undressing through binoculars, but that's not a police matter.'

And I'm not a policewoman, thought Carole, but what she actually said was, 'If you seriously believe that, Mr Southwest, then you haven't read a newspaper or watched the television news for the past twenty years.'

'All right,' he whined. 'But you don't know what it's like, having these urges that can't find satisfaction in a way that's publicly acceptable.'

Thank goodness Jude isn't here, thought Carole. His words echoed what her neighbour had said on the subject of paedophilia. Jude was quite capable of ending up feeling sorry for the little worm.

'I'd like,' Carole proceeded magisterially, 'to talk to you about Robin Cutter.'

'What? Look, for God's sake, you're not going to try and pin that on me, are you?'

'Were you questioned by the police at the time of his disappearance?'

'No, of course I wasn't! Why should I have been?'

'Mr Southwest, you have just admitted that you have paedophiliac tendencies.'

'Yes, but I'd never give them expression in that way. And, besides, I'm not on any register or anything. Nobody else knows that I have . . . you know, what you said.'

'If that were true, Mr Southwest, we wouldn't be having this conversation now. The person who "shopped" you knows. Why shouldn't a lot of other people?'

'But nobody knew back then, you know, when Robin Cutter disappeared.'

'And that was why the police didn't question you at the time?'

'Yes.'

'Something which the police might now regard as something of an oversight.'

It took a moment for the implication of her words to sink in. 'Are you saying that I'm likely to be questioned about that?'

'I would think it's a very strong possibility.'

He looked appalled at the idea. Sweat was now prickling on his pale brow as he repeated, 'But I'm not on any Sex Offenders Register or anything. I've never touched a child in that way.'

'We have only your word for that,' said Carole, rather enjoying the police 'we'.

'But if I'm questioned there'll be lots of publicity. I might lose my job at Fether District Council.'

'Mr Southwest, eight years ago a very serious crime was committed. By pure chance you weren't questioned about it at the time. But given the facts: A) that you have admitted to me that you have paedophile tendencies, and B) that the remains of Robin Cutter were found under a beach hut for which you have responsibility, I think the very least that will happen is that you'll be asked to prove that you had nothing to do with the boy's abduction.'

'I didn't. You have to take my word for it.'

'You'd say that whether you were innocent or guilty, wouldn't you?' Shiftily he avoided her gaze. 'Were you doing your current job eight years ago?'

'Yes.'

'So you could easily have been here at Smalting the day Robin Cutter disappeared?'

'I could have been, but I wasn't.'

'Could you prove that?'

'I don't know. We're talking about eight years ago, for God's sake. I could have been here. All right, maybe I was, but if I was I didn't see any small boy here and I certainly didn't abduct one. I'd already found a way of controlling my urges.'

'You've mentioned that more than once, Mr Southwest. Would you explain to me what you mean by "controlling your urges"?'

'Yes, all right.' He was reluctant and the words came out slowly. 'The fact is, Carole, that I've always felt like I do and there was a time when perhaps I did represent a danger to children, when perhaps my urges would have got the better of me. It was something I was always afraid of. I tried to avoid being in situations where I might be left alone with children, and yet at the same time I *wanted* to be in situations where I was left alone with children. I was afraid that I might touch one of them, and then I might not be able to stop myself and . . .' The sweat was by now pouring profusely down his brow and temples. 'Then I found that I could stop myself from thinking about actually doing things to children, actually touching them, by seeing images of other people . . .' His words petered out.

'Of other people doing things to children?'

'Yes.'

'You mean by watching pornography?' asked Carole in disgust.

'Yes, but don't be so dismissive of it. For me child pornography is a harmless release for—'

'But it's not harmless! The children who feature in that kind of material are being harmed. At the time they're filmed they're being abused by—'

'Listen, Carole. If the existence of that pornography is stopping one person – me – from abusing a child, then surely that's a good thing?'

'Well, it's—'

'All I can say is that it works for me. It controls my urges, it provides a release for me – and it stops me from actually harming a real child!'

There was a silence. Carole recognized that she was never going to see eye to eye with Kelvin Southwest on the subject. But, more importantly, she found she was beginning to believe his protestations that he had had nothing to do with the abduction of Robin Cutter. Her certainties of earlier in the day were melting away. But then again, she told herself, paedophiles were notoriously devious and plausible. As she had pointed out to him, a guilty Kelvin Southwest would say just the same things as an innocent one. She needed to find out more.

'So where do you get this pornography from?' she asked with a shudder. 'Do you download it from the internet? Are you part of some paedophile ring? Or do you have another source?'

'I have another very good source,' he replied almost smugly. 'A very good source indeed.'

'Where do you get it from?'

There was a note of pride in his voice as he said, 'You should know this, Carole, given your background in the Home Office.'

'Oh?' she asked, puzzled.

'Where does child porn go when it's confiscated?'

'Well, obviously it goes to the police.'

'Exactly. So if someone like me had a contact in the police, a contact let us say who owed one a favour . . . that person might be persuaded to access . . . to copy that kind of material for one, mightn't they?'

'And are you saying you have that kind of a contact?'

'I do.'

Carole didn't need to ask him for the name. Suddenly the whole shabby set-up was crystal clear to her. 'Curt Holderness,' she said.

Kelvin Southwest nodded, pleased with his own cleverness. 'Yes, and even though he's left the force, he still has a friend there who keeps up the supply.'

'And does Curt Holderness enjoy that kind of material too?'

He chuckled. 'Why do you think he left the force early? Under something of a cloud? He could have been charged with stealing and disseminating the stuff, but the local police bigwigs didn't want the adverse publicity. He was shuffled out unceremoniously but discreetly. And since he was doing a favour for me . . .'

'You organized for him to get the job as security officer for the Smalting Beach Hut Association?'

Kelvin Southwest gave another self-satisfied nod.

Carole Seddon's mind was reeling. Everything she had thought about the case was suddenly turned on its head. Earlier in the day she had contemplated ending her interview with the Fether District Council official by revealing that she wasn't really a police officer, but now no thought could have been further from her mind.

She also felt fairly convinced that Kelvin Southwest had had nothing to do with the abduction and murder of Robin Cutter, but she wasn't about to tell the man that. Let him suffer a bit longer.

And in the meantime she would get back in touch with Curt Holderness.

Chapter Thirty-Five

Unlike Kelvin Southwest, Curt Holderness wasn't under the illusion that Carole Seddon was attached in any way to the police force. Nor, given his career background, did she reckon he'd be fooled for a moment if she claimed she was. But she still didn't reckon he'd argue when she said she'd like to meet and talk.

He didn't. She rang him as soon as a very chastened and nervous Kelvin Southwest had left . . . with many pleas that she would not tell anyone else about what they had discussed. But she wasn't about to let that particular little worm off the hook by giving him any such undertaking.

When she passed on to Curt Holderness what she'd heard from the Fether District Council official, the security officer agreed instantly to a meeting. He asked where she was and said he'd come straight to Smalting. *Fowey* that morning was becoming a kind of 'Incident Room' and in Carole's view the beach hut served the purpose pretty well. Though there was no one near enough to overhear any conversations conducted there, it was in full public view and therefore safe.

As she had the thought, she remembered that it was in full public view, in a situation that anyone might have thought to be safe, that Robin Cutter had been abducted on that very beach. A little shudder ran through her.

But no feeling of fear could overpower the sense of excitement welling up inside her. She was finally making real progress on the case. And on her own. Jude might live to regret wasting her time at a Past Life Regression Workshop in Brighton.

'Funny, Carole. I hadn't got you down as a black-mailer.'

She looked up to see the stocky figure of Curt Holderness standing between her and the sun. She was sure he had chosen to approach from that angle to emphasize his menace. And he'd succeeded. In spite of the June heat, he was once again wearing his black motorcycle leathers, though he stripped off the blouson as, uninvited, he sat in the chair opposite her. Underneath he had on a Metallica tour T-shirt.

'I'm not a blackmailer,' said Carole, with a calm that she didn't feel.

'Then what is all this about?'

'I am interested in the disappearance of Robin Cutter.'

'You're not alone in that. Everyone on the South Coast has theories on the subject.'

'Yes, but I'm interested in your involvement in it, Curt.'

He shrugged, remarkably insouciant, given the implied accusation in Carole's words. 'All right. I was still on the force then. I worked on the case briefly. Went through some of the foot-slogging, house-to-house inquiry stuff. Didn't come up with anything useful. If you're hoping to get new information out of me, forget it. I don't have any.'

'That wasn't what I meant. Robin Cutter was assumed to have been abducted by a paedophile . . .'

'That was the general view, yes. After another high-profile local case, people were seeing paedophiles everywhere. God, the number of paranoid calls we got at the station round that time.'

'Are you suggesting you think there was another explanation for Robin Cutter's disappearance?'

He shrugged again. 'Not particularly, no.' His answers sounded laid-back, but Carole could sense the tension in him. He was on the alert, waiting to see which direction their interview was taking.

'I said on the phone what Kelvin Southwest had told me . . .'

'Uh-huh.'

'. . . about you supplying him with child pornography.'

'Okay, I'm not denying it. The little creep wanted the stuff, I had access to it, we made a deal. It was a business arrangement.'

'A business arrangement that led to your early retirement from the police force?'

'Yes, all right. I don't deny that either. And if you're planning to blackmail me over it, I don't think you'll find the top brass in the force any keener to bring that out into the open now than they were at the time.'

'No, but the fact that you dealt in child pornography has other ramifications, doesn't it, Curt?'

'Like what? I had access to the stuff. I had the technology to copy it. I saw a way of making a quick buck. Salaries in the police force aren't that generous, you know.'

'I do know. I used to work for the Home Office.' If she had hoped that Curt Holderness might be impressed by that, she was disappointed, so she went on, 'It's a well-known fact that paedophiles exchange pornography with each other, that they form rings.'

'So?'

'I'm just suggesting that when you and Kelvin Southwest exchanged pornography you might have discussed going a step further, to move from using images of the stuff to realizing your fantasies with an actual child.'

It took him a second to take in the full implication of her words. And when he did, he was furious. 'Are you saying that I'm one of them? That I'd be in a ring with a little perve like Kel? God, they repel me, people like that! Scum! Filth! So far as I'm concerned you could string up the lot of them today without a trial!'

'Given that's your view, you seem surprisingly friendly with Kelvin Southwest.'

'That's a business arrangement, nothing more. We've both done favours for each other in the past and they're the kind of favours that we don't want to become public knowledge.'

'Your continuing to supply him with pornography, him having organized the security officer job for you?'

'Exactly that, yes. The reason we spend time together is because we don't trust each other. He's keeping an eye on me and I'm keeping an eye on him.'

'Curt, you say you're not a paedophile—'

'Too bloody right I'm not.'

'But your police career was ended early and in disgrace because you'd been accessing child pornography.'

'*Accessing* it, yes. Not bloody using it for my own purposes! God, at times I had to watch some of the stuff for professional reasons, you know, when we were trying to nail some pervy schoolteacher or someone like that . . . and it bloody turned my stomach. I'm glad I don't even have to copy the stuff any more. My mate who's still in the force does that. He hands over the CDs to me, I pass them on to Kel. Thank God, I don't see any of the content now.'

'But,' Carole persisted, 'you were turned out of the police force for—'

'I was turned out of the police force for copying and selling the stuff. How many times do I have to tell you? I don't get any kick from watching filth like that. It's disgusting!'

'Then why did you come here so promptly when I reported what Kelvin Southwest had told me?'

'I came because I've got a good little business going, and I don't want a nosy bitch like you to bugger it up. The police wouldn't have any interest in prosecuting me – I'm ancient history – but if they found out about my mate on the inside who's keeping up the

supply for me . . . well, they'd close down the opera-
tion sharpish, and I could lose a lot of money out of
that.'

'Are you implying that Kelvin Southwest isn't the
only client you supply?'

'What if he isn't? The important point you seem to
be failing to take on board is that I deal in the stuff, I
don't use it myself.'

Carole found herself in a familiar dilemma. What
Curt Holderness said sounded very plausible. His re-
pulsion at the thought of watching child pornography
seemed genuine. But then again, as with Kelvin Southwest, someone who really was a paedophile would
make himself sound just as plausible.

'So,' she asked rather desperately, 'you have no
idea what happened to Robin Cutter?'

'Not until his bones were found under that beach
hut over there, no.' Curt Holderness suddenly turned
businesslike. 'Listen, Carole, I've got to know what
you're planning to do. That's why I came here. Are
you going to keep the information about my mate
supplying the porn to yourself? And if so, on what
terms? You say you're not a blackmailer—'

'And I'm not.'

'Then what do you want?'

'I want to find out what happened to Robin Cutter.'

He was silent for a moment, calculating. Then he
said, 'So if there was a piece of information I could
give you – something I'd found out while I was working on the case, something no one else knows – if I
were to give you that, would you get off my back?'

'I certainly would, Curt.' She wasn't sure whether what she said was true, but she knew it was the answer he required at that moment.

'Right.' Again he was silent, assessing his situation. 'Okay, try this,' he said at length. 'You know the boy was being looked after by his grandparents when he disappeared?' Carole nodded. Curt Holderness pointed along the row of beach huts. 'Those two old dears over there, as it happens – you know them?'

'Yes, we've talked to each other.'

'Okay, so you know that the old geezer brought the boy down here and he was snatched outside the ice-cream shop up on the prom.'

'I heard the circumstances.'

'Well, needless to say, the forensic boys pulled in the old man's car as soon as possible – took it from right here where he'd parked it in Smalting – and they ran every test they could on it. Of course they found Robin Cutter's DNA all over the interior. Well, they would, wouldn't they? Kid saw a lot of his grandparents, Lionel Oliver would have driven him around all over the place.

'Nothing odd in that. But there was something one of the forensic boys thought was odd and I remember chatting to him in the canteen about it.' He paused, fully aware of the command he had on Carole's attention. 'Now the boy – Robin Cutter – was like five, wasn't he, at the time he disappeared – and his Mum was always insistent that when he went in the car he was clipped into a child seat, you know, for safety reasons. She'd taken Robin's seat out of her car when she dropped the boy with his grandparents that morning and said, if they drove him anywhere, they were to make sure they used it. But when Lionel Oliver's car was taken from here to the labs, straight after the boy had been abducted, there was no car seat fixed in it.

'Okay, the old boy had an explanation. He said he was from a different generation, that he wasn't molly-coddled when he was a nipper . . . you know how that generation go on about stuff. There weren't any car seats around when he was growing up and it'd never done him any harm. And he said the boy Robin liked being free to move around in the car, and it was their little secret and he wasn't to tell his Mum, but his Granddad reckoned he was grown up enough not to need a car seat. Okay, the old boy's explanation could have been the truth, certainly everything else in his account tallied and rang true, but at the time I did think it a little odd.'

It was funny, Carole had always had a feeling that at some point the investigation would entail talking further to the Olivers.

Chapter Thirty-Six

Curt Holderness didn't exactly threaten her when he left, but Carole felt the undercurrent of menace in him. She wouldn't volunteer to spend any more time with him in the future, and was glad there was no reason why she should. A little shudder of relief ran through her body as he set off back up the beach to his motorbike.

Her morning in the *Fowey* 'Incident Room' had taken longer than she expected. When she looked at her watch once the security officer was out of sight, she was surprised to see it was ten past twelve. She looked along the row of beach huts. Outside *Mistral* the Olivers sat in their usual positions. Carole was undecided as to how her next step should be taken. In spite of her desire to solve the case and crow over Jude, she found herself wishing her friend was there. Dealing with the Olivers was likely to require a level of delicacy which she wasn't confident that she possessed.

With a synchronicity that Jude would have recognized and Carole herself pooh-poohed, at that moment her mobile phone rang. And of course it was Jude.

'Oh, I thought you were regressing to a past life?'

'Done that. Apparently I was once married to an Egyptian Pharaoh.'

'And how was that?' asked Carole sceptically.

'He was a bit of a Mummy's boy.'

'Oh, do shut up.'

'Anyway, tell me what's been happening. I'm agog.'

'So you should be. There's so much to tell you. All roads seem to lead to the Olivers.'

'Have you spoken to them?'

'Not yet.' Then in a rather small voice Carole added, 'I'd rather do it with you.'

'All right. I'll come straight away.'

'Where are you now?'

'Still in Brighton.'

'But how're you going to—?'

'I'll get a cab.'

'That'll be terribly expensive to—'

Jude had rung off.

Carole tried to concentrate on *The Times*, but her eyes kept slipping off the newsprint and homing in on the couple in front of *Mistral*. She didn't know what she would do if the Olivers moved before Jude arrived.

She tried to get her mind engaged by the crossword, but without success. Anyway, the prize crossword on a Saturday was always subtly different and Carole rarely bothered with it, even though completing the weekday ones was an essential part of her ritual. Maybe it was a kind of intellectual snobbery that kept her from the Saturday crossword. Even though she'd never enter for it, the idea of there being a prize seemed to cheapen the experience. Whereas by doing the weekday crossword she was engaging in a purely intellectual activity.

Jude arrived within the half-hour. 'I'm starving,' she announced. 'You can bring me up to date while we have something to eat.'

Rather than expose themselves again to the high prices of The Crab Inn, Carole and Jude went to one of the many cafés on the Smalting prom. They selected one which gave them a perfect view of the back of *Mistral*, so that they could see if the Olivers made any kind of move, and they sat outside in the sunlight. Jude said she was desperate for fish and chips and Carole found the idea rather appealed to her as well.

While they waited for the food, Carole gave Jude a virtually verbatim report of her interviews with Kelvin Southwest and Curt Holderness.

'I knew there was something odd about our Kel,' said Jude. 'I couldn't put my finger on it, but I sensed that women weren't his thing.'

With respect for her sensitivities in such areas, Carole asked Jude if she'd got the same feeling with Curt Holderness.

'No, he's very definitely normal hetero. Possibly a rather aggressive and bullying normal hetero – actually *probably* a rather aggressive and bullying normal hetero – but no way is he a paedophile.'

Their fish and chips arrived. Beautiful. Plump

fillets robustly battered and dripping with oil, not those cardboard-like scabbards of dry fish flakes which get served in so many pubs and coastal restaurants. And the chips they were served had had encounters with genuine potatoes quite recently, not in some Past Life Regression.

'Bliss,' said Jude. 'Is there anything in the world to beat sitting in the sun at an English seaside resort and eating good fish and chips?'

But they both knew there was still a cloud over their idyll – the death of Robin Cutter and the need for its circumstances to be explained.

Chapter Thirty-Seven

Lionel Oliver was, as ever, gazing abstractedly out to sea, but he looked up as they approached. He recognized Carole and rose politely from his chair when introduced to Jude.

His wife's chair was empty. He raised a finger to his lips and pointed to the inside of *Mistral*. 'Joyce is having a little zizz in there. Always does after lunch.' Carole and Jude could see her stretched out on the towel-covered bench seat at the back of the hut.

'We wanted to talk to you about Robin,' said Jude gently.

'Everyone suddenly wants to talk to me about Robin.' He gestured to Joyce's chair. 'If one of you wants to sit . . .'

'You take it, Carole. I'll be quite happy on the shingle.'

'Yes,' Lionel Oliver went on, 'there's been a lot of interest in Robin since . . . since what was found under *Quiet Harbour*.'

'Interest from the police?'

'Oh yes. From the police.'

He was silent. Carole wasn't sure how to move the

conversation along, but Jude's instinct was sure. 'You loved Robin, didn't you, Lionel?'

'Oh yes. I loved him very much. Still do love him, even though he's not here to love any more.'

'And you've talked a lot about him to the police?'

'I certainly have. A lot around the time he disappeared. And now a lot more. They rang this morning. They want to talk to me again.' He looked at his watch. 'They're going to pick me up here this afternoon. Inspector Fyfield's going to come. In a car. Very thoughtful of them to send a car for me, isn't it? But then of course you probably know that, don't you?'

Jude flashed a puzzled look at Carole, who sent a no-don't-say-anything one back. It seemed that Helga Czesky's assumption that they were police officers had spread as far as the Olivers.

'Different department I suppose you'd be,' the old man went on. 'They use a lot of women in this area, I believe, you know, when it concerns the death of a child.'

There was a strange calm about him, a kind of resignation, as if some great weight had just been removed from his shoulders.

'We heard about the fact that you didn't put Robin's car seat in the car.'

'No, I should have thought of that. In the panic I forgot. Invented some story on the spur of the moment that seemed to convince the police, but maybe they've been suspicious all that time.'

'And no one in Smalting saw him, did they, when he waited for you outside the ice-cream shop?'

'No.'

'I think I know why,' said Jude softly.

Carole looked at her neighbour in astonishment. She knew Jude was capable of making great – almost magical – leaps of logic, but had no idea what she was about to reveal this time.

'Robin never came to Smalting that afternoon, did he, Lionel?'

Slowly the old man shook his head.

'That's why he didn't need the car seat. He was already dead, wasn't he?'

A nod confirmed this. Carole couldn't work out how Jude had reached the conclusion she had, but it did make sense of a lot of anomalies in the case.

'When I saw he was dead,' said Lionel, 'I knew I had to hide the body. I couldn't leave him there. Miranda would never have forgiven us. I had to hide him somewhere temporarily, until the furore died down and I could make a more permanent resting place for him.'

'So what did you do?'

'I put his body on the back seat of my car. I knew it wouldn't matter if traces of him were found there, he'd been in the car with me often enough. And I drove him to work.'

'To the funeral parlour?'

'Yes. It was lunch hour. I knew the girl on reception, who was meant to stay there right through while all the others were out . . . I knew she was in the habit of sneaking off to the pub to meet her boyfriend and shutting the parlour up for an hour.

I'd been about to take her to task for it, but that day I was glad she was skyving. I drove in the back entrance, where we take the bodies in. Nobody saw me arrive and there's a big shutter comes down so nobody saw what I was doing.

'I took Robin's body out of the car. I'd wanted to embalm him, but I knew there wasn't time. So I wrapped him up tight in plastic sheeting and I took him through to the room where we display the coffins. There was a small one we had there, you know, for young children who die . . . like Robin. It's sad, that, always sad showing it to the parents.

'Anyway, I put him in and sealed the coffin lid. I thought he'd be safe there. After all, the last place anyone would look for a dead body would be in a funeral parlour.' He let out a dry, humourless chuckle. 'After I'd finished, I went back to the car and drove here to Smalting. I was in the parlour ten minutes top-weight.

'I parked the car near the prom. There were a lot of people around, all caught up in their own business. No one looked at me. I went into the shop to buy the ice cream. When I came out, I rang the police and told them my story, about Robin having been abducted, or at least having disappeared. I never thought they'd believe it, but they seemed to, and the more they questioned me about it, the clearer the details came in my mind. After a time I almost came to believe it myself.

'Obviously I couldn't leave Robin in the parlour for too long, but a week later I came in at night-time and embalmed him. That would preserve the body for a while.

'And all the publicity and the press conferences and the pleas on television from Rory and Miranda . . . well, that all died down after a time. And I was doing some work in the garden at home. Previously we'd just had the one pond, you know, but I was adding to that, making a great big water feature and that involved a lot of digging and—'

'So you took Robin's body from the funeral parlour back to your garden and buried him there?' suggested Jude.

The old man nodded a weary nod. He seemed to have aged during his narrative. 'So Robin was always close to me. I knew where he was. He was there, and it gave me comfort to know he was there.'

'And everything was fine,' said Carole, joining up the dots, 'until you had to move house?'

'Yes. I couldn't leave Robin in the garden there. Partly I was worried about a new owner finding his remains, though I didn't care so much about that. It's more I couldn't be parted from the child, from the boy I loved. We've no garden with the new flat we're going to, just a window box. So . . .' He gestured rather feebly towards *Quiet Harbour*. 'I knew we'd still come here. I knew if I put him under one of the beach huts he'd still be near me.' He let out a little mirthless laugh. 'I think I also knew that it couldn't last, that very soon I'd be found out. Which is, of course, what's happened.

'In fact, I was nearly found out earlier. Only a few nights after I'd taken the bones from our garden and reburied them under the beach hut, some idiot tried to set fire to it. Fortunately the fire didn't spread far – or someone put it out, I don't know.'

'And you put down an old offcut of carpet so that the damage wouldn't show from the inside,' said Carole, pleased to be filling in the gaps in the case.

'Yes, I did that.' Lionel Oliver sighed. 'I'm a stupid old man. I don't know why I thought I'd get away with it. Or perhaps I didn't think I'd get away with it. Perhaps I was just so tired of holding the secret inside me that I wanted to be found out. Yes, I think that's probably it.'

Jude broke the long silence that ensued by saying, very gently, 'You still haven't told us how Robin died.'

'No.'

'Are you going to?'

'Why not? You know everything else. I'd taken the day off work, that day we were going to look after Robin. I enjoyed playing with him.'

'When you say "playing with him" . . . ?' asked Carole tentatively.

That did make him angry. 'Oh, for God's sake! Don't you start! I went through all that with the police, time and time and time again. What I meant by "playing with him" was kicking a ball about in the back garden, hide and seek, showing him the goldfish in the pond, the kind of things you do with a five-year-old child. The games grandfathers and grandsons have played down the centuries.

'Anyway, it was a hot day and I'd been busy at work the last few weeks and I wasn't as young as I used to be, so I was very tired. And we were playing hide and seek, and it was a big garden and so Robin had introduced this rule that we had to count up to two hundred. He was a bright boy, very advanced for his age. He could count up to two hundred, no problems. And then he'd shout at the top of his voice, "Coming, ready or not!"'

For a moment the recollection was almost too emotional for him, but he managed to control himself and went on, 'Well, it was my turn to count and Robin's to hide. And, as I say, I started counting and . . . I fell asleep. Don't know how long it was for, probably only a quarter of an hour, but when I woke up, there was no sign of Robin.

'It didn't take me long to find him. I knew he was fascinated by the goldfish. He must have been peering down at them and lost his footing. There was a kind of rockery at the side, with a little waterfall running down it, and when he fell he must have hit his head on one of the rocks. It was only a small pond, but big enough to drown my grandson.'

The long silence which followed this was finally broken by the voice of Joyce Oliver from inside the beach hut. 'Except,' she said, 'that isn't what happened at all.'

Chapter Thirty-Eight

The expression on Lionel Oliver's face as he watched his wife walk out of the beach hut was a complex one, combining puzzlement, annoyance and protective-ness. 'What are you on about, Joyce? Of course that's what happened.'

'No, it isn't. I think it must be true that Robin drowned in the pond, as you said he did. I didn't know that till just now, Lionel. But if he did, it wasn't you who was meant to be looking after him. It happened on my watch.'

'That's ridiculous, Joyce.'

'It happened on my watch,' his wife repeated. She looked at Lionel, daring him to interrupt her, then turned firmly to Carole and Jude. 'I didn't know the half of what he's just told you. I just woke up and heard almost all of it. Lionel, why couldn't you have told me before?'

'There wasn't any point,' he mumbled. 'Why should you suffer too?'

'I should suffer because I deserved to suffer. I should suffer because it was my fault.'

'No.'

'Yes, it was. I don't know why you two are here, but since you've heard the rest of it, I think that you should hear the truth. My daughter-in-law, Miranda, didn't trust me. She didn't like me looking after Robin. And she was right. Because back then I had a serious problem. A drink problem. We tried to keep it quiet from everyone, but the family knew. Miranda certainly knew and that was why she would only let Robin stay with us if she knew Lionel was going to be there, that it wasn't just me on my own.

'Well, that day, the day that Rory and Miranda were going up to London to see the matinee of *Les Miserables*, I'd had a real blinder the night before. I was on more than a bottle of gin a day then, and that morning I woke up having slept very badly and with the kind of crushing hangover that can only be alleviated by a very large hair of the dog. But I'd drunk the house dry the night before. I was desperate for a bottle of gin. I managed to disguise how I was feeling from Rory and Miranda when they came to bring Robin over, but as soon as they'd gone I ordered Lionel to go and buy me a bottle of gin. I'm not proud of how I was in those days. I was a monster.'

'No, you weren't, love,' her husband protested feebly. 'You couldn't help yourself. It's an illness.'

'I was a monster,' Joyce reiterated. Jude began to understand the great hatred Miranda Browning had felt against her mother-in-law. 'So, I ordered Lionel to go and replenish my stocks of gin and I was in sole charge of Robin. Except I wasn't in a state to be in charge of anything or anyone. I remember that

I fell asleep at the kitchen table. Robin was around before I fell asleep, and I know the door to the garden was open, and the next thing I remember was Lionel waking me up.

'He seemed a bit agitated, but I didn't ask him why. All I cared about was the fact that he'd brought me a bottle of gin. I got stuck into that. Lionel said he was going to take Robin down to Smalting, get him an ice cream, maybe spend some time with the boy here at *Mistral*. The next thing I'm aware of is the news that Robin's been abducted and the police are coming round and . . .'

There was a long moment before Joyce Oliver turned back to her husband and said, 'Tell me the truth, Lionel. Did you come back that morning from buying the gin and find Robin drowned in the pond?'

There was nothing he could do but nod abjectly.

'But why did you do all you did? Why?'

'If Miranda had ever found out that I'd left Robin alone with you . . . If she'd found out that you were dead drunk and had let him go near the pond on his own . . .' He shook his head, unable to say out loud what would have happened.

Joyce Oliver looked at her husband with an expression of infinite pain and infinite respect. She realized the extent of his love for her. To put himself through all the trauma of police questioning, the inevitable suspicions that he might be a paedophile . . . all that for the woman who had allowed the child he adored to die.

'The only good thing to come out of any of it,' Joyce said, 'was that, although I didn't know the details of what had really happened, the shock of Robin's disappearance did stop me drinking. Maybe I felt guilty for the fact that the last time I'd seen him, I'd been almost comatose from the gin, I don't know.' A deep sigh trembled through her body. 'All of this is going to take a long time to come to terms with.'

They were aware of a young man in a crumpled beige suit hovering on the edge of their charmed circle in front of the beach hut. Lionel Oliver looked up and recognized him. 'Ah, Inspector Fyfield. The car's here, is it?'

'Yes, Mr Oliver. The Superintendant would like to talk to you back at the station.'

'Of course.'

'I think he ought to talk to me too,' said Joyce.

'I'm sure that'd be fine. If you wish to accompany your husband, Mrs Oliver . . .'

'Yes, I do. Lionel, if you'll just lock up *Mistral* . . .'

'Of course, love.'

'Carole and Jude,' Joyce went on, 'if you don't mind just walking up to the car with me, I'd like to get your contact numbers. I think there are a few things we're going to need to talk about.'

The two women reckoned that was probably an understatement. Joyce Oliver picked up her beach bag and the three of them followed Inspector Fyfield up the beach.

On the edge of the prom Joyce stopped by a bench, which faced away from the sea, and sat down. 'If I could just get those numbers from you . . .'

The simple process seemed to take a long time.

Joyce Oliver shuffled through the contents of her bag in search of pen and paper, but her hands were shaking so much Jude had to help her. In spite of her earlier apparent calmness, she was clearly in a state of shock.

But eventually one of her wordsearch books was found. Carole and Jude wrote down their contact numbers on the back of it. Then they followed the route taken by Inspector Fyfield, who was by now leaning against his car. Though he had his back to them, the women could detect the impatience in his body language.

It was an unmarked police car with a driver in civilian clothes, not a patrol car. After the shock of being a scene of crime, Smalting was not about to suffer any further affronts to its middle-class respectability.

Or was it? Jude, as ever hypersensitive to the mood of her environment, experienced a feeling almost of dread. She tapped Carole on the sleeve. Both looked out to sea. Lionel Oliver had put his suit jacket on, as if dressed for work. The water was already up to his chest as he continued to march steadily forward away from Smalting Beach. Carole and Jude knew that his suit pockets would be full of shingle.

Jude looked at Joyce Oliver, but the old woman's powdered face was unreadable. Had she deliberately created the delay in taking their phone numbers so that her husband would have the opportunity to make his escape before anyone could stop him? Had some secret message passed between the couple as they parted for the last time? Those were questions that Jude felt sure would never be answered.

BONES UNDER THE BEACH HUT

Inspector Fyfield contacted the coastguard. A rescue helicopter was immediately mobilized. But of course it arrived too late.

Chapter Thirty-Nine

The following day, as arranged, Carole Seddon's daughter-in-law and granddaughter arrived at High Tor just before lunch. Lily had slept in the car and was very lively. She had become much more mobile since Carole had last seen her and climbed the stairs unaided to inspect her bedroom, of which she approved. She was very excited by the folding cot that her grandmother had bought and by the two new cuddlies that had been put in it.

Lily's speech had also developed. She could now vocalize a very convincing 'Mummy', 'Biscuit' and 'No'. Gaby had clearly been tutoring her to say 'Granny', but she had only got as far as 'Gaga'. Which, Carole reckoned, would soon not be a million miles from the truth.

Her concentration over the previous week on the investigations into Mark Dennis's disappearance and Robin Cutter's death had had the beneficial effect of stopping her from worrying about Gaby's visit, and the two women were very relaxed over their Sunday lunch. Lily also ate well and when they had all finished Carole announced that they were going to a nearby village called Smalting, where she 'had a beach hut'.

Lily of course had no idea what a beach hut was, but as soon as she saw *Quiet Harbour* she caught on very quickly. She liked the idea of their having their own little house to live in, and she loved her own little pink director's chair. And she was even more pleased with the new red and yellow bathing costume that Gaby put her into. Even at that age, Lily had a real girlie fascination with clothes.

But of course she had no idea what a significant event she was witnessing when her grandmother stripped off her outer garments to reveal a sedate Marks & Spencer one-piece bathing costume in a flattering, deep red colour. Nor was the little girl aware how privileged she was to witness Carole Seddon removing her shoes and socks and letting the sand get between her toes.

Anyway, Lily was far too preoccupied to notice what anyone else was doing. She had become instantly busy with the plastic buckets, spade and shapes that her doting grandmother had bought for her. In no time she had worked out what the sea and the sand were for, and was trekking back and forth from the shoreline spilling buckets of water and preparing elaborate tea parties with sand pies for the two dolls she had brought with her.

Carole Seddon took in the scene and couldn't have been happier. It was all so archetypally English – except of course for the fine weather.

And as she watched Lily busily playing, it seemed

incongruous that that same beach had so recently been a witness to such tragedy.

There were a few changes in the world of Smalting that summer. Following complaints about misuse of his authority and an internal enquiry, Kelvin Southwest was relieved of his job at Fether District Council and someone else took over the administration of the beach huts. No complaints were made about his paedophile tendencies, but then very few people knew about those. And perhaps his use of child pornography did keep him from committing worse crimes.

But he had to find another source of such material. The same Fether District Council internal investigation removed Curt Holderness from his sinecure as security officer. And following an enquiry and a clean-up, Curt's pornography-copying friend in the local police also lost his job.

Kelvin Southwest (with his mother) and Curt Holderness both moved from the area.

So did Mark Dennis and Philly Rose. Their country idyll no longer seemed as attractive to either of them. Mark returned to work in the City, though at a much less high-powered level. The breakdown had burnt out most of his early promise.

Philly found more work as a graphic designer back in London. But she had genuinely loved Seashell Cottage and had been unhappy about moving.

Then, perhaps inevitably, her relationship with Mark broke up. It was a long time before either of them found anyone else. Mark certainly made no attempt to reignite his marriage, but Nuala would never completely let go of him. While she exploited other men, she would still come back to her undivorced husband from time to time, usually demanding more money.

A happier, though unlikely, romance did, however, come to fruition. It was announced in the September edition of *The Hut Parade* (with complimentary tide table for new members of the SBHA) that Reginald Flowers had married Dora Pinchbeck. So now he could dictate to her whenever he wanted to and she could polish his brass fittings.

Not a lot changed with the other members of the Smalting Beach Hut Association. Deborah Wrigley continued to use *Seagull's Nest* as just another chamber in which to torture her family.

And in *Shrimphaven* Katie Brunswick continued endlessly to rewrite her novel (except of course when she was off on courses instructing her about different ways of rewriting it).

Meanwhile up on the Smalting prom at Sanditon Helga Czesky continued to indulge her husband's middle-aged *enfant terriblisme*. And Gray Czesky, cushioned by his wife's substantial tolerance and substantial income, still didn't realize how lucky he was and would still maunder on to anyone foolish enough to listen about his world-shattering plans to *épater le bourgeois*. (The local bourgeois, it should be noted, remained remarkably unaware of and uninterested in his efforts to *épate* them.)

After his grandfather's suicide the police closed

the case of Robin Cutter. He was found by an inquest to have died of accidental drowning. His grandmother still used *Mistral* a lot, still always had a wordsearch book with her, but she now spent a lot of time, as her late husband had done, just looking bleakly out to sea.

There was never any thought of a rapprochement between Joyce Oliver and her daughter-in-law. Miranda Browning perhaps received some comfort from the discovery that her son had not been the victim of a paedophile, but the sense of loss remained ever present in her life. As it did in the life of her divorced husband Rory.

For the inhabitants of High Tor and Woodside Cottage everything continued much as before. Jude was occasionally restless, feeling that perhaps it was time for her to move on from Fethering, but she didn't confide these thoughts in her neighbour. Carole Seddon could always find sufficient imagined slights in her life, without being given any real ones to worry about.

And the general view in Fethering remained that the people in Smalting were a bit up themselves.

Ew

EW

EW

ℓw

NEATH PORT TALBOT LIBRARY							
AND INFORMATION SERVICES							
1		25		49		73	
2		26		50		74	
3		27		51		75	
4		28		52		76	
5		29		53		77	
6		30		54		78	
7		31		55			
8		32		56			
9		33					